If I Fall for You

If I Fall for You

A Montana Mercies Romance

MYRA JOHNSON

Cover by
Fawn Ridge Concepts

Mercy unto you, and peace, and love, be multiplied.

— JUDE 2, KJV

"You will not 'get over' the loss of a loved one; you will learn to live with it. You will heal and you will rebuild yourself around the loss you have suffered. You will be whole again but you will never be the same. Nor should you be the same, nor would you want to."

— ELISABETH KUBLER-ROSS AND
DAVID KESSLER

Chapter One

This couldn't be happening. This could *not* be happening!

Fists clenched at her sides, Shannon Halsey filled her lungs, held for a count of five, then blew out slowly. The calming technique Dr. Yoshida had taught her during therapy usually worked.

Today? Not so much.

"Ms. Halsey?" The auto mechanic hesitated, as if he sensed that one more word risked pushing her over the edge. "Ms. Halsey, I'm real sorry I can't give you better news."

She drew another shaky breath. "Are you saying my car isn't worth fixing?"

"Not unless you're ready to drop a few grand. For the same money, you could probably find a decent used car in considerably better shape than this one."

Either way, she didn't have *a few grand* lying around.

"Mommy?" Tate tugged on her wrist. "Grampy can fix our car. Why don't you call him?"

With a peek at her precious four-going-on-forty-year-old little boy, her heart swelled with love. Tate had inherited his daddy's warm brown eyes and dark hair, a contrast to her fair coloring and straw-colored locks.

She brushed aside a strand that had come loose from her ponytail. "I know, honey, but Mommy needs to figure this out herself."

Her dad wouldn't hesitate a moment to come running to her rescue, but relying on him—more than she already had these past few years—was the absolute *last* thing she wanted.

Unfortunately, it didn't appear she had a choice. She needed transportation for work, and she needed her job if she had any hope of giving her son the life he deserved.

Not that their life wasn't good. In the five years since her husband, Steven, had been taken from them without ever having met his baby boy, God had sustained and blessed them in too many ways to count. But what kind of woman—*mother*—was she if she had to run to her dad and stepmom every time something went wrong?

Looking up at the mechanic, she stifled a sigh. "Any chance you'd want to buy this junk heap for parts?"

"Couldn't offer much." An awkward silence lengthened as he stroked his jaw. "But seein' as how you're in a tough spot, I'll do what I can."

"Thank you. Any amount would help." Shannon resisted the urge to grab his greasy hand and give it a grateful shake.

While the man stepped into his office to do some figuring, Shannon walked to the front with Tate and made a call. "Hi, Maddie. I realize this is last minute, but I don't think I can help you at the arts and crafts fair this weekend after all. My car broke down."

"Oh, no. Are you okay? Where are you?"

"At the garage. We were on our way home after Tate's dentist appointment and somehow made it this far, but the Ol' Gray Mare"—her nickname for the ancient silver sedan she'd been driving since college—"has officially given up the ghost."

"Sounds like you're stranded," Maddie said. "I'm on my way to the venue right now. Let me pick you up, and you can help me arrange my booth while we figure this out."

"You don't have to—"

"No arguments. Besides, I really need you this weekend. Where am I going to find another assistant the day before the fair opens? Text me your location. I'll be there ASAP."

Accepting help from a friend felt less humiliating than having to call her dad. "Okay," Shannon replied weakly. "Thanks."

Julia, her late husband's mother and now her step-mother, had introduced her to Maddie Wittenbauer. Julia and Maddie had been best friends for years, and as Shannon had gotten to know Maddie, she understood why. There wasn't a sweeter, more caring person on the face of the planet.

Twenty minutes later, Maddie's Suburban pulled up. Shannon climbed in back to secure Tate's safety seat, then buckled him in. Falling into the front passenger seat, she released a groan. "This is so nice of you. I hadn't thought ahead to how we'd even get home from the garage."

Maddie cast her a sympathetic smile as she turned onto the street. "I take it your car is hopeless?"

"Utterly. Guess I'll be going car shopping next week. That's *if* I can qualify for a loan."

"Why can't you ask your dad and Julia? I'm sure they'd jump at the chance to help."

"'Cuz Mommy's gotta figure it out herself," Tate piped up from the backseat.

Maddie's burst of laughter set her strawberry-blond curls shimmying, but after one glance at Shannon's scowl, she grew serious. "I get it, honey. You've been trying hard to stand on your own two feet."

"Exactly. And I'll never make any progress if I go running to Dad and Julia for every little problem."

After a thoughtful pause, Maddie said, "Needing new wheels isn't what I'd call a *little* problem."

"I know." A frustrated sigh escaped. "I've been searching online for some kind of part-time work I could do from home in the evenings to earn some extra cash, but so far I haven't found anything."

Maddie patted Shannon's arm. "Don't lose faith. The right thing will turn up."

One more thing Shannon loved about Maddie—her encouraging, God-centered outlook.

A few minutes later, they arrived at the community center. Cars had already lined up near the entrance as other vendors unloaded their wares onto carts and hand trucks.

Maddie's supplies were much lighter—a small folding table and tablecloths, a hanging banner, informational brochures, and an art box packed with sketchpads and pencils. Her on-the-spot pet drawings had grown more and more popular as animal lovers in and around Missoula, Montana, discovered her talent. She used the income to supplement funding for Eventide Dog Sanctuary, the nonprofit rescue kennel she owned and managed in Elk Valley for senior or otherwise unadoptable dogs.

A volunteer directed them to Maddie's assigned space, where neighboring vendors were already getting organized.

Shannon had visited Maddie's booth at other fairs, but this was her first time as Maddie's assistant. For now, at least, nervous excitement helped to take her mind off her current problems.

Tate poked her with the long cardboard tube he'd carried in. "Where does this go, Mommy?"

"I think that's Miss Maddie's banner. We'll wait and let her tell us what to do with it." Shannon set the container of art supplies on a chair, then unfolded a pastel-yellow tablecloth and smoothed it across the six-foot-long table that fronted the space.

"Can I go look over there?" Tate pointed toward the booth next to theirs, where a brown-haired young woman was arranging and rearranging trays of something in baggies. "It looks like doggy stuff. We can buy something for Weena."

Shannon read the sign over the booth: Anika's Paw-fect Picks. Tate was always on the lookout for new ways to spoil his best bud, Rowena, a gangling Irish wolfhound mix. They'd been pretty much inseparable since Julia, a veterinarian, had convinced Shannon's dad to take the abandoned dog. Dad had been caring for Tate during Shannon's six-month hospitalization for depression. Once she'd recovered and could make a home for Tate again, there was no leaving Rowena behind.

"Please, Mommy? *Pleeease*?" Tate clasped his hands beneath his chin, those pleading puppy-dog eyes rivaling Rowena's.

"Okay, but don't touch anything or get in the lady's way. Just look. And stay where I can see you."

Maddie had finished setting up the folding table she used for posing smaller pets. "I haven't seen her before," she said, nodding toward their neighbor. "Must be new on the circuit."

Shannon cast a sympathetic smile toward the woman behind the table. "She does have a deer-in-the-headlights look about her. She's rearranged that same tray three times already."

"Once we get set up, I'll go over and introduce myself. Maybe offer a few tips." Maddie slid her banner out of the cardboard tube. "In the meantime, want to help me hang this?"

Already fifteen minutes later than he'd promised, Luke Daniels dodged a rolling cart stacked with boxes as he jogged down the wide center aisle. On either side, vendors bustled to set up fair booths and lay out their wares— stained-glass ornaments, scented soaps and lotions, framed art, handmade jewelry, just about anything anyone with an ounce of creativity could think up and offer for sale.

Luke couldn't claim much creativity of his own, unless he counted the arsenal of clever tricks he'd taught Fletch, his talented border collie. He'd rather work with dogs than just about anything else.

Lately, though, other responsibilities had stolen his time. Luke's father had been checking out more and more the last few years, as if he no longer cared about the family legacy that was Fox Pass Ranch. Unable to watch things fall into ruin, Luke had been trying to pick up the slack. Before his mad dash into town this afternoon, he'd been overseeing immunizations for the latest batch of calves.

He reached the end of the aisle and looked both ways.

Anika had shown him on a diagram where to find her booth, but with all the commotion and blocked passageways, he kept getting turned around.

Down another aisle, up the next one, and then he spotted her. She was talking to a little kid who couldn't be more than three or four. At least she was smiling—a good sign.

"Hey, Ani." Luke stepped behind the table and gave her a side hug. "Sorry I couldn't get here sooner."

"Did you get all the calves taken care of?"

"All done." He didn't say they'd have finished a lot sooner if Dad had pitched in. He tipped his head toward the kid. "Looks like you've got your first customer already."

"Yes, he's quite the big spender." Anika grinned. "This is Tate. He promised to bring his mom over later and buy eleventy-nine bags of treats for his doggy."

"Eleventy-nine, huh?" Luke wiggled his brows. "At that rate, you'll run out of merch before the fair's half over."

The little boy pushed out his lower lip. "'Cept my mommy broke her car, so maybe not that many."

"Aw, that's too bad. About your mom's car, I mean." Wondering what kind of mother let a kid his age roam unsupervised in a busy place like this, Luke glanced around.

His gaze locked on the wide-eyed blonde striding toward them. "Tate," she called. "I asked you not to bother the lady."

"He isn't bothering me at all," Anika said, warmth in her tone. "He's been telling me all about his big doggy— Weena, is it?"

"Rowena," the woman said. She set her hands protectively on the boy's tiny shoulders.

"That's such a pretty name." Selecting a bag of treats,

Anika handed it across the table. "Here you go, Tate. On the house."

The boy's lips puckered. "How are they on the house? My house isn't here."

Luke laughed. "It means you get a free sample to take home to your dog."

"Oh, that isn't necessary," the mom protested. "Let me get my wallet. I'll pay you for it." When her glance fell to the price tag, she faltered. "Or maybe we could buy one of the smaller bags instead."

"No, please, I insist." Anika extended her hand. "I'm Anika Daniels. This is my first time doing anything like this, and your little boy is just the icebreaker I needed to calm the jitters."

The mom's discomfort was obvious, and Luke felt bad that his sister had put her on the spot. Hoping to lighten the moment, he gave Anika a friendly poke. "I thought that's why *I'm* here."

"You were supposed to get here early enough to help with the heavy lifting. But that obviously didn't happen." Anika reached over to close Tate's fist around the bag of dog treats. "I mean it. Those are my gift to your doggy."

"That's really kind of you." The boy's mom released a breath as she accepted Anika's handshake. "I'm Shannon Halsey. I guess you've already met Tate."

"We did. And this is my brother, Luke." Anika slanted a brow. "He thinks I can't manage tying my shoes without him."

"I know the feeling." A look of understanding narrowed Shannon's eyes.

"You have an overprotective family member, too?" Leaning across the table, Anika said in a stage whisper, "We'll have to get together sometime and commiserate."

When both women chuckled, Luke stuffed down a twinge of irritation. Who was going to look out for his baby sister if not him? If Shannon Halsey had someone in her life who'd be there for her like Luke tried to be for Anika, she should consider herself fortunate.

Her husband, most likely, judging by the wedding band.

Unless she was married to an oblivious, apathetic, lose-himself-in-a-bottle recluse like his and Anika's father. Luke wished he could convince his sister to move out on her own, but she insisted Dad needed her.

As for Luke, he made it a point to keep his distance. Why invite trouble by wanting more from the man than he could give? Despite Dad's abdication from ranch management, he resented Luke plenty for seizing the reins. Luke doubted his father would ever forgive him for selling off the Herefords and investing in Angus cattle.

"Well, we should get back," Shannon was saying. She gestured toward the booth behind her. "I'm supposed to be my friend's assistant this weekend."

Luke looked past her. "You're with Maddie Wittenbauer?"

"Yes. You know Maddie?"

"Only by reputation. But I've worked with her husband, Witt, through Equipped and Empowered Ministries. I lead dog-training classes on weekends."

"Oh, right, the canine program for people in transitional housing. Maddie's told me about Witt's involvement."

"It's proving very successful. I'm glad to be a part of it."

Shannon nodded and smiled, then bent close to her son's ear. "Honey, we need to go. Thank the nice lady for Rowena's treats."

"Thank you!" The little guy waved his bag of goodies.

"By the way," Shannon continued, "if you have any questions about running your booth, Maddie said she'd be happy to share tips."

"That's sweet of her. Thanks!" As they walked away, Anika released a sigh. "Such a cute little boy. His mom's pretty, too, don't you think?"

"Don't start, sis. She's married. Didn't you see the ring?"

"Oh, too bad. I didn't notice. But of course it makes sense." Smile brightening, she went on, "One of these days, though, you'll meet someone special, and then ..."

He knew what she was thinking. If he developed a serious relationship, he'd have less time to keep tabs on his baby sister. Well, that wouldn't be happening anytime soon, so she didn't need to get ideas about playing matchmaker.

Feeling put out again, Luke roughly straightened a tray of treat baggies. "Just don't make a habit of giving products away for free. It's bad for business."

Anika slapped his hand. "It was one baggie. Is that what's got your jeans in a wad?"

"I want to see you succeed, that's all."

She crossed her arms and glared. "You honestly don't think I can succeed on my own, do you?"

"I think you're more than capable. It's just ..." He whipped off his baseball cap and twisted the brim. To say more would mean dredging up the accident that his sister barely remembered, anyway. Truth was, she was better off not knowing the details. "Forget it, okay? What else can I do to help you get set up here?"

"For starters, you can wipe that frown off your face. It's *bad for business.*"

"Touché." Luke slapped on his cap. "Anyway, the fair hasn't even opened yet."

"Whatever. But I don't need your doom-and-gloom vibes rubbing off on me." Anika unlatched the lid on a plastic crate and began laying out a colorful assortment of bandannas, braided collars, and doggy bow ties, every one of which she'd crafted herself.

Jaw clenched, Luke gave himself a mental talking-to. As talented as his sister was, he had no right to suggest she couldn't make a go of selling her pet treats and accessories. She'd come up with the idea all on her own, hadn't she?

It began during her weeks-long stay in a rehab hospital while she recovered from two broken legs, cracked ribs, and a traumatic brain injury. An activity director had brought in bags of fabric scraps and taught patients how to craft simple things like potholders, table runners, tea towels, and such. Anika chose instead to make cute collar accessories for Luke's dog. By the time she got out of rehab, Fletch's wardrobe was twice the size of Luke's and ten times more stylish.

Soon, Anika was adding homemade dog treats to her repertoire. The healthy recipes she concocted became a hit with Luke's obedience classes as well as all the dogs at the animal shelter where he volunteered. The shelter manager had even agreed to keep a few bags on hand for adoptive families to purchase.

This fair would be Anika's first attempt at large-scale sales, and she'd been preparing for weeks to build up her inventory. If the booth turned a sizable profit, Luke hoped he could finally convince his sister to get out from under their dad's roof. Victor Daniels's name still carried some weight in the Montana ranching community, but he'd failed miserably as a husband and father.

The simplicity of Maddie's booth meant setup took little time to complete. While Maddie arranged her drawing supplies, Shannon familiarized herself with the iPad app for tracking sales and accepting payments.

Adding a finer point to a pencil, Maddie asked, "What's the scoop on our neighbors?"

"Her name's Anika Daniels. She seems very sweet." Shannon cast a furtive look toward the guy in the ball cap. He emptied a crate with jerky movements, as if annoyed about something. "Her brother is Luke. He knows Witt."

"Luke Daniels, the dog trainer?" Maddie peered around Shannon. "Cute guy. I haven't met him in person, but Witt speaks highly of him."

"Cute? I guess so." She lowered her voice. "There seems to be tension between Anika and her brother. I got the impression Luke is almost as overprotective as my dad used to be—and still is sometimes."

Maddie scoffed. "Are you sure you aren't reading more into it than there is?"

"With them, or with me and my dad?"

"Both, maybe?" Pressing a hand to Shannon's arm, the older woman smiled. "People express love in different ways. What looks like overprotectiveness could simply be concern."

"Until it's taken to extremes." She glanced behind her, where Tate knelt on the floor and scribbled on the sheet of drawing paper Maddie had given him. Speaking in a whisper, she went on, "You don't know what my dad was like when it was just him and me on the mountain. I felt suffocated, and so incredibly lonely. It's why I couldn't wait to get away and start college."

"I'm not defending your dad, and I'm certainly not saying he made the wisest choices, but when Julia told me what had driven him into isolation, I could almost understand. You were just a baby when your mom died. Left to raise you alone, your dad was heartbroken. Scared. He was only trying to keep you safe."

"I know, I know." Laying aside the iPad, Shannon hunched over and covered her eyes. Her sessions with Dr. Yoshida, both in private and with her father, had helped tremendously in coming to terms with the past and mending their relationship.

Julia had helped, too, offering the motherly love Shannon had been craving. Sharing memories of Steven, they'd taken turns weeping and laughing together. It was both surreal and oddly comforting when Dad and Julia, bonding over their grandson, had fallen in love and married.

At her son's tap on her shoulder, Shannon sat erect. "Hey, Tater-Tot, whatcha got?"

"I drew Weena." He thrust the paper toward her. "She has a bow on her neck, and she's eating a treat."

"I see that. Good job." Shannon tousled Tate's mop of dark hair.

"Can I go show Anika?"

Looking toward the next booth, Shannon frowned. "Not now, sweetie. They're busy setting up their stuff."

"But I'm not coming with you tomorrow. 'Member? Grampy and Grammy are gonna take me and Weena to the cabin."

When Tate turned those big brown eyes on her, there was little she could refuse him. She sighed and turned to Maddie. "Mind if I desert you for a few minutes?"

"Not at all. We're almost done here anyway."

Taking Tate's hand, she led him back to Anika's Paw-fect Picks. When the young woman looked up with a smile, Shannon apologized for interrupting again. "My son wanted to show you his drawing. All your treats and pretty doggy things inspired him."

Anika accepted the paper Tate held out to her. "Oh, Tate," she said with a soft gasp, "this is a wonderful picture. Is this Rowena?"

"Yes, and she's eating the treats you gave us, and I also made a big purple bow." He aimed a stubby finger toward the display rack Luke was working on. "Like that one on top."

"Well, in that case ..." Anika reached around her brother and unclipped the purple polka-dot bow tie from the rack, then handed it to Tate. "You absolutely must take this home to your doggy. Then she'll look just like your picture."

Feeling trapped, Shannon pasted on a smile. "I'll get my wallet. How much—"

"No, it's a gift," Anika stated.

Her brother couldn't hide a scowl.

"Really, we can't accept," Shannon insisted. "The treats are more than enough."

"Please, Mommy?" Tate tugged the hem of her T-shirt. "Weena would look so pretty."

"I'll buy it for you, honey," she murmured, leaning down. "Run back to Miss Maddie's booth and bring me my purse."

When she glanced back at Anika, the girl looked distraught. "I feel terrible now. I never meant to make you feel obligated."

"It's okay. You have some cute things, and I wish I could afford even more." Shannon heaved a shrug. "It's just that my car died this afternoon, and I'm facing a major expense."

"Tate mentioned something about your car breaking down." Anika motioned her brother closer. "Luke, do you think Tobias could help? He's always working on some car or another."

Shannon waved her hand. "Thank you, but I'll figure something out." Tate had returned lugging her shoulder bag. She dug through it for her wallet. "Let me pay for the bow, and we'll get out of your way."

"Fifteen percent off, then." Anika keyed something into her cell phone. "That's the vendor-to-vendor discount."

"But I'm not officially a vendor."

"Close enough," Luke said, a reluctant smile turning up one side of his mouth. He scraped a palm across the stubble darkening his jaw. "Like Anika said, if you need a second opinion, Tobias, our ranch foreman, knows his way around an engine."

They owned a ranch? Luke did have an outdoorsy look about him that working as a dog trainer didn't quite explain. She shrugged. "It's too late for second opinions. I sold it to the mechanic for parts."

"I hope he was fair with you."

"Like I'd have a clue. I was thankful to get anything for the old clunker." Shannon's stomach lurched. The meager check tucked in her wallet wouldn't be much help toward her next vehicle purchase. More to herself, she muttered, "I should be scouring the classifieds and used-car lots for deals."

Anika elbowed her brother and shot him a meaningful stare.

Clearly not getting the message, he cocked a brow and frowned at her from beneath the brim of his cap.

"Luke," she snapped in a hoarse whisper. "What about that old VW you've been helping Tobias restore for the past six months?"

When he shot a wary glance toward Shannon, she looked away and pretended to search for something in her shoulder bag. Even so, she couldn't help overhearing.

"Yeah, it's almost done," Luke murmured, his face turned away. "But I think Tobias may want to hang on to it."

"Seriously?" Anika made no effort to keep her voice down. "What's a cowboy going to do with a Volkswagen Beetle?"

He scoffed. "I have no idea, Ani. But it's not up to me."

Noisily clearing her throat, Shannon held out a ten-dollar bill. "Thank you so much, Anika. I need to get back and help Maddie."

The girl's disgusted glare toward her brother morphed into an apologetic smile for Shannon. "Let me get your change."

While Anika counted out bills and coins from her money box, Luke came closer and crossed his arms. "Sorry if you felt pressured. Anika's got a heart as big as Montana, which is why—"

"Why you have to make sure she doesn't give away the farm—or ranch, as the case may be." Shannon quirked her lips. "It's okay. Really."

"If you need any car advice, though, or just somebody to tell you whether it's a good deal or not, please call. If I can't help, I can always ask our foreman." He tugged a small leather case from his jeans pocket and withdrew a business card. "Here's my number."

The card advertised his dog-training business,

Practically Paw-fect Pets. Shannon released a chuckle. "Clever."

"The name was Anika's idea. I would have gone for something simple, like Luke Daniels, Certified Dog Trainer. But she's my sister. What can I say?"

Heart softening toward the overprotective big brother, Shannon gave in to a grin. "Well, *I'd* say you're pretty lucky to have such a creative and talented sister."

Chapter Two

Luke had cleared his calendar for the weekend, rescheduling an obedience training session and making sure Tobias would be around to oversee things at the ranch. If things at the fair got too hectic and overwhelming for Anika, he wanted to be on hand to help.

He hated that almost four years later, she still suffered lingering effects from the accident. Hard as she fought not to give in to the occasional brain fog, migraines, and muscle stiffness, they could sneak up on her without warning and sideline her for days. Too much stress only increased the likelihood.

Pulling under the portico at the main house early Saturday morning, Luke glimpsed his dad pass the front windows. In no mood to deal with the man, he hoped Anika had seen him drive up and would be right out. Depending on traffic, the drive into Missoula could take almost an hour. They'd be pushing it to get there by eight o'clock to finish getting set up before the fair opened at nine.

He waited five minutes, and when Anika didn't show, he sent her a text.

> Out front. Don't want to be late for the big event, do you?

Another five minutes went by. Still no sign of his sister. Guess he'd have to go in and get her.

This wasn't his home anymore—a few years ago, he'd had a cabin built for himself on the ranch. He knocked, waited a few seconds, then rapped harder. "Anika? You coming?"

The door whooshed open, and Luke came face-to-face with his father. "She's in bed with another headache."

"What?" Luke shoved past. "Why didn't you call me?"

"I've only been up a few minutes and found her like that." Dad stomped after Luke as he headed upstairs to Anika's room. "She was up pretty late last night, still working at her sewing machine when I went to bed at two a.m."

"And you didn't stop her? You know what happens when she doesn't get enough sleep." No need to ask what his father was doing up in the wee hours of the morning. Most likely dozing in his recliner after polishing off another six-pack or bottle of Scotch.

Reaching his sister's bedside, Luke eased down on the mattress and brushed tangled strands of hair off her face. "Ani?" he whispered. "Did you take your meds?"

"Mm-hmm." A tear slipped from beneath her closed lids. She covered her eyes with her arm and mumbled, "Sorry. So sorry."

"It's okay, babe. Get some sleep. I'll check on you later."

Rising, Luke glimpsed the plastic crate next to Anika's sewing machine. Another couple dozen fabric bow ties and bandannas were piled inside. With a sad shake of his head, he scooped up the crate. After all the work his sister had put into getting ready for the fair, the least he could do was cover for her.

He ignored his father's crossed-arm stance and headed to the front door. When Dad grabbed his Stetson and acted as if he meant to follow Luke out, he spun around and blocked his path. "Uh-uh. You need to stay here with Anika."

"I'm meeting some pals in Elk Valley for breakfast."

"Call and tell them you have a family emergency."

His dad huffed. "Who died and made you king?"

Luke had no answer for that. None that would get through to his father, anyway. Marching down the porch steps to his truck, he waved without looking back. "Just do it."

A few minutes past eight, Luke arrived at his sister's booth and began folding the sheets they'd covered the merchandise with before leaving yesterday. One stall over, Maddie Wittenbauer and ... Shannon, if he remembered right, were getting organized for the day. Since he was on his own, about all he had time for was a brief smile and nod.

He peered into the crate of bows and bandannas Anika had stayed up half the night to complete and got angry all over again. Why'd she do this to herself? Worse, why did their father let her? All he could do now was hope for a good day in sales so that his sister's stubborn determination wouldn't be for nothing.

He already blamed himself for pushing her to give this a try.

When the fair opened at nine, shoppers began streaming in—mostly browsers at first, which gave Luke a little time to get familiar with the routine. Greet the customers, talk up the products, smile a lot. That last one was the hardest, especially with his brain ping-ponging between worrying about Anika and the urge to slap some sense into their clueless father.

Over the next hour, business steadily picked up. As Luke handed a customer her purchases and receipt, he looked up to find three more shoppers vying for his attention. They didn't seem to care that they were talking over each other or that he couldn't get a word in edgewise to answer their questions.

"Excuse me ... excuse me, please." One sharp female voice—Shannon's, he realized—cut through the noisy chatter. "Who was here first?"

"Um, I think I was," said the lady with the big green tote.

Luke had no choice but to make room as Shannon scooted next to him behind the table. She nodded toward the redhead with twin girls clinging to each arm. "She's next, I think."

He gaped. "What are you doing?"

"Lending a hand. Isn't it obvious?" Shannon turned her attention to Ms. Green Tote. "What kind of dog are you shopping for, ma'am? We have accessories in all sizes."

Luke had to drag his attention off his impromptu assistant long enough to help Twin Mom pick out color-coordinated bandannas for the two Yorkies she and her daughters described to him in minute detail. They purchased four bags of mini treats as well.

He finished with his customer about the same time as Shannon, after which they segued to the next two shoppers in line. The pace continued almost nonstop for the next forty-five minutes, which boded well for Anika's profit margin but had Luke's head spinning. He wasn't sure how he'd have managed if Shannon hadn't appeared out of nowhere to rescue him.

He said as much when at last they had a few minutes' respite.

Closing the lid on the cashbox, she smirked. "I could see you were about to be in over your head."

"Retail sales are definitely not my thing." He pulled over a chair and collapsed onto it, then took a long swig from his insulated water bottle. "Aren't you supposed to be Maddie's assistant this weekend?"

"I am. But her husband's here now, and she didn't need both of us."

Looking over his shoulder, Luke gave Witt a quick wave. "Never even noticed him until now."

"Where's your sister?" Shannon asked as she straightened the bows on a display rack. "She seemed so excited about her first arts and crafts fair."

"*Too* excited—that's the problem." Luke leaned forward, elbows on his thighs. "She must have been concerned about running out of inventory and stayed up way too late sewing last night. She ended up with a migraine and couldn't get out of bed this morning."

"That's awful. Does she get those often?"

"Ever since the accident, yes."

"Accident?"

"A bad auto wreck a few years ago." Luke clenched his jaw. "If she makes it in later, please don't bring it up with her. It's a tough subject."

"Of course." Twisting her wedding ring, Shannon looked away. "I understand, more than you know."

"Did you—I mean, it's none of my business, but—"

"Yes," she murmured, her lips tight. "That's how I lost my husband."

Her *husband?* He winced. "I'm sorry."

Before he could think of what else to say, more shoppers arrived. Shannon pasted on a smile and helped a silver-haired woman select a bag of treats and a bright red braided collar for her beagle. Luke had his hands full with a trio of tittering teenagers who couldn't pick between bow ties and bandannas, and then asked if they could try samples of the dog treats.

It took him a minute to realize the girls wanted an actual taste for themselves. But since Anika used only quality ingredients, why not? The girls agreed the treats were oaty-peanut-buttery and flavorful, and they each bought a bag.

By the time they finished with that round of customers, it was nearing the noon hour. Witt ambled over to say hello. "Maddie told me she saw you here yesterday setting up with your sister."

"Yeah, she wasn't feeling well this morning. I appreciate you sparing Shannon to lend me a hand."

"Not a problem. The handyman job I had scheduled for this afternoon got canceled. I'll be able to stick around." The fifty-something gentleman turned to Shannon. "That is, if you're okay bailing this guy out for the rest of the day. I can vouch for his character," he added with a wink.

"I don't mind." She shrugged. "I worked my way through college as a clerk in a department store. This is right up my alley."

Luke nodded appreciatively. "That explains your natural way with customers. Maybe you can teach me a thing or two."

A pink flush crept up Shannon's cheeks. The way she smiled and dipped her chin evoked an unexpected twinge in Luke's belly, a feeling he hadn't experienced since he'd kissed his date goodnight after high school senior prom.

Not that he hadn't had other relationships since then, although none recently. And *definitely* none he could recall that had made his heart race with quite the same first-crush intensity.

Crush? At thirty years old? Uh, no. Not happening.

He caught Witt studying him, a funny gleam in his eye and a grin spreading across his face. The man's lips twitched as he schooled his features. "I'm heading over to the snack bar to order grilled chicken wraps for Maddie and me. Can I bring y'all back anything?"

"That'd be great." Glad for the distraction, Luke took a twenty-dollar bill from the cashbox and handed it to Witt. "I'll take one of those chicken wraps. Shannon, what sounds good to you? My treat for bailing me out."

"Thanks. The same is fine." She blushed again, but this time with an expression that implied more regret than self-consciousness.

Snippets of yesterday's conversation came back— Shannon's cash flow problems and her broken-down car. Plus, she was raising that cute little kid, apparently as a single mom.

Those issues alone should be enough to quell any sparks of attraction. What with overseeing Fox Pass Ranch, holding dog-training classes, and doing his best to look after his baby sister, didn't Luke have enough on his plate already?

Shannon hadn't expected Luke to buy her lunch.

For that matter, she hadn't expected to spend almost the entire morning working in his sister's booth instead of Maddie's. No question he'd needed her help. Shannon hated to imagine the disaster that would have ensued if Witt's arrival hadn't freed her to assist.

The shopping frenzy had tapered off. While they waited for Witt to return with their sandwiches, Shannon excused herself for a much-needed trip to the ladies' room. After washing up, she stepped outside the building and texted her dad to see how Tate was doing. With cell service on the mountain too weak for most voice calls, phoning was futile. Today, she didn't mind so much, because a text would make it easier to avoid bringing up her car situation. Good thing Tate had been too sleepy to say anything last night when Dad and Julia had come to town to pick him up.

She opened the message window and typed:

> How's it going? Having a fun day?

A few seconds later, her dad replied:

> Tater-Tot and Rowena are playing tag in the yard. BTW, what's up with your car? Tate said it went bye-bye???

Great. Naturally, her little boy couldn't wait to regale his grandparents with yesterday's drama. She chose her next words carefully.

> Not worth repairing, but the mechanic bought it for parts. We'll be fine. Give Tate a hug for me. Gotta get back to the fair!

She tucked the phone in her pocket and hurried inside. There'd be time enough later for her father to pepper her with questions and try to throw money her way. Much as she hated the idea, if a decent moonlighting job didn't materialize soon, she might have to accept.

Witt had just dropped off the chicken wraps, along with two lemonades. As she settled into a chair, Luke asked, "Everything okay?"

"Yes, fine." Shannon peeled back the waxy paper around her wrap.

"It's just ... for a minute there, you looked bothered about something."

Was she that easy to read? Trying for a smile, she took a quick sip from her drink. "I needed to get some fresh air and check on my son. His grandparents are looking after him this weekend, and I already miss him."

Luke nodded. After swallowing a few bites, he said, "Raising your little boy alone can't be easy. It's good you have family close by."

"They help a lot." More than she wished sometimes. "Do you and Anika have family in the area?"

"Anika lives with our dad at the ranch. I have my own place on the property." The downward drift of his gaze implied he and his father didn't have the best relationship. After a sip of lemonade, he went on, "Our mom passed away a few months after Anika's accident."

"That's too bad." She sighed and picked at a piece of lettuce poking out from the tortilla. "I never really knew my mother. She was killed when I was a baby."

Brows lifting, Luke tilted his head. "Killed?"

"There was a robbery at the law office where she and my dad worked. Losing her is why my dad chucked city life and moved us into the mountains to live off the grid."

"Wow."

Shannon snorted. "Yeah. Wow."

She hadn't planned on opening up about her past to a virtual stranger, but her instincts, combined with Witt's seal of approval, told her Luke could be trusted. That maybe he could even relate.

Conversation paused while browsers slowed to look over the merchandise. They didn't appear interested and soon moved on.

After another few minutes, Luke asked, "How long did you live off-grid?"

"Until I could finally escape to college. That's where—"

"Luke, I'm so, so, *so* sorry!" Anika breezed in and wrapped her arms around Luke's neck from behind. Her long ash-brown hair cascaded across his shoulder. She looked pale behind big, round sunglasses. "Thank you from the bottom of my heart."

"Hey, it's okay." He set aside the remains of his lunch and stood to face her. "How's the headache? Are you feeling better?"

Removing her sunglasses, she motioned with them toward the display table. "Better enough to feel absolutely horrible about leaving all this to you." Turning to Shannon, she gave her a quick hug. "You've been helping? How can I ever thank you?"

"No thanks necessary. Your brother was concerned about you."

Anika puffed out a sharp breath. "What else is new?"

The building was humming with a fresh influx of shoppers. With Anika here, Shannon wasn't sure she'd still be needed. "Are you feeling up to taking over, or would you like me to stay?"

"I appreciate the offer, but this was supposed to be my

thing, and I'd better take responsibility." Anika glanced around with a thoughtful frown. "I think we'll be okay."

She sounded more like she was trying to convince herself, but Shannon knew all about how that felt. "All right, then. I'll be over at Maddie's booth if things get really busy."

With another heartfelt thank you, Anika pressed a large bag of dog treats into Shannon's hand. "For Tate to give Rowena."

Shannon surmised it would be pointless to refuse. "He'll be thrilled."

Two chatty older women approached, and with Anika turning on the sales charm, Shannon excused herself and edged around the table.

She'd taken only a few steps when Luke caught up with her. "You saved my bacon today. When you're ready to go car shopping, I hope you'll take me up on my offer to assist."

"That's totally unnecessary."

"Please, it's the absolute least I can do."

She gnawed her lower lip. Getting car advice from someone other than her overprotective dad would certainly make the process less painful. "I need to do something quickly, because I've got to have transportation for work."

"Can you make do until Monday afternoon?"

"I think so." Dorothy and Martin Frasier, Julia's parents, had retired from their veterinary practice and had been watching Tate while Shannon worked as a receptionist at the clinic. Dorothy wouldn't mind giving her a ride for a day or two. "I usually work until five, but I'll see if I can get off a few minutes early."

"Great. Let me know when, and I can pick you up."

Shannon furrowed her brow. "Are you sure? I mean, with the ranch and your dog classes and all ..."

"I can be flexible. That's one perk of being my own boss."

The idea of such freedom made Shannon envious. Would she ever be free to make her own choices and live life on her terms? Before Steven's death, she'd been working toward a journalism degree with visions of traveling the world while writing stories, articles, and entire books about her experiences.

But after Steven's death at the start of her senior year, she'd dropped out of college and never went back. Nothing had mattered anymore. Even after Tate was born, she'd struggled to cope, which led to those six long months under a doctor's care in a mental health facility. Now here she was, almost back where she started, and with nothing to show for the big dreams only Steven had ever known about.

Luke tilted his head. "Was it something I said?"

Startled, she forced a light laugh. "My mind was wandering, that's all." She gestured over her shoulder. "I should see if Maddie needs me. Witt could probably use a break."

"Right. And I should help Anika." He inched backward a couple of steps. "You have my number. Text me about Monday, okay?"

"I will. Thanks."

Chapter Three

"Yes, ma'am, the bow ties come in three different sizes and are fully adjustable." Anika hid a grimace as another stab of pain pierced her right temple.

She'd stretched the truth a bit when she'd told her brother she was feeling much better. Though the headaches waxed and waned, she'd rarely been completely pain-free since awakening from a coma two weeks after the accident.

The migraine had subsided enough by late morning that guilt had set in for leaving Luke to manage her booth. Ignoring the throbbing as best she could, she'd showered and dressed. Dad had offered to heat a can of soup, but her stomach rebelled at the idea. After forcing down a few saltines, she'd headed to the community center.

Three hours later, her leg muscles ached from standing on the hard floor all afternoon, and she was wishing for that bowl of soup.

The frowning customer held up the small bow tie and compared it to the medium. "Fritzie is very persnickety. He won't be happy unless it fits just right."

The *dog* was persnickety? Anika pressed a finger to her lips. "Tell you what. I'll only charge you for one, but you can take both sizes and try them on Fritzie. I'll be here again tomorrow afternoon, and you can return whichever one you—I mean, *he* doesn't care for."

"Aren't you the sweetest thing!" The woman patted Anika's hand. "I wish more salespeople were as accommodating as you. I'll take the turquoise in a small and a medium. Since I drive right by here on my way home from church, that'll work out just fine."

Handing the woman her purchase, Anika sensed her brother's disapproval. As her customer walked away, she muttered, "Don't say it."

"Don't say what?" Luke took a few more bows and bandannas from the crate and began replacing the ones recently sold.

"That I'm an easy mark. That giving stuff away is bad for business." She snatched a bow tie out of his hand and clipped it onto the display rack. "You don't believe she'll return the one that doesn't fit, do you?"

"I didn't say that."

"But you thought it."

"Anika ..." He got that look on his face, the one she despised. The one that meant he didn't think she could make competent decisions about her own life.

Holding back angry tears, she busied herself straightening bills in the cashbox. "No need for you to stick around. I've got it from here. We close in an hour anyway."

"Anika," Luke said, more firmly this time. Coming up behind her, he set his hands on her shoulders. "I'm sorry. This is your business. I heard your stomach growling. If I bring you a giant pretzel from the concession stand, can I stay?"

She glowered at him. "Only if you keep your critical comments to yourself and the judgment off your face."

He crossed his heart, then raised one hand, palm outward. "I will do my very best."

She wasn't sure how long his commitment would last, but she loved that he intended to try. "Just hurry back with my pretzel. I'd like a ginger ale, too, if they have some."

Saluting, he sped down the aisle.

Luke had always been there for her, and maybe she didn't appreciate him enough. He'd been the one to sit at her hospital bedside hour after hour, day after day, week after week. Mom came when she felt up to it, but the lupus drained her both physically and mentally. She'd passed away only a few months later.

As for Dad? He knew cattle and horses, no question about it. Relationships? Not so much. Grandpa Daniels had been that way, too, and likely Dad had learned nothing different. Mom must have seen something in him worth loving, though. Too bad he rarely showed that side to his kids, instead withdrawing whenever life got too hard to handle.

The flow of shoppers ebbed as closing time neared. After devouring her snack, Anika neatened and replenished the product displays to prepare for tomorrow, while Luke tallied the profits. She was almost afraid to ask for the results, but the jingle of coins and the rustle of bills and receipt copies sounded reassuring.

When a loudspeaker announcement informed stragglers that doors would close in five minutes, Anika exhaled with relief. She hadn't put in a full day but was already exhausted. Part of it she could blame on the lingering headache, but even more on anxiety about attempting this new venture.

Arms wrapped around one of the folded sheets for covering the display table, she plopped into a chair. "I can't stand the suspense. How'd we do?"

"Minus what we had in the till to make change ..." He narrowed one eye, his mouth quirking into a grin. "We ended the day with three hundred eighty-seven dollars and fifty cents."

"Really? That much?" All thoughts of fatigue vanishing, Anika felt like she could hyperventilate. "I'll have to wait until I get home to check the exact figures, but I'm certain I didn't spend anywhere near that amount on materials and supplies."

"Way to go, Ani." Luke pulled her into a one-armed hug. "You did it."

"*You* did most of it today—the selling part, anyway. I hate to think what would have happened if you hadn't covered for me this morning."

"I had help, don't forget."

"Yes, I'm glad." Anika glanced past her brother to where Shannon and Witt were helping Maddie close for the day. "Did you two have a chance to get to know each other?"

"Some, when we weren't busy with customers." Luke shut the cashbox, then helped Anika unfold the sheet and spread it over the table.

"And?" Anika cast him a *tell me more* look.

"And ... what?"

Anika waved as Shannon walked out with Maddie and Witt. When they were out of earshot, she turned back to her brother. "Oh, come on, Luke, she must have told you something about herself."

"A little. She's a single mom." He shifted, a frown forming. "Her husband passed away."

Guilt skewered her for the momentary thrill of hope. "Oh, how sad. How long ago?"

"She didn't say, and I didn't ask." With the table covered, Luke took out another sheet to drape over the standing displays. "Pretty sure you have plenty of merch left for tomorrow. I'd better not hear you stayed up late again doing more sewing or baking."

"No worries," she murmured. This morning's vicious migraine and the weariness in her limbs were more than enough incentive to get a decent night's sleep.

Chapter Four

On Sunday morning, a colicky horse required Luke's attention, providing a timely excuse to decline Anika's repeated invitations to go to church with her. While their mom was alive, he'd been a regular at Larchwood Glen Fellowship, a small congregation about halfway between Elk Valley and Missoula. After Mom died, he'd drifted away and couldn't seem to find his way back.

Leaving the recovering horse in Tobias's care, Luke arrived at the fair venue shortly before noon. He was relieved to find his sister looking much more bright-eyed than yesterday.

She offered a perky smile as she added more treat baggies to a tray. "You missed a good message today. The pastor preached on how much we need the family of believers to hold us accountable and encourage us in our faith."

Luke knew how these conversations always went, and he didn't feel like getting into it. He set his backpack on a chair. "I brought my computer today. I started a spread-sheet to help you track income and expenses."

"More micromanaging. Can't wait." She tipped her head toward the next booth. "Shannon's here with Maddie again. You should go over and say hi."

He'd chosen a different path through the building to avoid passing Maddie's booth. Why, he wasn't sure. Maybe because he could tell his sister was hoping something might develop between him and Shannon?

More likely, because he'd decided his initial spark of interest in the attractive young mom was a bad idea.

Interest he was pretty sure she didn't return. No matter how long it had been since she'd lost her husband, he sensed she was still grieving.

Still, they'd sort of made a date to go car shopping. Which was not a *date*-date by any stretch of the imagination. But it would only be polite to say hello.

Stifling a sigh, he strode over. "Hey, how's it going?"

Maddie answered since Shannon was busy straightening the cloth over the small table at the back. "Hi, Luke. We had a great day yesterday. How about you and Anika?"

"Not bad for our first experience. At least Anika's better enough to get in on some of the *fun*." He surrounded the last word with air quotes.

Maddie laughed. "I understand. Witt had to work at convincing me to try selling my pet portraits at a fair."

"Speaking of Witt, he didn't join you today?"

"We give our sanctuary volunteers Sundays off, so he's taking care of things at the kennel."

Shannon joined Maddie at the front table. "Anika looks like she's feeling much better today."

"She is." Luke tried to ignore the tingling in his chest. Shannon seemed more relaxed today, not nearly as stressed as when he'd first met her on Friday evening. He edged closer. "How are things with you?"

"More hopeful, I think. Tate's great-grandparents picked us up for church this morning, and the pastor's message helped me focus on God's mercies instead of my problems."

"That's ... good." Apparently, the area pastors had conspired to make sure Luke got the message, whether he wanted it or not. "I'd better get back before the shopping frenzy begins."

"Right. I hope you and Anika have another successful day."

"You, too."

Slipping behind Anika's table, he sank into a chair and pressed his fists into his eye sockets.

"What's wrong?" His sister patted his shoulder. "It looked like you and Shannon were having a pleasant conversation."

"We were, I guess." With a sigh, he straightened. "But you both seem determined to remind me how far I've drifted from God."

"I know you've been struggling since Mom died."

"It's been ... hard." Rising, he looked around for something to busy himself with. After uncovering the displays, Anika had tossed the sheets into a crate. He pulled out a sheet and attempted to fold it properly.

Anika took one end from him and matched up the corners. "It's only hard because you let it be. How do you think I've made it this far? Without God, I couldn't have survived any of what we've been through these past few years."

"I admire your faith, I truly do. But I—"

An announcement interrupted him. "Doors are opening. Vendors, please man your booths."

He finished folding the sheet and laid it in the crate. "Here we go. You ready?"

Lips pursed, his sister studied him for a moment. Just like it used to be with Mom, Anika didn't have to say anything to get her point across: *We'll take this up again later. I'm not letting you off the hook.*

He didn't really want to be let off the hook. He knew he needed God, but he didn't care to be lectured or guilted into getting his faith act together. In that respect, he was probably a lot more like his dad than he wanted to admit.

The afternoon brought a fresh surge of shoppers, which was both rewarding and worrisome as Anika's stock dwindled. The next time she signed up for a fair booth, she'd better start much earlier building up her inventory—and as profitable as this event was turning out, he hoped there *would* be a next time.

It'd be great if one of these days Anika mustered the resources to open her own shop—if not in Missoula, then in one of the smaller surrounding towns where rent might be cheaper. Luke would do just about anything to help her rebuild the life the accident had robbed her of.

The one thing he *didn't* want was to see her languishing under their dad's roof, essentially nothing more than his housekeeper, secretary, cook, companion, and—if he continued drinking himself to death—full-time caregiver.

Anika deserved more. So much more.

* * *

Once the fair shut down, Shannon was eager to get home. Dad and Julia should be there with Tate by now, and she could hardly wait to wrap her arms around her son and tell him how much she'd missed him.

Except she'd also have to face her father's interrogation about the car. After working at the fair all weekend, she wasn't sure she could scrape up the energy.

When Maddie dropped off Shannon a few minutes after six, her dad's maroon truck sat in the driveway. She groaned. "I'm already dreading how I'm going to turn down my dad's bailout."

Maddie patted her arm. "Don't be too quick to say no. He loves you, and you need help. Remember, this is only a temporary setback."

"Temporary? How about continual?" The measure of hope she'd gained at worship that morning was fading.

"I won't hear that kind of talk," Maddie chided. "'There is a time for everything, and a season for every activity under the heavens.' You're in a season of leaning on others, but that will change someday. Count on it."

Shannon knew the passage from Ecclesiastes well. "I know you're right." She released a long sigh. "And by the way, thank you for the money. I wasn't expecting anything."

After Maddie had tallied her receipts, she'd handed Shannon $200 from the cashbox. "You put in a solid day and a half, most of it standing on your feet, plus helping me set up on Friday. Need I quote the verse about the worker deserving his—or, in your case, *her*—wages?"

"Yes, but I spent a good part of yesterday in Anika's booth."

"No matter. Witt could easily have been called away on an emergency handyman call. I was thankful to know you were there if I needed you."

Shannon stretched her arms toward Maddie for a hug.

"The better I get to know you, the more I understand why you're Julia's best friend."

"I hope you consider me your friend, too." Maddie gave her a nudge. "Now, go on inside and hug that sweet little boy you haven't seen all weekend."

After another burst of profuse thanks, Shannon climbed from the vehicle. Steeling herself, she marched up the walk to the front door.

Before she could insert her key in the lock, a little boy's screech and the scramble of dog toenails reached her ears. The door burst open and Tate barreled into her, while Rowena barked and pranced in circles around them. Julia's two frisky dachshunds, Daisy and Dash, made their presence known as well.

"Mommy, did you have fun? Did Miss Maddie draw lots of doggy pictures? Did Miss Anika give you any more presents for Weena?"

Shannon's laughter rang as she hefted her son to her hip. Goodness, he was growing so fast! "I'll tell you all about it, I promise. How about after we go inside? Because I smell pizza, and I'm starved."

"We figured you wouldn't feel like cooking." Julia ushered Shannon through the door. "Your dad's just bringing it out of the oven."

"Wonderful. Let me wash up, and I'll be right there." Shannon lowered Tate to the floor, then hurried to the bathroom to freshen up, take out her scrunchie, and run a brush through her hair. She used those moments to inhale a few steadying breaths and to anchor her thoughts in the scriptural wisdom Maddie had shared in the car.

This is only for a season ... only for a season ...

Gathered with her family at the table while they ate, she enjoyed another brief reprieve from her dad's questions.

Between bites, Tate chattered about everything he'd done and seen while at Grampy and Grammy's mountain cabin over the weekend.

Half an hour later, one lone slice of pepperoni lay congealing on the pizza pan. Shannon had downed at least four hefty slices, along with two tall glasses of iced tea. When Tate's head began to bob, she scooped him up and carried him to the bathroom for a quick cleanup. Getting him into his jammies and tucked in for the night gave her that much more time to gear up for the conversation with her dad.

She returned to the kitchen, where her father and Julia had just finished loading the dishwasher. "Thanks again for supper," she said. "I was hungrier than I thought."

"Room for ice cream?" Dad asked. "We brought a carton of pecan praline for dessert."

"Maybe later. Right now, I'm stuffed." She plopped into a chair. Deciding to be proactive, she swallowed and said, "Look, I know you're dying to ask me about the car. Let's get it over with."

Dad and Julia exchanged glances as they joined her at the table. "You've been driving that pile of junk forever," Dad said. "What happened, exactly?"

She described leaving the dentist's on Friday when the car began making grinding noises and smoke poured from under the hood. "It was sputtering and jerking so badly that I drove straight to the mechanic."

Julia stroked Shannon's arm. "That must have been scary. Thank goodness you and Tate made it there safely."

Shannon agreed. With a sigh, she went on, "The repairs would have cost more than replacing the car, but he was kind enough to buy it for parts. Now I need to find something else. Something I can afford."

"But something reliable." Her father frowned and massaged his jaw. "I never liked the idea of you and Tate riding around in that old rust bucket. What if you'd broken down on the interstate ... or gotten stranded in a risky part of town?"

"We didn't. As always, God was watching over us." She said it more to remind herself—just as He watched over them now, meeting their every need.

Even if that comes as another handout from your father?

"I can go car shopping with you in the morning," Dad said. "In fact, we're prepared to stay the night since Julia has to work at the clinic tomorrow anyway. I've already arranged with the Vernons to tend the livestock and check on things at the cabin."

"You're welcome to spend the night, of course. But Dylan is getting a root canal tomorrow, which means I'll be on my own at the reception desk for most of the day. Anyway," Shannon went on, "a ... a friend has already offered to look at cars with me. He has some contacts, and—"

"*He?*" The outburst came from Dad and Julia in unison.

Shannon couldn't mistake the hopeful surprise on their faces. She locked her arms across her chest. "It isn't what you're thinking. Luke is an acquaintance of Witt's. He trains dogs for the Equipped and Empowered Ministries program. His sister had a booth at the arts and crafts fair next to Maddie's."

"Oh. That's nice." Julia's smile softened. Voice cracking, she went on, "But you know it would be okay for you to ... to ..."

"I do know, and thank you for saying so." Shannon twisted in her chair to offer Julia a grateful hug. As Steven's mother, she still grieved, too. Straightening, Shannon used her knuckle to brush away an escaping tear. "I'm not sure I'll ever be ready to move on. For now, I only hope to support my son and myself as best I can."

"And you're doing a great job," Julia stated, flicking away moisture from the hollows alongside her nose.

"Absolutely." Her dad cleared his throat. "Okay, if you'd rather your friend help you find a car, I understand. But safety and reliability should be your top priority, no matter the cost. Find something you like, and I'll take care of it."

"Dad, you can't keep doing this." She seized his hand and cast him a pleading look. "Give me a chance to handle things myself."

"But—"

"I mean it. I promise I'll come to you if necessary, but only after I've done what I can on my own."

Her father glanced at Julia, then nodded. "Can't argue with that."

"Thank you." She pushed up from her chair. "And now I'm off to bed. My six a.m. alarm will come all too soon."

Chapter Five

After the hectic weekend, Luke welcomed a quiet day—even if he needed to spend it at his computer. By noon, he'd entered most of last week's financials into the ranching software. Tobias had done a good job of staying within budget on feed expenses. Plus on Saturday, the astute foreman had successfully wrapped up negotiations for purchasing the prize-winning Angus bull they'd had their eye on.

Necessary or not, desk work had to be the most tedious job in the universe. When Luke stood from his desk to ease the kinks out of his back, Fletch read the signals. The black-and-white border collie pranced over and dropped a Frisbee at Luke's feet, then settled on his haunches and looked up expectantly.

"I agree, time to get off my you-know-what." Luke snatched up the plastic disc and headed out the back door.

He'd built his four-room log cabin on the far side of the horse barn from the main house. It put distance between him and his father but was close enough that he could pop in on Anika regularly. The backyard sloped down to a stand of towering cottonwood trees along a rippling creek. A few early orange-gold leaves peeked through the green, a sign that shorter days and cooler weather would soon arrive.

Above the tree canopy to the north, a growing mass of gray clouds suggested a front could be on the way. Luke hoped any precipitation would hold off until tonight and wouldn't interfere with taking Shannon car shopping.

At the thought of seeing her again, his stomach flipped. How many times did he have to remind himself that he was only helping a new friend?

Fletch pranced and let out a high-pitched bark.

"Okay, okay." He cocked his arm and let the Frisbee fly.

Already halfway across the yard, the dog locked his gaze on the disc and matched its speed. In one graceful leap, he caught the disc in his teeth, then circled back, ready for another throw.

Luke obliged. Over, and over, and over. His arm grew tired long before Fletch ran out of steam. It was a relief when the buzz of his cell phone interrupted the game with a text from Shannon.

> If we're still on, I can leave work at 3:30.
> No worries if something else has
> come up.

There went those confounded butterflies again. Maybe it would be wiser all around if he invented an excuse not to meet her.

But no, he wasn't the type to renege on an agreement.

> No prob. Text me your location. I'll be
> there to pick you up at 3:30 sharp.

She replied she worked at Frasier Veterinary Clinic and included the street address. He'd taken Fletch there a while back when the dog had injured his paw at a Frisbee-dog demonstration in Missoula. The small-animal vet Luke normally used in Frenchtown was more convenient, but the ridiculous thought suddenly came to him that if he transferred Fletch's records to the Frasier clinic, he'd have more opportunities to see Shannon.

No. His responsibilities to the ranch and his sister left no room for romance. Any chance for his own happiness would remain on hold until Anika was ready to spread her wings and no longer felt tethered to their father.

He returned to the cabin and threw together a ham sandwich, then added a pickle spear and a pile of sour-cream-and-onion potato chips to his plate. Grabbing a bottled iced tea from the fridge, he carried his lunch to his desk. He wanted to research an idea he'd been mulling over.

An idea his cattle-breeding father would absolutely hate.

Fletch had already proven his worth around the ranch as a cattle dog and was accumulating points in Mountain States Stockdog Association cattle-herding competitions. Next, Luke wanted to invest in a small herd of sheep to gain even more experience. If Fletch continued moving up in the rankings, Luke hoped to eventually branch out from teaching dog obedience classes and open a school here on the ranch to train herding dogs and their handlers.

When his phone alarm chimed at 2:30, he added a bookmark to the website he'd been perusing and then shut down his computer. He saw no reason not to take Fletch along for the ride, and the two of them climbed into Luke's truck. For about five seconds, he wished he'd allowed enough time to run the dirty blue RAM 1500 through a carwash and vacuum Fletch's dog hair off the seats and floorboards, but too late now.

Forty-five minutes later, he parked outside Frasier Veterinary Clinic. After instructing Fletch to hop over to the rear seat, he marched inside.

Shannon stood behind the reception counter. She glanced up with a tentative smile as she ended a phone call and replaced the receiver. "I'll let the office manager know I'm leaving. Be right back."

She disappeared through an inner door, and Luke ambled over to the seating area. In the staff photo on the opposite wall, he recognized Dr. Julia Frasier as the vet who'd treated Fletch's paw. She also took care of the Wittenbauers' dogs, and Witt said once that she'd cut back on her hours after getting married a couple of years ago.

Shannon returned with a light sweater and shoulder bag. As a man with graying sideburns took her position behind the front desk, she called, "Thank you, Brad. See you tomorrow."

"Good luck car shopping," the man replied.

On the way out, Luke said, "My dog's with me. Hope you don't mind."

"Not at all. I can't wait to meet him. Or is it a her?"

"He's a he. Name's Fletch." They reached Luke's truck. He opened the passenger door, then brushed a few dog hairs off the seat.

"That's okay, I'm used to it," Shannon said as she climbed in. "For a dog as big as she is, Rowena doesn't shed horribly, but my vacuum cleaner gets a workout every weekend."

"Tell me about it," Luke said with a snort. "Fletch, say hi to Shannon."

The dog raised his right foreleg and pawed the air in a semblance of a wave.

Looking over her shoulder, Shannon laughed. "Hi to you, too. Nice to meet you, Fletch."

Easy on the eyes, pitching in like nobody's business on Saturday when he was drowning in customers, and a dog person to boot. Luke liked this woman more and more.

And that was dangerous.

Shannon had no reason to feel ill at ease in Luke's company, but she couldn't help herself. It was almost a blessing that he'd brought his dog along. Fletch gave her something to focus on besides the attractive guy behind the wheel, something neutral they could talk about while keeping the conversation from drifting too far into personal areas.

Quite the contrast with how comfortable she'd felt with Luke on Saturday, when she'd revealed things about her life she rarely mentioned to anyone except family or her therapist ... and sometimes, not even to them.

Today felt different somehow. She sensed hesitation in Luke as well, perhaps because they were meeting for the first time away from the pandemonium of the arts and crafts fair. There, they'd shared the common goals of making sales and satisfying customers.

This felt ... too much like a date?

Only it wasn't. Not in any way, shape, or form. No matter that Julia had given her blessing for Shannon to move on after losing Steven. She still missed him something fierce, and she'd always regret that he hadn't lived to see his son's birth and would never watch their precious little boy grow up.

"Everything okay?"

Luke's question startled her from her thoughts. "Just

wondering where we're headed. You said you had some car contacts."

"I do. But I'd also like you to look at the VW Beetle Anika mentioned on Friday. I checked with Tobias, our ranch foreman. He has a few minor fixes to make, and then it'll be ready to go."

"Oh. I thought you said he may want to keep it."

Luke scoffed. "Tobias has zero use for a little car like that. When I told him about your situation, he said he'd be willing to let it go for a fair price."

"It'd have to be a whole lot better than *fair* for me to afford it." She hugged herself and stared straight ahead.

"He isn't looking to get rich off the deal. He just enjoys working on cars."

Shannon wasn't in a position to be choosy. "All right, guess it can't hurt to look."

"I was hoping you'd say that. Figured you'd rather not ride all the way out to the ranch to see it, so Tobias is bringing the car to town. He's supposed to meet us at four thirty outside the venue where the arts and crafts fair was held."

"That's very nice of him." She sniffed. "And you."

"No problem. In the meantime, we can check out the deals at a used-car lot where I know the owner."

A prickle worked its way up Shannon's spine. The last thing she needed was to be hustled by a slick car salesperson who thought he could take advantage of a clueless female. "How do you know the owner?"

"Bruce Chapman is an old family friend. He and his wife are Anika's godparents." Luke briefly looked away as he made a left turn. "He's a straight shooter. No worries."

They arrived at a concrete-paved lot, and Luke steered between a row of vehicles with big green price tags on the windshields. He braked in front of a low stucco building and shifted into park.

"There's Bruce now," he said as a plump, grandfatherly looking man slapped on a felt cowboy hat and marched out to greet them. "If he goes in for a hug, don't let it scare you. He's just that kind of guy."

"Thanks for the warning." Shannon eased open her door and stepped onto the pavement.

Coming around the front of the truck, Luke thrust out his hand toward the man. "Hey, Uncle Bruce. Good to see you."

"Been too long a time, young man. Put that handshake away and git yer sorry self over here." Bruce Chapman stood a good two inches taller than Luke and probably outweighed him by forty pounds. He grabbed Luke in a crushing embrace and lifted him off his feet.

Luke wheezed a laugh. "Okay, okay! If you put me down, I promise I won't stay away as long next time."

The dog had followed Luke from the truck and now danced circles around the two men. Shannon could only chuckle at the sight they made.

Once he'd caught his breath, Luke made the introductions. Mr. Chapman accepted Shannon's extended hand, then pulled her in for a much gentler hug than he'd given Luke. "Any friend of this fine boy is a friend of mine. Now, missy. What can I do you for today?"

They spent the next half hour strolling through the car lot as Mr. Chapman reeled off the pros and cons of any vehicles he thought might meet Shannon's needs. A twelve-year-old compact SUV with relatively low mileage and several safety features captured her attention. It would be the perfect size for her and Tate, and with plenty of room in back for Rowena.

The only problem was the price. "I'm afraid it's more than I can afford right now."

"Can't come down much if I'm gonna make a profit." Mr. Chapman stroked his jaw. "Could you swing it if we stretched out payments over five years?"

"I'm pretty sure I could never qualify for a loan that big." A quaver had entered her voice. She turned away to inhale a steadying breath.

"Let's take another look at that blue sedan over there. It's got a few more miles on it, but—"

"I'm sorry. This was a bad idea." Whirling around to face the two men, Shannon forced a smile and hoped they wouldn't notice the moisture filling her eyes. "Luke, can we go now? I'll have to pick up Tate soon from his great-grand-parents'."

"Uh, sure." He angled her a concerned look before turning to Mr. Chapman. "Thanks for your help, Uncle Bruce. I'll talk to you soon."

In the truck, Shannon dug through her purse for a tissue. The tears were coming hard and fast now. "I'm sorry," she murmured. "I didn't know how hard this would be."

"Not your fault." Luke turned the truck around and headed to the street. "We can try this another time."

"But I need a car *now*." Straightening, she released a harsh laugh. "Oh, the irony. I can't afford to be without a vehicle, and I can't afford to buy one."

After a thoughtful silence, Luke said, "I can take you straight over to get your son, if that's what you want. Or we can head to the community center. It's almost four thirty. Tobias should be there with the VW by now."

She was grateful he hadn't offered syrupy words of false comfort. His directness gave her the strength to pull herself together. She blew her nose, then tucked the damp tissue into the front pocket of her purse. "Since your ranch person was kind enough to come all this way, I should at least take a look."

❧

The woman was scared and desperate, no question. It took some doing for Luke to hold back from patting her arm and offering useless platitudes. He'd learned the hard way during Anika's recovery. She'd wanted support and encouragement, yes, but not sympathy. She'd told him flatly that if he didn't wipe the pitying expression off his face, she'd ban him from her presence.

Instead, he'd taken the practical route. Prodding his sister to keep pushing through the pain of PT. Setting up a home gym at the ranch house with a treadmill and weight machine. Making her do more and more for herself instead of jumping in with his big-brother-in-shining-armor act. And she'd risen to the challenge. Her battle toward self-sufficiency amazed him.

Or would, if only he could get her off the ranch—away from their self-absorbed father and into a life of her own. Why she insisted on wasting her time trying to maintain a relationship with the man, Luke couldn't fathom.

Ahead on the right, he spotted the community center, then the canary-yellow Beetle parked nearby. Tobias had the hood up and was adjusting some engine part. As Luke halted the truck nearby, Tobias straightened and closed the hood. Lifting one hand in greeting, he shook back his too-long dark hair, then reached inside the car for his dusty tan Resistol. Palming the crown, he settled the hat on his head.

Ridiculously curious about Shannon's reaction to the

lean, muscled cowboy who was every pretty woman's favorite dance partner at Rattlesnake Jack's, Luke braved a glance her way.

She wasn't even looking at the guy. Instead, she had her phone out and appeared to be reading a text. Her frown suggested it wasn't good news.

"Something wrong?" Luke asked.

"I was just reminding Tate's great-grandmother that she doesn't have to pick me up at the clinic." Her frown lines deepened into a scowl. "She asked how the car shopping is going. I can't say too much without having to fend off another offer to bail me out."

Obviously a touchy subject. Expelling air through tight lips, Luke pushed open his door. "Ready to take a look at the VW?"

When Tobias greeted Shannon with a tip of his hat and his most alluring grin, Luke nearly gagged. The former Texan sure knew how to turn on the cowboy charm. "Howdy, ma'am. Luke here tells me you're in the market for a reliable used car."

She replied with a curt nod, her gaze already locked on the Beetle. Moving past the cowboy, she peered in through the open driver's-side door, then circled the outside. "Can I drive it around the parking lot?"

"Be my guest. Key's in the ignition." As Shannon drove away, Tobias came up beside Luke and gave Fletch's ears a quick rub. "Not very talkative, is she?"

"She's a single working mom with limited income and a lot on her mind. And don't get any ideas." As much as Luke liked Tobias, the guy didn't need to complicate things by making moves on Shannon.

"I read you loud and clear. But you have to admit she's mighty pretty."

He did have to admit it. Just not out loud. "Did you decide what you want for the car?"

"For her, I'd be happy to recoup what I've spent restoring it."

Luke shot him a piercing look. "What do you mean, *for her*?"

"Nothing, man. Nothing more than what you told me. She's a single mom in a bind." Tobias gave his head a disgusted shake. "Sheesh."

"Sorry." He didn't know where these protective feelings for Shannon were coming from.

The car stopped a few feet away, and Shannon climbed out. "It's a nice-looking car and drives pretty well, but I can't waste time haggling. What's your price?"

"Prob'ly less than you're thinkin'." Tobias pulled a folded yellow paper from his shirt pocket and spread it open. "I picked up the car for a song, and this is an itemized list of everything I've put into it so far. If you can swing another hundred over my total outlay to cover the last few fixes, I'll be a happy camper."

After a cursory glance at the figures, she gnawed her lip and studied the page more closely. "This ... this is all you're asking?"

"That's it, ma'am. I work on cars for fun, not to make my fortune."

Shannon turned her gaze to Luke, an *Is he serious?* expression in her eyes. When he replied with a smile and a nod, she inhaled a shaky breath. "I—I need to think about it. Can I let you know in a day or two?"

"Not a problem," Tobias said. He tapped the top of the page he'd given her. "That's my number. Call me whenever."

"I will. Thanks." She marched to the truck and climbed in.

Tobias whistled. "The lady doesn't waste words, that's for sure."

"Give her a break. She's having a tough day."

Hands on his hips, Tobias narrowed one eye. "You're falling for her."

"What? No!" Luke scoffed. "I only met her three days ago."

"And you're already helping her shop for cars? In dating lingo, that's almost the equivalent of rounding second base." He snapped his fingers. "Actually, no. It's edging up there close to fiancée territory."

"And you're out in left field." Luke rolled his eyes and groaned. "Gotta go. I'll see you back at the ranch."

He opened the rear door for Fletch to jump in, then scooted behind the wheel. Shannon faced forward and hugged her purse. She looked like she'd been crying again.

This time, he couldn't keep from reaching across the console to squeeze her shoulder. "Hey. It's gonna work out."

He wasn't sure how, but he intended to make certain it did.

Chapter Six

Anika came up behind her father's recliner and draped her arms around his neck. "It's almost suppertime, Daddy. What are you hungry for?"

"Don't matter." He gestured in the general direction of the barn. "Where'd your brother take off to earlier? If he's that dead set on running the ranch, he ought to stick around more."

"He and Tobias went to meet our new friend from the arts and crafts fair. She might be interested in that little yellow car Tobias is finishing up." Easing onto the arm of her dad's chair, Anika sighed. "Luke won't admit it, but I think he's already got a thing for Shannon."

Dad took a long swallow from his beer. "Who's Shannon?"

"Shannon Halsey, from the fair. She's a widowed mom with the cutest little boy ever."

"Halsey," he muttered, as if trying to place a face with the name.

"Do you know any Halseys, Dad?"

"Huh? No. Bring me another beer, would you?" He

handed her the brown bottle he'd just emptied, then upped the TV volume on the remote. It was a sports channel, talking heads loudly rehashing the results of one of last weekend's pro football games.

Rising, Anika gave her dad's shoulder a pat. A few minutes ago, she'd browsed through the contents of the fridge in search of ideas for supper. Hard not to notice the almost empty beer carton on the lower shelf. Lately, Dad had been going through at least a six-pack a day, sometimes two—plus the tequila shots he liked to finish with.

The drinking had been worrisome before Mom died. Since then, it had only gotten worse. Anika had given up pleading with him to stop, or even to cut back. He wasn't a mean drunk, thank goodness, just a morose one.

On her way to the kitchen, she called, "I think I'll make salads with grilled chicken. How does that sound?"

No response.

She decided to ignore his request for another beer. He'd probably already dozed off and wouldn't miss it—not for a while, anyway. By then, she hoped to get something in his stomach.

With the evening news playing on the under-counter TV, she rinsed a head of romaine at the sink. A motion through the window caught her eye—the yellow Beetle zipping up the lane, Tobias behind the wheel.

Her heart did a little jump. She'd had a secret crush on the cowboy for close to twelve years, ever since he'd first shown up at the ranch looking for work. Of course, she had no chance with the guy. He was a good ten years older and a lot more experienced in the ways of the world. Luke described Tobias as a serial dater, never asking the same girl out more than two or three times before moving on. "World champion commitment-phobe," he'd called him.

Anika could almost say the same about her brother. Except not really, because Luke flat didn't date. Three things held his utter devotion: his dog, the ranch, and looking out for his sister.

His unexpected interest in Shannon Halsey was an encouraging sign, though. Good grief, volunteering to help a virtual stranger shop for a car? And an attractive female at that. It was so unlike Anika's brother that she couldn't help but laugh—and pray! If only Shannon could be the woman who finally captured Luke's heart.

While the lettuce drained on a clean dishtowel, Anika set a cast-iron skillet on the gas range to preheat. She pounded out two skinless chicken breasts, sprinkled them with seasoned salt and a dash of lemon pepper, then laid them in the skillet. Keeping an eye on the browning chicken, she sliced and diced a selection of fresh veggies from the crisper drawer.

As she turned the chicken, the image behind the TV news anchorman switched to a fiery wreck. Frozen in place, she stared at the screen.

"This just in," the man was saying. *"Reporter Phil Delgado is on the scene of a collision on Interstate 90 in the Frenchtown area. What can you tell us, Phil?"*

The reporter stepped into the frame. *"Right, Stu. According to witnesses, approximately fifteen minutes ago, a semi hauling roadwork equipment swerved to avoid merging traffic. The semi sideswiped a truck in the left lane and caused it to flip over several times into the median. Emergency personnel are on site. No word yet of any casualties."*

Heart racing, Anika dropped the tongs and sucked air into lungs that didn't want to fill. She spun in circles in search of her cell phone, then found it in her jeans pocket.

She jabbed the call button next to Luke's name. *Please, God. Please, God. Please, God.*

Her ears were ringing now, almost as loud as the ringtone coming from her phone speaker. "Answer. Answer!"

An eternity passed before Luke's voice came on the line. "Hi, Ani. What's up?"

"You're okay?"

"Of course I'm okay. Just heading home from dropping off Shannon."

Every muscle went limp. She slid down to the cold tile floor. *Breathe, Anika. Just breathe.*

"Okay, good," she said, fighting to control her pitch. He mustn't suspect how horribly she'd panicked. "Be careful, though. There's something on the news about a crash on I-90. Traffic might be backed up."

A pause. "Are *you* okay?"

"Oh, yeah, sure. Just making supper for Dad and me." The smell of burning chicken reached her nostrils. She scrambled up to shut off the burner.

Too late. The smoke alarm screeched.

"Anika?"

"Gotta go. Sorry!" Disconnecting, she threw open the back door, then grabbed a dishtowel and fanned the air until the alarm went silent.

If a mere news report could shake her up this badly, no wonder her brother felt like he had to keep tabs on her. It wasn't the first time since her accident that she'd learned of a wreck or passed one on the highway, but they rarely affected her as strongly as this one had.

It's because you knew Luke should be on his way home, and they said a truck was involved. That's all.

That had to be it. She wasn't losing her mind. She was only worried for her brother's safety.

Still, she knew her reaction hadn't been healthy. It might be time to meet with her pastor again. He'd counseled her almost daily during the early stages of her recovery and through the aftermath of Mom's death, then once a month for the next year while she worked toward some semblance of normalcy. Pastor Keegan and her doctors had told her she shouldn't try too hard to remember the accident, that the memories would return in their own good time ... or not.

Luke and Dad—Mom, too, before she died—kept telling her the same thing. But it seemed inconceivable that she couldn't recall where she'd been before the wreck or where she was going. All she'd been told was that she and Dad were in the truck together on the way home from a cattle auction, and she'd been driving. Everyone had urged her to focus on her own recovery and not to press for details.

Maybe they were right. Maybe she was better off not remembering.

Chapter Seven

On her lunch break the next day, Shannon phoned the Frasiers to check on Tate.

"We just finished morning story time," Dorothy said. "At the rate he's progressing, our little guy will be reading at a first-grade level by the time he starts kindergarten."

Shannon's heart swelled with pride. "He's always been a smarty-pants."

"After lunch and naps, we're going for a nature walk to learn about different kinds of trees and their leaves."

"Sounds fun. Wish I could go along." Being a working mom and having to miss these special times with her son was hard. She would hate it even more if not for how loving and attentive Tate's great-grandparents were. They'd made their home Tate's own private preschool—extra nice since a reputable paid program wasn't in Shannon's budget.

Thoughts of finances reminded her she had yet to decide about the car. The SUV at Bruce Chapman's dealership would be much more practical than the Beetle. Roomier, too, and she had to consider how their long-legged Irish wolfhound would fit whenever they took her anywhere.

All you have to do is ask, a voice in her head urged. *You know they'd front you the down payment.*

As if on cue, Dorothy asked, "Are you planning to look at cars again today?"

"I'm still considering a couple I saw yesterday that looked promising, and I don't want to inconvenience you any longer than necessary." She refused to hit up Steven's grandparents for a loan.

"It's no inconvenience. I'm happy to get you to and from work until you find something."

"I appreciate it so much, Dorothy—"

"Now, honey, how many times do I have to remind you?" the woman chided with a gentle laugh. "Martin and I consider ourselves your grandparents as much as we ever were Steven's. We love you."

"I love you, too, Dor—I mean, Gram." She swallowed over the catch in her throat. "Before I get back to work, can you put Tate on for a minute?"

"Hi, Mommy!" came her little boy's chipper greeting. "I can read almost all the words in *Big Red Barn*. Do you think we can visit Luke and Anika's ranch sometime? Maybe they have a big red barn, too."

The boy had a memory like a steel trap. Shannon had mentioned only in passing that Luke and his sister lived on a ranch. "We hardly know them, sweetie."

"Yes, we do. 'Member? I went to see them when you were helping Miss Maddie set up for the fair. And then you shopped for a new car with Luke yesterday. Are you gonna buy one today?"

"I haven't decided on the right one yet. Maybe tomorrow." Unless she decided before then.

Or won the lottery.

She smothered a frustrated sigh. "I have to go, sweetie. Have fun with GiGi and Pop-pop this afternoon."

As she stood to dispose of her sandwich wrappings, Amy, the senior tech, peeked in. "I heard you on the phone and didn't want to intrude."

"It's fine. I was just checking in with Tate."

"He's such a cutie." Amy took a plastic container and canned drink from the fridge, then pulled up a chair. "I didn't know Steven well—he was a few years behind me in school—but Tate sure looks like the pictures of his dad Dr. J keeps in her office."

"I see his daddy in him every day." Shannon offered a wistful smile. "I'd better get back out front. Enjoy your lunch."

Taking over reception duties from Brad, the office manager, she checked in the next patient, a tan-and-white Jack Russell with attitude. "Looks like Sparky's due for his annual checkup, heartworm test, and vaccines."

The scruffy-looking dog owner leaned across the counter and stroked the full beard that brushed his shirt collar. He cast Shannon a suggestive grin. "If you're doing the checkup, maybe I need an exam, too."

Meeting his gaze, she arched a brow. "Does that line usually work?"

"Just kidding, okay?" The man stepped back. "C'mon, Sparky. Lady can't take a joke."

Nikki Ramirez, one of the veterinarians on duty this afternoon, joined Shannon behind the counter. "Is Mr. Grose bothering you?"

"Not in the least. Here's Sparky's file. Room two is available."

Following Dr. Ramirez to the exam room, the bearded

guy gave Shannon the side-eye. "Don't know what you're missin', babe."

I know exactly what I'm missing, she wanted to reply, *and it isn't you.*

Some days, she wondered how she'd survive the rest of her life without Steven. They'd had so little time together—less than a year of dating, then barely five months of marriage. And in secret, no less, because Steven didn't know how to tell his mother that he'd decided he no longer wanted to stick to *the plan.*

Julia's plan for her son meant finishing veterinary college with top grades and no distractions, including no girlfriends, and she expected him to join the family practice as soon as he passed his boards. But before he'd even met Shannon, Steven was having second thoughts about veterinary school. He'd enrolled in a journalism class, mainly to explore something different, and found himself seated next to her. They paired up to work on a class writing project together, and then another. Study dates turned into real dates, and within weeks, Shannon knew she'd met her soulmate.

She twisted the thin gold band on her left ring finger. It wasn't even her wedding ring—she'd bought it at a pawnshop after Steven died, so lechers like Mr. Grose would leave her alone. When Steven had proposed, he'd presented her with an heirloom ring passed down by his great-great-grandmother, an emerald-cut amethyst with an intaglio Rose of Sharon and a tiny diamond in the center. It was beautiful, but too precious for everyday wear, and Shannon only took it out for special occasions.

But those had been few and far between. She tried hard to stave off the threat of another deep depression, but it lurked in her peripheral vision like yesterday afternoon's rain clouds on the horizon. Only faith and prayer had sustained her during those dark months. She had stronger family connections now, plus Dorothy and Martin Frasier's supportive friends from the church she and Tate attended with them.

Why, though, when she had so much to be thankful for, did happiness—true, deep-down, soul-healing joy— continue to elude her?

Riding Zorro, an agile black cutting horse, Luke turned up his collar against the brisk northerly wind whistling down from the higher elevations. He'd ridden into the foothills with Tobias and a few ranch hands to move fifty-plus heifers and their calves to a more sheltered grazing area before the first snows of fall arrived.

Tobias motioned toward the mountains behind them. "It's not even September yet, but there's already a fair amount of snow coverage on the peaks. Wouldn't surprise me if winter sets in early this year."

"That's what they're predicting." Luke signaled Fletch with a wave of his arm. "Come by! Let's keep 'em moving, boy."

As the dog circled the herd from the left side, Luke and Tobias came around from the right, with the two other riders bringing up the rear.

"He's doin' all right," Tobias called with a nod toward Fletch. "Got another competition coming up anytime soon?"

"I'm thinking about taking him to one over near Boise next month. Depends on how things are going here."

"Don't worry about the ranch. I can always cover for you."

Tobias was more than capable, but that wasn't Luke's most pressing concern. He didn't like how Anika had sounded yesterday when she'd called to make sure he was safe. The closer he'd gotten to the scene of the wreck, the more the traffic had backed up. When he finally drew even with the jackknifed eighteen-wheeler and the smoke billowing from the overturned truck, he glimpsed several EMTs frantically treating someone on a gurney.

No wonder his sister had freaked out. If she ever remembered the details of her own accident, it could be devastating for her.

They'd ridden on a little farther when Tobias reined closer. "What's up, Luke? You've been preoccupied with something all day."

When he wasn't working on cars or flirting with the ladies, the cowboy could be downright perceptive. "I'm a little worried about Anika, that's all."

Tobias snorted. "When are you *not* worried about your baby sister? You've hardly let her out of your sight since the day she came home from the rehab hospital. What's it been now? Three years since the crash?"

"Almost four, but who's counting." Luke called another command to Fletch, and the dog went after a straggler to get her back with the herd. "Were you already home yesterday before that collision on I-90?"

"Just missed it. Heard on the radio as I was turning in at the ranch gate." Growing thoughtful, Tobias reached forward to pat his horse's neck. "Aw, man, I just realized. The similarities between Anika's wreck and this one ... no wonder it shook you up. Is *she* okay?"

"I think so. A little quieter than usual, that's all. She was baking dog treats all morning. It's her happy place."

Spotting the turn into the valley they were heading for, Luke waved his Stetson and yelled, "Come by, Fletch!"

The dog yipped at the cows' heels, angling them to the right and across a shallow stream between two hills. With Fletch and the ranch hands taking it from there, Luke and Tobias fell back. Giving Zorro's reins some slack, Luke let him drink from the creek, then swung his leg over the saddle horn and dropped to the ground.

Tobias did the same. After doing some stretches, he plopped down on the straw-colored grass and leaned back on his elbows. "Big Sky Country doesn't look so big when you're this deep in the hills."

Luke joined him on the grass. "Ever sorry you left Texas?"

"Every now and again. But there wasn't a whole lot left for me there, and nowadays, nothin' to go back to. I decided Montana and Fox Pass Ranch would be my happy place, and it's working out just fine."

Tobias never talked much about where he came from. Seemed he was content to close the book on that chapter of his life and live in the present. Sometimes Luke wished he could do the same and forget everything that had happened before today. The bad parts, anyway.

Chewing on a stalk of grass, Tobias shifted to look over at Luke. "You got a happy place?"

He didn't even have to think about it. "Working with Fletch. When we're in sync, everything else fades into the background."

"That's pretty obvious when I'm watchin' you two." Heaving a groan, Tobias pushed to his feet. He grabbed a canteen from his saddlebag and took a long swallow as he gazed between the hills. "Here come the boys and Fletch. Plenty early to clean up and head over to Rattlesnake Jack's."

Luke could only shake his head. "How many girls you planning to dance with tonight?"

"Many as I can. Maybe sing some karaoke, too." Laughing, Tobias hoisted himself into the saddle and turned his horse toward the barn. "You should tag along."

"No way I can keep up with you." As Luke mounted Zorro, Fletch bounded over, tongue and tail both wagging. Luke didn't have to ask what his dog's happy place was. Whether chasing Frisbees or chasing cows, the border collie thrived on doing his job.

Doing his job. Some days, Luke felt like his life was all and only about the work. Since he'd taken on more and more responsibility for the ranch, the things he loved most —working with dogs and volunteering at the animal shelter —got less and less of his time. Plus, he did everything possible to nudge his sister toward a better life while protecting her from the terrible thing he hoped she'd never remember.

Was he wrong to think he could? Because, like it or not, the day was bound to come when something like yesterday's wreck on I-90 would flip the switch on Anika's buried memories. And the truth could destroy her.

Luke and Fletch arrived at the ranch about ten minutes behind Tobias. As Luke led Zorro into the barn, Tobias came out of the tack room with his phone to his ear.

"Yeah, yeah, I can do that," Tobias was saying. He shot

Luke a thumbs-up. "I'll get Luke to follow me to your place. We'll complete the deal, and I'll hand over the keys. It'll be about an hour and a half before we can get there." He paused, then nodded. "All righty, see you soon."

Luke secured Zorro in the crossties and began unbuckling the saddle. "Was that Shannon?"

"Decided she wants the Beetle. I told her we'd deliver it this evening."

"Thought you still had some work to do on it."

"I do, but she needs it right away. I'll go over on Saturday and finish up. It's mostly cosmetic stuff, no effect on drivability." Tobias removed his hat and combed his fingers through his sweat-dampened hair. "We gotta hit the road pretty quick. Grab a shower and put on a clean shirt and jeans. Maybe slap on some aftershave while you're at it."

"Since when are you giving the orders around here?" Luke hollered as the cowboy walked away.

"Since I know how you been hankerin' to see the little lady again—even if you can't admit it." With a wave of his hand, Tobias sauntered out the barn door. "Hoo-boy, watchin' you fight your attraction will more than make up for skipping a night at Rattlesnake Jack's."

Now the cocky ranch foreman thought he could read Luke's mind?

He wished he could say the man was wrong, but he couldn't deny how often Shannon's image had danced behind his eyes since last weekend—or how many times he'd forcefully blinked it away. Hadn't he reminded himself numerous times already that he wasn't relationship material?

After giving Zorro a quick brushing, he led the horse

into his stall, then carried the saddle and bridle to the tack room. Since Tobias hadn't left him much choice about going along for the car delivery errand, he'd better get a move on. The smart-aleck Texan was right about one thing —it wouldn't be polite to show up at Shannon's smelling like cows and horse sweat.

"Let's go, Fletch." He left the barn and strode toward his cabin. "I'll dish you up some supper and then let you hang out with Ani while I'm gone. How does that sound?"

The dog answered with a happy bark before dashing ahead.

A steamy shower and clean clothes made him feel more presentable. He skipped the aftershave, though. No need to go overboard. On the way out, he grabbed his phone and keys and slapped on his Colorado Rockies baseball cap.

Minutes later, glimpsing Anika in the kitchen window of the main house, he let himself in through the back door. Chatter coming from the den TV assured him Dad was otherwise occupied.

Hands tucked into quilted oven mitts, Anika smiled at Luke as she removed a baking sheet from the oven. "Just in time to sample my latest recipe creation."

Luke eyed the miniature bone-shaped dog treats. "I'm sure that offer was meant for Fletch, not me … right?"

"Of course. Although they do smell yummy, if I do say so myself." She set the tray on a cooling rack, then slipped off the oven mitts and took a treat from an open plastic container. "These have cooled already. Here you go, Fletch. Ready?"

The dog sank onto his haunches and held steady as she balanced the treat on his nose. Once she gave the okay, he flicked the treat into the air and caught it in his mouth.

"Yay, good boy!" Anika bent to ruffle the dog's cheek fur.

Observing his sister, Luke heaved a mental sigh of gratitude. She seemed like her usual cheery self again, unfazed after yesterday's scare. Maybe he should take up baking for whenever the stress of everyday life got to be too much.

Nah, he'd rather just snuggle on the sofa with his dog, a bowl of popcorn, and a good movie on TV.

Which wasn't happening tonight.

He explained to Anika about delivering the Beetle to Shannon. "Can I leave Fletch with you for a couple of hours?"

"That's fine. Say hi to her for me. And her little boy, too. Oh, and wait!" She yanked open a drawer and took out a baggie. After stuffing it full of freshly baked treats, she handed the baggie to Luke. "For their doggy. And do not, under any circumstances, allow Shannon to pay for them."

"Yes, *ma'am*." He saluted. "You're getting to be almost as bossy as Tobias."

His sister drew her lower lip between her teeth. He could have sworn she was blushing as she turned to look for something in the fridge. "I'm making stuffed peppers for supper. I'll keep one warm for you."

"Thanks. Sounds a lot more tempting than another can of beef stew from my cupboard." He tugged on her arm until she pulled her head out of the fridge and faced him. "I love you, kiddo."

"I love you, too, big bro." She hooked an elbow around his neck. "Now go. You don't want to keep Shannon waiting."

Ignoring the gleam in her eye, he instructed Fletch to behave and not to eat too many of Anika's treats.

He reached his truck about the time Tobias pulled up in the yellow Beetle. Tobias honked and waved, then headed toward the gate.

Seconds later, Tobias texted a GPS link to Shannon's address. Luke programmed it into the truck's navigation system.

The sun was a melon-colored ball on the western horizon by the time he parked in front of the simple but attractively landscaped one-story house. Tobias had pulled into the driveway and was already striding toward the front door.

Luke caught up with him as the porch light blinked on. The door opened, and a dog the size of a small Shetland pony greeted them with an ear-shattering bark. Luke and Tobias both jumped back.

"It's okay, she's harmless. Come on in." Shannon slid her fingers under the dog's collar. "Rowena, give them some room."

"Wow." Luke whistled through his teeth. "You mentioned she was a big dog, but ... wow."

"My exact reaction the first time I met her. And she eats more than Tate and me put together."

"Maybe these will help." Luke handed her the bag of treats. "Fresh baked today, with Anika's compliments."

"Yay!" Tate reached around his mom to grab the bag. "Mommy, can I give Weena one now?"

"Okay, just one, but take her to the kitchen." When the dog lumbered after her young master, Shannon returned her attention to Luke and Tobias. "Thank you for bringing the car—and the treats, too. I know it was short notice."

Tobias removed his Stetson and held it over his heart in a gesture that made Luke stifle an eye roll. "Glad we could oblige, ma'am. Anything to assist a lady in distress."

Discomfort flickered across Shannon's expression. She cleared her throat. "I suppose we have some papers to sign?"

Luke edged around them. "Okay if I visit with Tate while you guys handle business?"

"Sure, he'll enjoy the company." Shannon nodded in the direction Tate had gone.

"Shouldn't take long," Tobias said.

Luke stepped into the kitchen to see Tate fishing a handful of treats out of the bag. The big dog appeared to be chewing several the boy had just given her.

Luke scoffed. "Thought your mom said only one."

Tate looked up with a sheepish grin. "But Weena likes them so much. Look, she's wearing her purple bow, too."

"Indeed she is." Pulling out a chair from the dinette, Luke straddled it and folded his arms across the back. "You know how important it is to obey your mom, though, right?"

"I know. I'm mostly a good boy."

His solemn expression brought a chuckle to Luke's throat. "I have no doubt you are."

"I hafta be 'cause I don't have a daddy an' someday I'm gonna be the man of the house. That's what Pop-pop says."

Seemed like a heavy load of responsibility to lay on a kid this young. Although Luke hadn't been much older when it dawned on him that his father had begun checking out from the family, both emotionally and physically. Anika was only a few months old when their mother received her lupus diagnosis. When symptoms flared and Mom struggled even to get out of bed, she counted on Luke to handle simple chores and help with his baby sister.

As for Dad? The sicker Mom got, the more time he spent working in the barn office or riding into the hills to check on the cattle ... or drowning his sorrows in a bottle.

"Mr. Luke?" Tate patted his knee. "Don't look sad, Mr. Luke. Here, give Weena a treat. She'll lick your hand and you'll feel all better."

"Thanks, kiddo."

If only all life's problems could be solved as easily.

Chapter Eight

Laying her checkbook open on the coffee table, Shannon inhaled a slow, calming breath. She'd agreed to give Tobias a check for half the selling price tonight as a sign of good faith. Tomorrow, she'd meet him at the Missoula County Treasurer's office to complete the sale and title transfer.

"I'll go online first thing in the morning to get us in the queue," Tobias explained. "Once I get us an estimated time, I'll text you."

"Let me know as soon as possible, and I can have someone cover for me at work. I can't be gone any longer than necessary." Shannon's pen hovered over the blank check. "I also need time to transfer the funds into my account."

"No worries. I'll hold your checks until you let me know they're good."

She couldn't understand why he seemed so uncon-cerned. Was he expecting her to return the favor somehow?

A shudder crept up her spine. "I'll make sure the

money is in the bank within the next couple of days. How should I make this out?"

"Tobias Flynn." He spelled it as she wrote.

After filling in the amount and signing her name, she ripped out the check and passed it to him.

"And here are your keys." He stood and dropped them into her palm, then gently closed her trembling fingers around them. "Hey, nothin' to be nervous about. I stand behind my work. If you find anything wrong with the car, you call me and I'll make it right."

Looking into his eyes, she didn't detect any ulterior motives. Luke had vouched for Tobias, and Maddie's husband had vouched for Luke. Shannon could only trust that God had brought both men into her life for His purposes.

"Thank you," she said, meaning it. "It's a relief to have reliable transportation again."

Scuffling sounds behind her announced Luke, Tate, and Rowena returning from the kitchen. Tate climbed onto the sofa beside her and peered up with a pout. "Sorry, Mommy. I didn't give Weena just one treat, like you said."

At the moment, that was the least of her concerns. "Well, did she like them?"

"She liked them very much. I let Mr. Luke give her some, too, because he was sad."

Luke released a self-conscious laugh and stuffed his hands into his pockets. "Not sad, just thinking about ... stuff. Are you done here?"

"All set. Ready to go whenever you are," Tobias shifted his glance between Shannon and Luke. "But no hurry," he added with a wink. "I'm just gonna step outside and make sure I didn't leave anything of mine in the Beetle."

Lips skewed, Luke waited for the front door to close

behind Tobias. "Nothing subtle about the guy. Sorry if he embarrassed you."

From Shannon's perspective, Luke seemed more bothered by his friend's matchmaking ploy. "It's fine. But you can tell him I'm immune to setups and flirtatious remarks. I have no room in my life for anything but my son and my job." She didn't add that she was still deeply in love with her late husband and probably always would be.

"I get it," Luke said. "Tobias and my sister are always trying to set me up. I keep telling them it's pointless, but they don't listen."

Tate scooted closer. "But Mommy, you have room in your life for Weena, right? And Grammy and Grampy, and Pop-pop and GiGi when they come over?"

"Of course, honey. Of course." Wincing, she gave a helpless laugh. She always forgot how literally Tate could interpret her words.

Luke reached over to tousle Tate's hair. "That's one smart boy you've got there."

"Too smart for his britches."

"If I could give you some unsolicited advice ..."

Shannon stiffened. "What about?"

"Don't let him grow up too fast."

Luke's softly spoken words jolted her back to that dark and despairing time after Steven's death, when grief and clinical depression had stolen all joy from her life, even that of caring for her little boy. The memory of the many times as a toddler he'd cupped her tear-streaked cheeks and whispered, *"No cwy, Mommy. It be otay,"* nearly undid her.

"I know," she murmured as she rose from the sofa. "Believe me, I know."

Luke cast her a thoughtful look before moving toward the door. "I should let you get on with your evening."

"Thanks again for helping me find a car." Shannon followed. "And say hi to your sister for me. Tell her how much Rowena loved her treats."

"I'll do that."

Tate rushed forward and grabbed Luke's jacket sleeve. "Will you come back and see us, Mr. Luke? Mommy said you teach doggies how to do stuff. Can you teach Weena some tricks?"

With an apologetic glance at Luke, Shannon set her hands on her little boy's shoulders. "Now, Tate, what have I said about asking people for things?"

"It's okay," Luke said with a snicker. He lowered to his haunches and tugged on Tate's shirt collar. "It's true, little guy, I teach dogs all kinds of stuff. Mostly how to be good companions, but also how to have fun and do tricks. But you want to hear a secret?"

Tate nodded.

Leaning close to Tate's ear, Luke dropped his voice to a whisper. "I'm not actually teaching the dogs at all. I'm teaching their humans how to communicate."

"Co—commu—"

"Communicate. It means to get your message across. To let someone—or some dog—know what you mean and what you want."

"Like a trick I want Weena to do?"

"Exactly. And when you two are communicating like a boy and his dog should, she'll know what you want, and she'll want to do it just because it makes you happy."

Tate spun around and looked up at Shannon. "Mommy! I want to com—commun-ticate with Weena like that. Please can you let Mr. Luke teach us?"

"Oh, honey." One hand to her abdomen, she pressed

against a pang of regret and no small amount of embarrassment. "It's ... it's not in the budget right now."

Tate's little mouth worked. He dipped his chin and mumbled, "I guess cars cost too much money."

In one smooth move, Luke pushed up from the floor and scooped the boy into his arms. "You're right, cars cost a lot, and your mom's got to be careful how she spends her money so she has plenty left over to take care of you and Rowena."

Braced on Luke's hip, Tate gave a solemn nod.

"But I can see you're a smart little guy who wants to be a good helper for his mom," Luke went on. "I'll make a deal with you."

"Luke—" Shannon stretched her hand toward him. If he was about to offer more charity, the answer would be a flat no.

"Now, hold on. You haven't heard the deal yet." He winked at her, evoking a whole different response in her chest than when Tobias had done the same. "I'm planning on teaching my dog, Fletch, to herd sheep. But before I invest in real sheep for him to practice with, I could use some volunteer pretend sheep. Tate, do you think you could help me out?"

"You mean play like I'm a sheep?"

"Right. And run around a little pen while Fletch tries to get you to go where he tells you."

"Oh, yay! Mommy, can I?"

What was she supposed to say, now that Luke had snagged the boy's interest? She pursed her lips. "What's the rest of this so-called *deal* you're offering?"

"Well, that's the best part. After we spend a little time giving Fletch some sheepherding lessons, we'll work on teaching Rowena some simple tricks. Does that sound like a fair trade?"

Tate's beseeching pout dared her to say no, and when Rowena chimed in with her deep, happy bark, Shannon knew she was outnumbered. "I work Monday through Friday and sometimes on Saturday mornings. Where and when would we do this?"

"I've got obedience classes on Saturday mornings. How about this Saturday afternoon, if you don't mind a drive out to the ranch? You could say for an early supper. Anika's a great cook, and I know she'd enjoy seeing you again."

Now Luke was looking almost as hopeful as Tate. If he hadn't made it clear he wasn't interested in relationships, she might read something else entirely into his expression.

"Mommy," Tate drawled. "Stop thinking so hard and just say yes."

Luke snickered. "Yeah, 'Mommy,' it's not rocket science."

"Okay, okay. Yes." Shannon heaved a defeated shrug. "We'll plan on Saturday afternoon. Text me directions."

Luke strode down the front walk and wondered with every step what had gotten into him. He could easily have said good night and goodbye, with no expectations of ever seeing Shannon or her son again.

Or at best, not until the next local fair Anika signed up for, and only if Maddie Wittenbauer also had a booth and again enlisted Shannon as her assistant.

Tobias sat waiting in the truck. "Took you long enough," he said as Luke slid behind the wheel. His self-satisfied grin rankled. "You kissed her, right?"

"What? No!" Luke jammed his seatbelt clip into the buckle. "For crying out loud, is romancing women all you can think about?"

"All *I* can think about?" Arms crossed, Tobias snickered and turned his face toward the window. "'You foolish and senseless people, who have eyes but do not see.'"

As he pulled away from the curb, Luke shot Tobias a quick glance. "What's that from?"

"The Book of Jeremiah. Seems to fit your situation real well." Tobias may have the reputation of a ladies' man, but he knew his Bible.

Which was no comfort to Luke at the moment. "How many times do I have to tell you? I am *not* interested in Shannon that way."

Maybe before Saturday, he should come up with a logical reason to back out of their—

No. He would not, under any circumstances, call it a *date*.

"Well, if you weren't kissing her goodnight, what *were* you doing in there all that time?"

"Will you stop with the kissing already?" Luke huffed and turned at the next intersection. "We were talking, is all. Her little boy asked if I could teach his dog some tricks, and somehow ..." He'd regret saying this, but too late now. "Somehow I ended up suggesting they come to the ranch on Saturday."

Tobias roared and slapped his thigh. "This just gets better and better."

In Luke's mind, things were getting progressively worse. How had he let a pretty young mom and her adorable son sway him this easily?

He figured he'd just answered his own question.

Because Shannon was definitely attractive, and not

merely because of her looks. Something about her candid mixture of vulnerability, determination, and tenacity entranced him. In those ways, she reminded him of Anika. But the feelings he was developing for Shannon Halsey were anything but brotherly.

As for her little boy? He was a charmer in his own right. Smart, perceptive, outspoken, and he sure knew how to use those puppy-dog eyes and pouty smile to his advantage. If Luke were ever to have a son of his own—

Stop right there, Daniels. It's never gonna happen.

He glanced over at Tobias, who chuckled to himself as he looked out across the darkened landscape beyond the window. The smart-aleck ranch foreman was about as close to a best friend as Luke had, but Tobias had better get it through his thick head that the topic of romance—Luke's, at least—was off the table.

After they'd driven a few miles in stiff silence, Tobias heaved a sigh. "Look, man, sorry for razzing you. I get it, I do."

"Do you?" Luke cast him a sidelong glance.

"I get that you haven't been the same since Anika's wreck. I get that your mom's passing so soon afterward couldn't have come at a worse time. I get that you're angry with your dad for drowning his sorrows in booze and not stepping up like he should. And I even get that, for some strange reason, you believe the ranch, your sister's recovery, and everything else you're dealing with rests entirely on your shoulders."

Luke fought to keep his focus on the road ahead when what he felt like doing was pulling over and punching Tobias's lights out. Which was beyond comprehension, because the man spoke the truth. Every last word.

He sniffed hard and ran his sleeve across his face. "Who

else is gonna be responsible? Who else is gonna care like I do?"

"How about the Lord?" Tobias asked gently. "Ever think of letting Him carry these burdens for you? His shoulders are mighty big ones."

"Don't. Not that I don't appreciate what you're trying to do, but ... don't go there."

"All right, if you say so." Crossing his arms, Tobias returned his gaze to the window. "But you can't stop me from prayin' for you."

More miles ticked by. Judging by his friend's silence, Luke figured Tobias was praying for him right this minute. Since he didn't have the faith to pray himself, what could it hurt? But only on the off chance a friend's prayers could actually make a difference.

In the meantime, he wasn't holding his breath.

He took the Elk Valley exit, then headed north along the winding road and through the blinking yellow light marking the tiny town's main intersection. Oncoming headlights made him squint, and when it appeared the vehicle was about to veer into his lane, he swerved and hit the horn. The right-side tires kicked up loose gravel.

Tobias startled and grabbed the dashboard. "Easy, man!"

By then, the other driver had whizzed by. With all four wheels back on the pavement, Luke exhaled sharply. "Sorry. I thought he was coming right at us."

"Prob'ly texting, or else high on something. What's wrong with people?"

Luke eased his foot off the gas. "You okay?"

"Yeah. You?"

Luke wasn't sure. He'd encountered plenty of unsafe drivers on the roads and had his share of close calls.

Normally, he could blame their stupidity and let it go. But not tonight. Maybe the crash yesterday, combined with Anika's reaction to it, had gotten to him more than he realized.

They were nearing the turnoff that would take them farther into the foothills toward the ranch. Luke made the turn and drove another hundred yards before pulling over. He shut off the engine and hit the switch for the emergency blinkers. Better safe than sorry.

In the dim light of the cab, Tobias shifted to face him. "Not as okay as you thought?"

"The wreck yesterday—the eighteen-wheeler, the truck on fire—too close for comfort, I guess."

"I remember seeing those awful pictures in the news after Anika's crash. It's a miracle she and your dad survived."

"To this day, I don't understand why neither of them was wearing a seatbelt. Dad, maybe. But not Anika, especially considering how nervous it made her to drive Dad's truck. If they hadn't been thrown clear, if the snow on the ground hadn't softened their impact, they'd have—they'd—" His throat closed. He couldn't finish the sentence.

Tobias squeezed his shoulder. "Like I said, it's a miracle. The Lord was watching over them that night."

Fighting for control, Luke forced down a swallow. "Guess He wasn't paying as much attention to everybody involved. To this day, Anika remembers nothing about the guy in the car behind her who died. If she ever realizes she might have been responsible, it'll break her."

Based on their dad's muddled recollection, vague statements from the few witnesses, and evidence at the scene, the cops had pieced together their best guess about what had happened. It was late one snowy January night, and

Dad and Anika were heading home from Idaho. Anika was driving because Dad, as usual, had a little too much to drink at the cattle auction.

Avoiding a stalled car parked too close to the edge of the highway, Anika must have swerved, only to sideswipe an eighteen-wheeler passing them in the left lane. Skidding on the icy pavement, the truck went into a spin and careened into a vehicle that had come up too close behind them. The truck flipped over several times and burst into flames. The fire burned so hot that by the time the highway patrol and fire engines arrived, nothing remained but a shell.

For as long as he lived, Luke would never forget answering the knock on their front door at three o'clock in the morning, or his mother's ashen face as she'd fallen to her knees—first in shock when the patrolmen broke the news, then sobbing with relief and gratitude that her husband and daughter had survived.

Breaking through Luke's memories, Tobias pushed open the passenger door. "Get out," he gently instructed. "I'll drive us on home."

"Thanks, Tobe." Luke cast him a weak smile. "In case I haven't told you lately, you're a pretty good friend."

Chapter Nine

It felt good to wake up Wednesday morning and picture her shiny new—well, new to her, anyway—little car in the garage. Knowing the Frasiers would be eager to see the car, too, Shannon allowed a few extra minutes when she dropped off Tate for the day.

"Well, isn't this fancy!" Gripping the handlebars of his rolling walker, Martin tottered around the vehicle. Stability issues caused by Parkinson's had forced his retirement from the veterinary practice. "How's it handle?"

"Very smooth," Shannon replied, though from her house to the Frasiers' was the farthest she'd driven it. "Much nicer than the Ol' Gray Mare. And the radio even works."

Dorothy gave her a squeeze. "It's adorable, and so *you*. Plan to stay for supper this evening. Afterward, you can take us for a spin."

"Sounds good." Watching the time, Shannon knelt to give Tate the usual instructions about minding his great-grandparents.

He responded with his usual exaggerated eye roll. "I *know*, Mommy."

Arriving at the vet clinic a few minutes later, Shannon glimpsed Julia's neon-green SUV in the rear parking area and pulled in next to it. She'd forgotten Julia would be in this morning to assist with the surgical schedule.

This could work in Shannon's favor. She still needed to come up with the balance she owed Tobias for the car, and it would be much less stressful presenting her request to Julia without Dad present.

And—finally—she had a plan of action. After Luke and Tobias left last night, and with Tate tucked in bed, she'd continued her internet search for a job that would allow her to work from home and set her own schedule. This time, a local business popped up—Zootown Tech Writers, a company looking for remote workers to edit and proofread instruction books, user manuals, corporate documents, and the like.

Technical knowledge helpful but not required, the description read. *Must be detail-oriented, with clear communication skills, and possess a strong command of grammar, punctuation, spelling, and usage.*

If Shannon had completed her college degree, she'd probably be teaching high school journalism right now, and she'd always gotten straight A's in her English and journalism classes. Since the starting pay rate looked good and they needed someone right away, she'd filled out the online application.

Apparently, the person in charge of hiring set his own hours, too. Shortly, a man named Ravi Kapur had phoned, asking if she could meet him at the Zootown Tech Writers office for an in-person interview. She'd promised to call back today after she knew her schedule.

In the meantime, she was waiting to hear from Tobias about when to be at the county office to transfer the car title. His text came through shortly after eight.

> Got us in the queue. Meet me there at
> 10:45?

She replied with a thumbs-up, then reminded Brad, the office manager, that she'd be gone through her lunch hour.

As soon as Julia was out of surgery, Shannon peeked into her office. "Got a minute?"

"Hi, sweetie. Sure, come on in." Julia lifted a steaming mug from her single-serve brewer. "Like some coffee?"

"No, thanks." Once they were both seated, Shannon went on, "I need to ask a big favor."

"Is this about buying a car? Because you know your dad and I are more than willing to help."

"Actually, I found an affordable car and bought it last night." She locked her fingers together. "But to cover the cost, I ... I hate to ask, but I need an advance on my paycheck. Today."

"Oh." Julia's brows lifted. "Is that wise? How will you make it through the month?"

"I have an idea about that, too." Shannon explained about the work-from-home job she'd applied for.

Julia's closed-off posture implied her disapproval. "I realize the receptionist job here doesn't pay all that much, but your dad and I hoped you'd eventually go back to school—which we're more than willing to finance. We both want you to have a career someday that you'd be happy and fulfilled in."

Shannon chose her words carefully, because she really needed Julia on her side. "I'm not even sure what I want to do with the rest of my life. Before ... before I lost Steven, I

thought I had things figured out. We both did. Then ..."
Eyes filling, she looked toward the ceiling and took a breath.

Lifting the photo of Steven from the credenza, Julia gave a slow nod. "Losing him changed everything for me, too."

"Which is why I'm just trying to be a good mom and take care of Tate the way Steven would want me to. The way he would if he was still alive." Shannon snatched a tissue from the box on Julia's desk and blotted her cheeks. "This job will give me a chance to do that without leaving Tate with somebody else all the time."

After several moments of silence, Julia gave a soft laugh. "You remind me a lot of myself when I was younger. After Steven's father and I parted ways, I was determined not only to be the best mother possible but successful in my career as well. Which means I understand how important it is for you to prove you can do it on your own—even more, how hard it can be sometimes to ask for help." She pulled open a drawer and withdrew a memo pad, then scribbled something on it and passed it to Shannon. "Give this to Brad. It's my authorization for an advance on your salary. He'll cut a check for you today."

Inhaling past the lump in her throat, Shannon circled the desk to wrap Julia in a hug. "Thank you. This will help tremendously."

By the time her conversation with Julia ended, Shannon had only a few minutes before leaving to meet Tobias. She gave Brad Julia's memo and apologized again for taking more time off. "I promise, after this week, things should be back on track."

On her way out to the car, she phoned Ravi Kapur and asked if he would be available for their interview over her lunch hour.

"No prob," he said. "Pick something up and bring it with you. We can eat while we talk."

Wow, must be a really casual office atmosphere. "Okay. Thanks."

Tobias was waiting for her outside the Missoula County Courthouse. "Ready to get this done?"

Feeling empowered, she hiked her chin. "Yes, I am."

When their turn in line came, the clerk efficiently handled the paperwork and registered the title transfer. Back at the car, Shannon wrote Tobias a check for the balance. "I'll have the funds in my account by tomorrow."

"Sounds good. And I'll be over to your place on Saturday to wrap up those last few items."

"Actually, there's no need for you to make a trip into town. Tate and I are coming out to see Luke on Saturday afternoon."

"Right, he mentioned your dog-training trade-off." Tobias's lips skewed in a quirky grin before his expression turned serious. "A word to the wise: Go easy on the guy. He's ... well, he's goin' through some family stuff."

Recalling their conversations during the fair last weekend, Shannon smothered a sigh. "Yes, I know he's been very protective of his sister since her auto accident."

"That, and a few other issues."

Curious that Tobias felt it necessary to point this out. "If you're concerned I'm going to ask Luke a bunch of nosy questions, don't be. My only reason for accepting his invitation is because my son asked Luke to teach our dog some tricks."

"The only reason, huh?" Tobias narrowed his eyes in a bemused expression.

"Yes. What else would it be?"

"Oh, nothin'." Grin returning, he pulled a set of keys from his pocket. "Guess I'll see you at the ranch on Saturday."

Could the flirtatious cowboy be any more inscrutable?

After stopping at a convenience store for a bottled water to have with the sandwich she'd brought from home, Shannon drove to the address Ravi Kapur had given her. She found the office for Zootown Tech Writers in a strip shopping center along Reserve.

A lanky, olive-skinned man with a shock of thick black hair ambled toward her as she entered. "Shannon?"

"Yes. Mr. Kapur?"

"Just Ravi." He showed her to a small worktable at the far end of the long, narrow room. "Have a seat. Be right back."

At desks nearby, she glimpsed a tattooed young woman and a red-haired guy with a long braid, both busy at their computers. The woman glanced Shannon's way and smiled. She took a long swig from an insulated mug before getting back to work.

Ravi returned with a takeout container. Popping it open, he said, "Please, let's eat."

She felt awkward at first, trying to sound competent and professional while dabbing mayonnaise off her lips. Her prospective employer didn't seem to mind, though. He asked about her education and previous work experience, and she answered honestly, including the fact that she was a single mother who'd dropped out of her final year of college after her husband's death.

"I think you'd be a good fit here, Shannon." Ravi

pushed aside his empty food container and leaned back in his chair. "Do you have time to do a test edit so I can assess your proofreading skills?"

She checked the time. "How long would it take?"

"Fifteen minutes, twenty at most. It's a one-page Word document with several strategically placed errors. I can set you up at an unused workstation. You're familiar with Track Changes, I hope?"

"I haven't used it much recently, but yes."

Ravi showed her to an empty desk and brought up the test document. Stomach in knots, Shannon prayed for God to restore the proficiency that had earned high marks in her college classes.

"Start whenever you're ready," Ravi said. "I'll check it as soon as you finish, and if it looks good, you have a job."

Shannon nodded and set to work. At first glance, the test document looked clean, but a closer inspection revealed several problems—misused or subtly misspelled words, misplaced modifiers, sentence fragments, punctuation errors, and other grammar mistakes.

Almost exactly fifteen minutes later, Shannon scooted her chair away from the computer station. "I'm finished."

Back at the table where they'd had lunch, Ravi accessed the file from his laptop. "Mm-hmm ... mm-hmm ... Wow. Excellent. You even caught a tiny mistake my test writer overlooked."

A surge of anticipation filled Shannon's chest. "Am I hired?"

"Absolutely." Frowning at his computer screen, Ravi tapped some keys. "Okay. I just forwarded some employment docs to your email address. Get those filled out, and be sure to sign the confidentiality agreement. Once I have all the paperwork, you'll be getting your first assignment."

Reminding herself to breathe, Shannon stood and offered her hand. "Thank you for this opportunity, Mr. Ka —I mean, Ravi. I can't wait to get started."

Luke stayed close to home for the next few days. He must have checked on Anika a few too many times, because after his third trip to the house on Friday, she called him on it.

"I am not your project, Luke Daniels. I'm a twenty-six-year-old woman. Intelligent and capable. *Not* an invalid, either mentally or physically, who has to be coddled and protected."

When she looked at him that way, fists planted on her hips and wearing an imperious scowl, she reminded him of their mother. Mom had worn that same glower when she caught them playing at something dangerous, like leaping out of the hayloft while pretending to be Superman and Wonder Woman.

Smothering a bittersweet smile, Luke spread his hands. "I know, Ani. I'm sorry. It's just that ..."

They were standing in the laundry room, where Anika was sorting dirty clothes into batches. She shook out one of their dad's undershirts.

Mouth hardening, Luke pointed at the shirt. "Actually, it's that right there. You're *too* smart and capable to spend your life taking care of Dad. Doing his laundry. Cooking for him. Fetching him another bottle of beer. You deserve more. You deserve *better*."

Her expression shifted to something akin to pity, and she looked more like Mom than ever. "I wish for once you'd quit hating him and try to understand him."

"I don't hate him." He couldn't look at her and focused

on the pile of laundry instead. "What I hate is how he's let us down. How he let Mom down. How he's disappearing into himself more and more every day."

"Which is why he needs me—*us*." She ran her fingers down the sleeve of a well-worn plaid flannel shirt before dropping it onto a pile. "He's hurting, Luke. Can't you see that?"

"Drinking himself into oblivion isn't going to help. Neither is you waiting on him hand and foot."

Anika arranged a load of clothes in the washer. She lowered the lid and selected a cycle, then faced him and tiredly shook her head. "I'm ending this argument right now, before it gives me another headache."

"Ani—"

"I have some sewing to do. Go do ranch stuff. Or play with your dog." On her way out, she paused and frowned over her shoulder. "Better yet, get a life. Get a *girlfriend*."

Feeling sucker-punched, he stared from the doorway as she marched out through the kitchen. Seconds later, her footsteps sounded on the staircase.

What was it with both his sister and Tobias always trying to match him up with someone?

And lately, not just anyone. Shannon Halsey's name had come up often this week, no thanks to the news he'd let slip that Shannon planned to bring her son and their dog over tomorrow. Didn't matter that he'd clearly stated it was only a friendly exchange—they'd help Luke give Fletch some "sheepherding" practice, and he'd teach their humongous Irish wolfhound a few dog tricks.

Friendly exchange. Right. Keep telling yourself that.

Giving a huff, he left through the back door and strode toward the barn. His piercing whistle brought Fletch bounding toward him across the nearest pasture.

"What have you been up to, boy?" Luke knelt to give the dog a brisk rub behind the ears. "Chasing rabbits and squirrels again?"

"We were looking over those bred heifers you bought last month."

At the sound of his father's voice, Luke pushed to his feet. He hadn't noticed the man shuffling along behind Fletch.

Dad leaned on his cane as he gestured toward the pasture. "One of 'em's got a cut on her leg that needs attention."

"I'll get the first-aid kit and go check on her." Luke started for the barn.

"Hang on, son."

Stomach clenching, Luke hauled in a breath. "What?"

His father cleared his throat. "I'm taking off for a few days. You'll have to look after things here."

What else was new? "No worries. Got it covered." He kept walking, then decided it wouldn't hurt to know how to find his dad—or where to go pick him up if he got too drunk to drive himself home. "Where are you headed, in case I need to reach you?"

"The hunting cabin. Cell service is spotty up there, so don't bother trying."

Aha. Dad *was* planning to get roaring drunk. Luke's anger seethed. He spun around, marched up to within inches of his father, and jabbed a finger into the man's chest. "You want to drink yourself to death? Sure, go ahead. But while you're at it, consider how your actions affect Anika. For reasons I cannot fathom, she's devoted to you. As long as she thinks you need her, that she's somehow keeping you from losing yourself altogether, she'll never be free to live her own life. Is that really what you want for your daughter?"

Jaw muscles working, Luke's dad took several shallow breaths. All kinds of emotions flickered across his expression, none of them settling into anything Luke could identify. Without another word, Dad pivoted and trudged to the house.

And Anika wanted Luke to try understanding the man? Impossible.

He picked up his pace toward the barn. "Let's go, Fletch. We have a cow to tend to."

First-aid kit in hand, he was hiking to the pasture when his cell phone rang. Shannon's name flashed on the display. He gave his pulse a moment to adjust before he answered.

"Hi, Luke." Her tone held a regretful note. "About tomorrow, I—I don't think we can make it after all."

Sounded like she'd been having second thoughts, too. Considering he'd come close to reneging on his invitation, why should he feel this disappointed? "I hope everything's okay."

Her delayed response gave him the sense that everything was *not* okay. "The timing isn't good, that's all. I have a new part-time job, and I'll probably have to work most of the weekend to get my first assignment completed on time."

Shannon worked at a veterinary clinic five or six days a week, and now she'd taken on a second job? His thoughts rushed to the kid. "How are you managing with Tate?"

"I'll be working from home, proofreading and editing. So far, I've been doing my work after he's in bed at night."

"Oh. Well, that's good, I guess." Reaching the pasture gate, Luke set down the first-aid kit and leaned against the fence rail. Before he could think better of the idea, he said,

"Come out tomorrow anyway. I'll keep Tate occupied, and you can set up in my study."

"Really, I couldn't."

"Why not? Anika was looking forward to seeing you again."

"Because—" She released a shuddering breath. When she continued, a tremor came into her voice. "It's just not a good weekend for me."

His concern deepened. "Shannon, what's really going on?"

A couple of muted sniffles gave way to a humorless laugh. "Tomorrow is one of those grief anniversaries I have to face. Every year I think it'll get easier, but this one never does."

"Your husband?"

"It'll be five years tomorrow since he died."

"Shannon, I'm so sorry." Eyes squeezing shut, he pinched the bridge of his nose. "Are you sure you should be alone?"

"After I make some progress on this proofreading assignment, I may drive up to see my dad and stepmom. Did I tell you she's Steven's mother? It's always a hard day for her, too."

"They live a little farther into the mountains, right? If you come here first, you'll be that much closer." Why he'd developed such a strong hero complex where Shannon was concerned, he couldn't say. But the woman was definitely getting under his skin. "Please. Let's stick to the plan. Maybe we can attach a few happier memories to the day."

When she didn't answer right away, he hoped it meant she was considering it. "I suppose I shouldn't disappoint Tate. Taking Rowena to a real ranch and playing 'sheep' is all he's talked about this week."

"There you go." Anticipation swelled Luke's heart. "We can't let the little guy down, now, can we?"

A more genuine laugh rang through the phone speaker. "All right, we'll see you early tomorrow afternoon. I'll text when we're on the way."

Ending the call, Luke pushed back his Rockies cap and palmed his forehead. He might as well quit lying to himself, because this unplanned attraction for Shannon was only getting stronger. He could either accept it and see where things led, or else close that door, lock it securely, and get on with the no-nonsense life he'd consigned himself to.

A wry chuckle escaped. As wired as he felt at the prospect of seeing Shannon tomorrow, he figured he was in for a whole lot of nonsense. And he didn't care.

Chapter Ten

Anika awoke Saturday morning with the beginnings of another migraine. Determined not to let the pain steal more hours from her life, she took her meds right away and then crawled back into bed with an icepack pressed to her temple.

An hour later, both the headache and the brain fog were lifting. *Thank You, Lord!*

With Shannon and Tate expected this afternoon, it would be a busy and fun day. Anika had all the ingredients for her mother's eggplant lasagna, along with salad fixings and a fresh sourdough baguette for garlic bread. For dessert, she planned to whip up a chocolate mousse cheesecake.

A shame Daddy had left for the hunting cabin yesterday and wouldn't be here to meet Shannon and share a meal of some of Mom's favorite recipes.

Maybe it was just as well. Anika loved her daddy with all her heart, but most days, she felt like she had to walk on eggshells around him. She worried about how much he drank, and her little tricks to distract him or pretend to forget he'd sent her for another beer only went so far.

More than likely, he was snoozing off another bender at the cabin right now. The only positive thing about it was that he wasn't on the roads. He'd seemed sober enough when he'd told her goodbye yesterday—another good thing, because the roads up to the cabin got pretty narrow, and the drop-offs were steep. The cellular signal was just strong enough that she could see on the Find Friends app that he'd arrived safely.

As she set out two packages of cream cheese to soften, a memory fragment surfaced. She and Daddy were at the cattle auction in Idaho. They hadn't come to bid, just to check out the competition. Daddy told her he was going to the concession stand and to come get him when a certain breeder's stock came up for auction. But as the time approached, she couldn't find her father anywhere.

Giving up, she'd gone back to her seat in the stands and settled for taking notes and snapping a few photos with her phone. Several more cattle were auctioned and sold before her father returned. By then, he was staggering so badly that two other ranchers had to help him up the steps and into his seat.

Anika recalled being angry and embarrassed and wishing she could disappear. She only knew they had to get home somehow, because Mom would wait up for them and she'd be worried. It seemed like maybe the same ranchers helped her get Daddy to the exit. After that, her memories got fuzzy.

She released a sharp sigh and grabbed the package of Oreos from the pantry. Pulverizing chocolate cookies for the cheesecake crust would be therapeutic, because she'd rather think about other things today than her near-fatal accident.

Even so, she prayed it was a good sign that parts of her memory were returning. Once she could put all the pieces together, maybe the nightmares and headaches would finally stop.

Chapter Eleven

Luke's Saturday-morning obedience class at Hope House wrapped up a few minutes after ten. He exited the fenced yard with Witt, who often observed the classes in his role as transitional housing assistant for Equipped and Empowered Ministries.

"I'd say this is the best group yet," Luke said. "It's obvious the men have put in the practice time with their dogs this week."

"They're highly motivated." Arms folded, Witt leaned against the fender of his dusty white pickup. "The guys thought up an informal competition between Hope House and the other two men's transitional homes. The class voted least improved at the end of this session has to host the other two groups for a cookout."

Luke snorted a laugh. "Reverse psychology? Whatever works, I guess."

"They're also trying hard to make Carl Anderson proud and ensure the canine program continues. It was his brainchild, remember?"

"I do." Hard to forget how Hope House's previous

counselor-in-residence had wrangled with the board of directors, not only over the canine initiative but the fate of the entire transitional housing program. His efforts had brought a reprieve and also earned him a promotion to Director of Transitional Housing.

Luke had to admire such tenacity, especially when his own dreams seemed to drift farther and farther out of reach.

He opened his truck door to let Fletch jump in, then waved to Witt. "See you next Saturday?"

"Hold up a sec." Witt pushed off his pickup and ambled over. "If you're not in a rush, I was hoping to check some dates with you for the next class session."

"Actually, I need to head home pretty quick." Luke hid a bemused smile. He still couldn't believe he was going through with this. "Shannon Halsey and her son are coming out to the ranch."

Witt cocked a brow. "Interesting."

"They're helping me with a project." He explained about training Fletch to work with sheep. "Shannon almost backed out, though. She told me today's the anniversary of her husband's death."

"Ah." Giving a slow nod, Witt drew a hand down his jaw. "That's tough."

"How much do you know about it? How he died, I mean." Wouldn't hurt to get a few more details so he didn't put his foot in his mouth. "Shannon only said it was an auto accident."

"Motorcycle, actually. Maddie knows more about it than I do. She's best friends with Julia Frasier Bromley."

"Right, Shannon's mother-in-law–slash–stepmother." Luke harrumphed. "Talk about complicated."

"It's quite the story. They've both had to work through some stuff, but they've developed a real special closeness."

"What kind of stuff?"

Frowning, Witt shared how Julia's son had kept his marriage to Shannon a secret. He was supposed to study veterinary medicine and join the family practice, but meeting Shannon changed everything. "He knew his mom would be hurt and disappointed that he no longer wanted to become a veterinarian. But when they found out Shannon was expecting, he couldn't put off being honest with his mother any longer. On the night of the accident, he was heading home to tell her everything."

Arm resting on the steering wheel, Luke gazed through the windshield. "Wow. He never even met his son."

Silence fell between the men for several somber moments. Witt broke it with a soft expulsion of breath. "It'll be good for Shannon and Tate to do something fun with you."

"If I can help take her mind off what day it is, it'll be worth it."

Witt's eyes narrowed as a meaningful smile formed. "I have a feeling it's definitely going to be worth it, for both of you."

Leaving the vet clinic shortly after noon, Shannon drove over to get Tate at the Frasiers', then rushed home for a quick lunch and to change from her office khakis to jeans and sneakers.

Next was finagling how to fit Rowena in back next to Tate's safety seat. She was a big dog, but she could scrunch up pretty small when necessary—although Tate's hair might be drenched with dog drool by the time they got to Luke's place.

"How far is it, Mommy?" Tate sputtered and pushed Rowena's ear out of his face.

She tried not to laugh at the sight in her rearview mirror. "About an hour, I think. Will you two be okay back there?"

"Uh-huh. I'm gonna read my storybooks to Weena so she won't get bored."

"Good idea. But keep those paper towels handy in case she drips on the page." With the directions queued up on her phone, she secured it in the cup holder. Shortly, they were on their way.

A full appointment schedule at the clinic had kept Shannon's thoughts occupied this morning. Now, between Tate's singsong voice as he read to his dog and the clipped tones of the GPS announcer dictating her route, she continued to hold the painful memories at bay.

She'd actually begun to look forward to this afternoon. Even though she'd grown up around livestock on her dad's plot of land in the mountains, a real working ranch would be a new experience for both her and Tate.

The drive into the foothills flew by. Turning in through the stately wood-and-stone entrance to Fox Pass Ranch, Shannon felt like she was entering the set of an Old West movie. On one side of the lane, black cows lazed or grazed in the afternoon sun. Farther along, two horses trotted up to the fence and craned their sleek necks to see who'd ventured into their domain.

"Mommy! Horses!" Tate sucked in an excited gasp. "Do you think Luke will let us pet them? Or *ride* them?"

"We'll have to wait and see. Remember, he asked us out to help him train his dog."

"And pretend like we're sheep. But maybe after."

"Maybe." Shannon eyed her son in the rearview mirror. "But don't pester him about it. Promise me?"

He nodded but gave her a smile that said he wasn't promising anything.

Luke had texted that she should park in the driveway next to the big house—*mansion* was a more fitting description. Natural stone pillars at ground level supported the second-story balcony. West-facing floor-to-ceiling windows on both levels reflected sky and sun and the expansive terrain.

As Shannon eased the car to a stop at the detached three-car garage, Luke strode out from behind the house. He opened the Beetle's passenger-side door and leaned in. "Hi, you made it. Any trouble finding the place?"

"None at all." The rustic beauty of the house enthralled Shannon. "You ... you *live* here?"

"Not for a few years. That's my place over there." He nodded toward a cabin just beyond the enormous barn they'd passed on the way in. "Anika lives here at the house with our dad. But he's away for the weekend."

"Mom," Tate interrupted. "Can we get out now?"

"Okay, hold your horses." Shannon undid her seat belt and pushed open her door.

"But I don't have any horses yet. Just Weena."

Luke burst out laughing. "All this big girl needs is a saddle." He pushed the passenger seat forward and leaned in to release Tate's buckles. "I'll get the kiddo, Mom. Monster-dog is all yours."

"Gee, thanks." Shannon grabbed Rowena's leash from the floorboard and snapped it on her collar, then guided the lanky dog to the ground. Ludicrous to believe she could control an animal of Rowena's size with a flimsy strip of woven nylon.

Tate bounded around the front of the car, his head swiveling in all directions. "Where's your dog, Luke?"

"He's in the house with Anika. I didn't want him over-whelming Rowena until the dogs got acquainted."

Shannon scoffed. "Sure you weren't worried our big ol' monster-dog might overwhelm your cute little border collie?"

"Well, maybe a tiny bit." Luke grinned and winked. He showed them to the back terrace, then said he'd be right out with Fletch.

While they waited, Shannon inhaled fresh air scented with grass and pine while she took in the incredible view. The ranch had a much more open feel than her father's cabin. Growing up surrounded by towering trees and mountains on every side, she'd often suffered a simmering sense of panic, as if the world were closing in on her, burying her alive.

Or perhaps it was merely her father's overprotective-ness, his belief that as long as they remained isolated up there on the mountain, no harm could reach them.

What if he'd been right? What if she'd never left the mountain? Never met Steven? Never had to hear from a highway patrol trooper that the love of her life was never coming home?

The grief she'd been stifling all day slithered up through her chest and tightened around her throat like a boa constrictor. Silently choking, she clapped a hand over her mouth and turned away. Tate mustn't see her lose control, not again. Not like before. She had to stay strong. She *had* to.

Somehow—she didn't know how, or why, or when—

she found herself in Luke's arms. He was cradling her head against his chest, stroking her hair, keeping her from falling.

"It's okay," he murmured. "Let it out. Let it all out."

She noticed the front of his cotton henley was damp. *From my tears?*

"Oh. Oh!" Embarrassed, she pressed her palms against his solid shoulders and stepped back. "I—I didn't mean to—"

He used his index finger to lift a strand of hair off her cheek. His smile held warmth and compassion. "Hard day, huh?"

"I was doing all right until I let my thoughts wander." Blinking, she looked around. "Where's Tate?"

"In the house. He and Anika are playing with the dogs."

"Thank you." She sniffed hard. "I hate he had to see me break down like this."

"As I was coming out with Fletch, I could see you were struggling. I got him and the dog inside right away. I don't think he noticed."

"Oh, you'd be surprised what that observant little boy can notice." How could she forget the countless times during her darkest days when her toddler son had tried to comfort her?

Luke guided her into a padded patio chair. "Anika made a pot of chai tea just before you arrived. Stay here, and I'll bring you a cup."

She nodded her gratitude. When the door closed behind him, she drew a long breath, counted to five, then released the air to a count of ten. Twice more, and she felt her frayed emotions beginning to settle.

Glimpsing Luke through the window as he prepared her tea, she sent up a prayer of thanks for the new friends

God had brought into her life. Except for Maddie and Witt, she hadn't had many opportunities to develop friendships outside of work. Not to mention, most of the women her age from church were married, engaged, or desperately hoping to be. Few could relate to a struggling young widow whose only goal was to make sure the rest of her son's life made up for how badly she'd failed him in the beginning.

Luke cast his sister a silent smile of thanks for keeping Tate and the dogs entertained. Fletch stood in awe of the gentle giant who'd invaded his territory, but he'd made quick friends with Rowena. Tate had taught all of them a game he liked to play with his canine companion. Sitting on the kitchen floor opposite Anika, he'd gotten the dogs to lie down at the other two corners of the square, and now they were taking turns rolling Fletch's tennis ball back and forth.

Chuckling, Luke decided the boy displayed all the makings of a first-class dog trainer. No doubt he'd someday make for tough competition.

Luke added a few of Anika's fresh-baked chocolate-chip cookies to the tray he was preparing. Not usually a tea drinker, he'd make an exception this time, even if he had to use the dainty bone-china teacups Anika was fond of. Maybe Shannon would feel less like she was being coddled if he made it appear they were merely two friends sharing refreshments together.

Two friends ...

His stomach twisted. The part of him that insisted on imagining something more—*much* more—had become irrepressible. And he'd only met her last weekend, for crying out loud!

But the memory of holding her moments ago, the surge of awareness that had made it hard to release her as she pulled away ...

A groan slipped out before he could contain it.

"You okay?" Anika looked up from their game with a concerned frown.

He hefted the tray. "Just thinking I hope this doesn't spoil Shannon's appetite for the dinner you've been working on."

Excusing herself to Tate, Anika clambered to her feet. Getting down on the floor like that couldn't have been easy, the way her legs stiffened up sometimes. She linked her arm through Luke's and whispered, "Spoil her all you want to. She needs it today." Poking him in the ribs, she added, "And while you're at it, go ahead and spoil yourself."

He looked at her askance. "What's that supposed to mean?"

"It means you deserve a little self-indulgence now and then, too." She nodded toward the door. "So go out there and don't try to be anything but a cute guy spending time with a pretty girl on a pleasant September afternoon."

Face warming, he ducked his head. "Don't read more into this than there is."

"If you say so." Anika heaved an exaggerated shrug before gingerly resuming her position for the game. "Dinner will be ready at four. Plenty of time to take a leisurely stroll and show Shannon around the ranch."

And give himself even more opportunity to cross that invisible line into relationship territory? Not that it mattered. Five years may have passed, but Shannon clearly wasn't through grieving her late husband. Was that even healthy? Or had she been so distracted by supporting herself and her son that she hadn't allowed enough time to mourn her loss?

Luke gave an annoyed eye roll. What business did he have trying to psychoanalyze Shannon or anyone else? He was just an ordinary guy, trying his best to manage his own family issues—and not doing such a great job.

He stepped out to the terrace to find Shannon on her knees, plucking weeds from a neglected flowerbed. She smiled over her shoulder. "Sorry, couldn't resist."

"It's fine." Luke set the tray on the glass-top table and then stooped to gather up the pile Shannon had started. "But I'm afraid it's hopeless. Nobody's done much gardening around here since our mother passed away."

"That's too bad. I'm sure your mother kept a beautiful garden." She stood and brushed off her jeans.

"She did, as long as she was able. Her last few months were pretty hard ... for all of us." He gestured toward the table. "Tea's getting cold. Anika made cookies, too."

Shannon held up her dirt-covered hands. "And now I'm a mess. Oh, dear."

"There's a powder room just off the kitchen where you can wash up."

"Be right back."

She returned a few minutes later and joined him at the table. Taking a sip of tea, she closed her eyes with an appreciative moan. "Mmm, perfect."

Relieved she seemed to have shaken off her sadness, Luke spent a moment just watching her. She held the delicate teacup with both hands, as if savoring the aroma. Another honey-blond curl had worked free from her hair clip and drifted across her cheek. Luke ached with the desire to touch those silky strands again, to let his fingertips graze her temple and the curve of her ear ...

Grabbing a cookie, the safest thing he could think to do with his hands at the moment, he devoured it in three quick bites.

Shannon cast him a strange look as she took a cookie and bit off a much more refined morsel. After another sip of tea, she said, "Tell me more about your family. You said your father's away for the weekend?"

Luke didn't care to talk about his dad, but he also didn't want to sound rude. "Sometimes he likes to escape to his hunting cabin."

"It must be difficult for him after losing your mother." Traces of melancholy returning, she looked toward the horizon.

"Difficult for all of us." Luke gulped down the last of his tea. "You said you needed to do a little work on your project this afternoon?"

Jaw dropping, she shifted to face him. "Oh, no. We left in such a hurry that I forgot to bring my laptop."

"Uh-oh. Will you have time to finish the work tomorrow at home?"

"Guess I'll have to. Maybe I can leave Tate with Dad and Julia for the weekend." She set down her teacup and palmed her forehead. "I'm a terrible mom. This job was supposed to bring in extra income without stealing more time away from my son."

"It's just one day. This won't scar Tate for life." Leaning closer, he pulled her hands away from her face and covered them with his own. "You're here now, with nothing better to do than enjoy the afternoon. What do you say we get Tate and the dogs and head over to my pretend sheep pen? That'll give us just about an hour before Anika's ready to get dinner on the table."

Chapter Twelve

Shannon leaned against the fence rail and hugged her aching sides. It had been far too long since she'd laughed this hard. Who knew getting herded around a pen by an overzealous border collie could be this much fun?

"That'll do, Fletch," Luke called with a chuckle. When the dog came and sat at his feet, he fed him a few treats.

Tate gave a disappointed huff. "Can't we do it some more?"

"Oh, honey, I don't think so." Shannon pressed her sleeve against her damp forehead. The early-September sun had warmed her quickly.

"Looks to me like your mom's worn out." Luke reached for Tate's hand, but he kept his gaze on her. A tantalizing smile played across his lips. "How about we go to the house, get something cold to drink, and wash up for dinner?"

A different kind of warmth heated her skin. "Yes, I'd love a cold drink."

"Okay," Tate said, "but then will you help me teach Weena a trick?"

"You bet."

Tate raced ahead with Fletch and Rowena, leaving Shannon and Luke to follow at a more leisurely pace.

Luke tipped back his baseball cap. "Hope that wasn't too much of a workout for you."

"I'll survive. And I definitely needed the exercise."

Slowing a bit more, Luke said, "I couldn't help noticing Rowena's limp. Is she okay?"

"She's fine. Before we got her, a car had hit her, and she had a badly broken leg. Julia did surgery, but Rowena will always have a slight limp."

"That's too bad. It doesn't look like it bothers her much."

"She's never let it get her down." *Unlike me*. Fresh waves of regret washed over Shannon at the memory of how she'd fallen into utter despair after losing Steven.

"Dogs can be a lot better than people at letting go of the past," Luke said, "especially when they trust you."

Maybe that was part of Shannon's problem. Steven's death had undermined her ability to trust in hopes and plans and a future she could count on. At least she hadn't lost her hope in the Lord. If not for the solid faith foundation Steven had nurtured in her during the short time they'd shared, she hated to imagine where she'd be today ... or if she'd even be around to think such thoughts.

The reminder that she'd once considered giving up on life caused her to stumble. When Luke reached for her hand to steady her, an electric current zinged from her fingertips to her shoulder.

"Sorry." Suppressing a shiver, she put a little more distance between them. "My mind was elsewhere."

Luke stuffed his hands into his jeans pockets. "Anything you feel like talking about?"

Looking toward the mountains, she sighed. "I've burdened you enough already with my personal problems."

"I don't consider it a burden." When she glanced back at him, sincerity shone in his brown-eyed gaze. "In case I haven't made it crystal clear, I'm glad you came out today, and not only because of your help with Fletch's training." His gentle smile stretched into a grin. "Although watching you and Tate dart around the pen while making sheep noises was definitely the highlight of my afternoon."

Gloomy thoughts evaporated as a burst of laughter escaped. She gave Luke a friendly punch in the arm. "I'm glad we kept you entertained."

"You certainly did." His smile became boyish, like the look on Tate's face when he'd done something cute and Shannon teased him about it. He sprinted ahead. "Hey, Tate, don't let the dogs in the house with their dirty feet, or Anika will be all over my case."

Shannon picked up her pace to catch up, but as she neared the terrace, she glimpsed Tobias in the driveway doing something to her car. She'd almost forgotten he'd promised to complete his fixes while she was here this afternoon.

He caught her eye and waved. "Almost done. I was about to come looking for you."

Changing direction, she strode over. "Do you need me to get the key?"

"Nope, almost done." Kneeling inside the passenger door, he tightened something with a screwdriver. "That should do it."

"I thought I heard a vibration somewhere in that area."

"The door panel needed some adjusting. It's tight as a drum now."

Shannon ran her hand along the upper edge, noting the solid feel. "I appreciate your attention to detail."

"I pride myself on it." Unfolding his long legs, Tobias reached for the cowboy hat he'd laid on the seat. "Looked like y'all were having all kinds of fun out there."

"We were." She cast a wistful glance toward the sheep pen. "It was exactly what I needed today."

"What Luke needed, too, more'n likely." He gave her one of those mischievous winks he seemed so good at. "Yep, saw you two flirtin' like a couple of teenagers."

Her brows shot up. "I think you have the wrong idea."

"Pretty sure I don't." Arms folded, he leaned against the Beetle's fender. "'Cause when it comes to flirting, I'm a consummate professional."

She had no doubt.

"Meant no offense," he said with a lazy grin. "Just the opposite, in fact. In my humble opinion, you're the best thing to happen to Luke in a real long time."

And yet, the other day at the DMV, he'd warned her to be cautious with Luke. Which was it, then?

"I should go inside." She gestured toward the car. "Thanks again for ... everything."

Pivoting, she smacked into Luke's firm chest. He caught her by the shoulders. "Wondered where you'd gotten to. Anika's calling us to the table."

"Just on my way in." Slipping out of his grip, she managed a brief smile before edging past him. "I hope Tate hasn't been pestering her to death."

Hurrying around to the terrace, she halted outside the back door to give her pulse rate a chance to slow. She wasn't supposed to be feeling these feelings—especially not today!

Her mind replayed the events of the afternoon and her interactions with Luke. If it looked like flirting to someone who hardly knew her, then what must Luke himself think? Because if she'd given him the wrong idea, led him to believe she was available ...

But aren't you? She could almost hear Steven's voice whispering through her thoughts: *It's been five years, babe. You know I wouldn't want you spending the rest of your life alone, grieving for me, mourning the future we were supposed to have. Be happy. Live your life. For our son. For yourself.*

❦

Luke planted himself in front of Tobias and fisted his hips. "What did you say to Shannon?"

"What? Nothing!" The lanky cowboy sidestepped Luke and began gathering up his tools.

"I warned you about coming on to her."

Tobias burst out laughing. "*Au contraire, mon ami.* If anyone was coming on to her—"

"Cool it with the French, okay? Besides, your accent's terrible." Luke followed Tobias around the car. "And what —you're implying I was flirting with Shannon?"

"If the shoe fits." Tobias shrugged and bent to secure the latches on his toolbox. "And unless my practiced eye deceived me, I'm pretty sure she was giving as much as she got."

Was she? No way. Tobias had to be mistaken. Besides, knowing what today meant to Shannon, Luke would never have been so forward. He'd wanted her to have an enjoyable day, but that's all. How could sharing a few laughs constitute flirting?

Because you're a guy and she's a girl. Not to mention, Shannon was the first woman to cause a noticeable blip on his romance radar in too long to remember.

"Hey, man." Tobias's hand landed on his shoulder. "Ain't nothin' wrong with letting a pretty lady know you're interested in getting to know her better."

"Okay, yes, I'd definitely like to get better acquainted with Shannon. But only when she's ready. In case you haven't noticed, she's still hung up on her late husband."

"Then give her a reason not to be." Tobias pivoted to grab his toolbox.

Fisting his hips, Luke called after him, "And how am I supposed to do that?"

With a look that implied Luke's utter incomprehension, Tobias heaved a sigh. "Be the living, breathing, in-the-flesh man in her life right now. Show her you have tons more to offer than the memory of a guy she'll never get back, no matter how much in love they were. And don't give up until she believes it."

Luke could only stare open-mouthed and shake his head. "How in the world can you claim to be this savvy about relationships and somehow still be single?"

"'Cause I'm holding out for the woman who makes my heart jump just like Shannon does for you." With a sly wink, Tobias turned and marched across the yard toward the bunkhouse.

⬥

"Luke. Luke!"

He spun around, startled to find his sister standing in the breezeway and wearing an impatient glare.

"What's up with you?" she demanded. "I've called your name at least five times. Dinner's getting cold, and you're being rude to your guests."

"Sorry." He felt like he'd been jerked back from somewhere far, far away. Maybe because it was true? "Be there in a sec."

Anika flung her arms in annoyance before tromping back inside.

He couldn't say for sure where his thoughts had taken him—much less how long he'd been there. But Tobias's remarks got him thinking. No, *imagining* was a better word for it. Imagining what it would be like if he ever made room in his life for something more.

If he made room in his life for Shannon.

Without a doubt, the woman intrigued him. Vulnerable yet strong. Tender but resolute. Beautiful inside and out.

And, he reminded himself, emotionally unavailable as long as she clung to the memory of her late husband.

Was Tobias right, though? If Luke could open her eyes and heart to the fact that *he* was here, right now, ready to be there for her in every way, would it be enough?

Before Anika came looking for him again, he set his feet in motion and strode around to the kitchen door. He drew a deep breath, then threw his shoulders back and pasted on an apologetic smile. Inside, he found everyone seated around the table. The dogs snoozed, tuckered out after their stimulating afternoon.

Luke closed the door behind him. "Sorry I kept you waiting. I was talking to Tobias and lost track of time."

"Typical." Anika smirked. "We were five seconds away from starting without you. Hurry and wash up."

He noted the only remaining seat placed him at Shannon's left. His sister's doing, no doubt. He should thank Ani later, but he'd rather not give her the satisfaction. Apologizing again, he made a quick trip to the powder room, then scooted into his chair and reached for his napkin.

Anika offered a blessing. As she began serving the lasagna, Luke passed the salad bowl to Shannon. She smiled and added some to her plate, then turned her attention to helping Tate with his food.

The kid stuffed a mammoth-sized bite of lasagna into his mouth. His eyes lit up as tomato sauce dribbled down his chin. "Yum!"

"Tate, honey, don't talk with your mouth full." Shannon used her napkin to mop up the drips before they landed on his T-shirt. "Be careful, sweetie. I'd rather not have to change your clothes again before we leave for Grampy's cabin."

"I can fix that." Luke went to grab a dishtowel from one of the kitchen drawers. He tied one end around Tate's neck and tucked the rest between the little boy's tummy and the table. "There, now you won't drip on your shirt."

"Thank you," Shannon murmured as he returned to his chair. "I never leave home without extra clothes for him, but what can I say? He's an active little boy."

"Luke was the same way. Still is, actually." Anika smirked as she sprinkled grated parmesan over her salad. "Mom could never keep him in clean shirts or jeans. As soon as she could teach him how to run the washer and dryer, she put him in charge of doing his own laundry."

Face warming, Luke cast his sister a snarky glare. "How about we don't air our dirty laundry in front of our guests?"

The muted sound of Shannon's chuckle drew his head around. She poked her salad fork into a black olive. "I think it's cute the way you two rag on each other." With a sad smile, she lowered her gaze. "I didn't grow up with siblings. I feel like I kind of missed out."

"We get along ... most of the time." Anika grinned and gave Luke's shin a playful kick under the table. "Can't help it—gotta love this guy."

"Ow!" He doubled over as if she'd actually hurt him. "If that's how you show love, I never want to get on your bad side."

"Already are, fella. You were late for dinner, remember? Just for that, you get to do dishes."

"Mommy?" Worry creased Tate's forehead. "Are they fighting? You should give them a time-out."

Shannon's laughter nearly caused her to spew the sip of iced tea she'd just taken. She pressed her napkin to her lips. "It's okay, Tater-Tot. They're grownups. They can work out their own disagreements."

"And we will." Catching Tate's eye, Luke winked and stole a piece of garlic bread off Anika's plate. Dodging her attempt to slap his hand, he stuffed the whole hunk of bread into his mouth.

Tate's jaw dropped. "Luke. That was very naughty! Be nice to your sister."

"Okay, okay, you're right, little man." Time to bring the curtain down on the dinner-table entertainment. He passed Anika a fresh slice of garlic bread. "My apologies, Ani."

"Accepted. But you're still doing dishes."

A peek at Shannon revealed her near-futile attempt at a more sedate expression. She cleared her throat and focused on finishing her lasagna.

Seemed the brother-sister act had done its part in easing tensions, and dinner continued with relaxed conversation. Once they'd finished the main course, Luke cleared the table while Anika served chocolate mousse cheesecake and decaf. Good thing for Tate's dishtowel bib, or the little guy's shirt front would have ended up a red-and-brown abstract art masterpiece.

Shannon took Tate to the powder room to wash up and returned with his face and hands looking pink from scrubbing. "Dinner was delicious, Anika. I hate to eat and run, but we'd better be on our way to my dad's."

"No worries." Anika gave her a quick hug. "We'll have to do this again soon."

Luke snapped on Rowena's leash, then scooped up Shannon's tote. "I'll walk you out."

At her car, he gave Tate a boost into his car seat and helped him with the buckles. Rowena squeezed in beside him.

"Thanks again for today," Shannon said as he joined her next to the driver's door. "I had a wonderful time, and I'm sorry for being such a downer earlier."

"You weren't. Not at all." The urge to offer a reassuring embrace became almost irresistible. He settled for taking her hand. "And Anika's right—we should do this again. How about next weekend?"

She cast him a crooked smile. "You mean another pretend sheep practice day for Fletch?"

The memory made him chuckle. Then his expression softened. "Or something else. Anything else. A leisurely drive up to Flathead Lake. A hike in the foothills. We could even do dinner and a movie."

She tensed, her hand slipping from his. "I—I'm not sure that's a good idea."

"Which part—dinner, or the movie?" He hoped his silly grin would bring back her smile. "I know you eat dinner, and I'd definitely let you pick the movie."

"Oh, Luke." Shaking her head, she took a step that placed the open door between them.

He wished he had Tobias in his ear right now, feeding him the words to say, because he was about to blow it. "Please, Shannon. Don't get the wrong idea. It's just ... I'm enjoying getting to know you. As a friend." *For now, anyway.* He leaned sideways to wiggle his fingers at Tate. "And I think the little guy likes me, too."

"I do, Mommy," Tate called from the back seat. "I like Luke a whole bunch."

He mentally pumped his fist. *Way to go, kid.* "You and Rowena just keep practicing those commands I showed you."

"We will!"

Shannon's shoulders relaxed, and she quirked her lips. "It's been fun getting to know you, too, Luke. But I've just started a second job, and I'm still working out my schedule —which, so far, I'm a miserable failure at. This isn't the best time for"—she swallowed hard—"new relationships."

"We can take it slow. No pressure. Just don't block my number if I call or text from time to time to see how you're doing." He laid his fingertips atop hers where they rested on the car door. "Because I care."

Dipping her chin, she murmured, "Okay, I promise I won't. And ... thank you."

Moments later, she drove away, leaving Luke standing in the driveway and wondering how soon was too soon to send her the first of many just-checking-on-you texts.

Chapter Thirteen

"Stop pacing, Fletch." Anika shook her finger at the hyperactive border collie. "He'll be back soon."

She hadn't meant to spy on Luke and Shannon while they talked in the driveway, but curiosity got the better of her. Luke may as well stop denying his interest in the pretty single mom—and Shannon would never convince anyone she wasn't equally attracted to Luke. Anyone with eyes could read what was going on beneath their surface expressions.

As Anika put away the last of the leftovers, her cell phone jangled. She plucked it off the counter to see Daddy on the lock screen.

Stomach knotting, she pressed the green answer icon. "Hi, Dad. Everything okay?"

At first, all she heard was rustling. Maybe he'd only pocket-dialed her. Then, "Ani, I—I'm real sorry, hon." His words slurred so badly that she struggled to understand him. "You"—a hiccup and a sob—"don't deserve what happened."

"Daddy, it's okay." Eyes filling, she sank into a chair.

"Please, Daddy. Don't do this to yourself. Alcohol won't fix anything."

Luke had just returned, his furrowed brow suggesting he'd immediately sized up the situation. He motioned for Anika to give him the phone.

She firmly shook her head. Getting her brother involved in this conversation would only make things worse. "I mean it, Daddy. Why don't you drink a big glass of water and eat one of those sandwiches I packed for you? Then get some sleep. Things'll look better in the morning."

"Can't eat, can't sleep." Another sniffling sob, then the screech of tires.

"Daddy, where are you?" With such clear phone reception, she should have realized he wasn't at the cabin. "Are you driving somewhere?"

"Aw, Nina." Her mother's name. "I done wrong, babe —messed up real bad." Dad was crying in earnest now. His rambling became too distorted to make out.

She pressed the mute button and faced Luke. "He's making no sense, and he's on the road. We've got to go find him."

"Not a smart idea." He shook his head. "No one can reason with him when he's this drunk."

Her brother's lack of concern irked her. "You're okay with the possibility that he might drink himself to death, either accidentally or on purpose?" She stood and held the phone at her side while her dad's incoherent blather continued. "And driving in that condition—are you willing to risk him killing somebody else?"

Luke's face paled. Jaw working, he looked away. "All right. But I'll handle it. You stay here."

"Are you kidding? No way! I know how you two fight. It's even worse when he's had too much to drink."

"Exactly why I don't want you in the middle of it." Luke started for the door. "Keep him talking for as long as you can. I'm guessing he's headed for the general store to grab another six-pack. It'll take me about an hour to get there."

Anika grabbed his arm. "At least take Tobias with you. If Dad gets belligerent, you might need help."

Luke gave a curt nod, then dropped his gaze to Fletch, who stared up at him with an expectant look. "Not this time, fella. You don't need to be in the crossfire either. Keep Ani company, okay?"

Fletch yipped and went to stand at her heel.

As soon as the door closed behind her brother, Anika took her phone off mute. Her father's mumbling had faded to wordless whimpers. "Dad? Daddy, can you hear me?"

A loud sniff. "Nina?"

"No, Daddy. It's Anika."

"Ani. My sweet, sweet girl."

"Daddy, tell me where you are. Did you go to the general store?"

The truck noises stopped. "The store. Yeah."

"Okay, good. Now please just stay put. You need to get your head clear before you drive again." She wouldn't mention that Luke was on his way for fear her father would take off.

More crying. "You shoulda come with me, Nina. I need you, babe."

Tears welled in Anika's eyes. She covered them with one hand and tried to keep her voice steady. "Mom's gone, Daddy."

"Gone?"

"Remember, we scattered her ashes beneath the larch

trees along the stream. It was three years ago, when the leaves were starting to turn."

"Jus' like she wanted, under those pretty golden leaves." His sobs were coming hard again. "Nina, my Nina!"

Anika ached to wrap her daddy in her arms and speak comforting words into his ear. She'd noticed the larches up in the mountains were already showing tinges of pale copper and gold. Was that what had sent her father down this path of fresh grief?

She should have insisted on going with Luke. Why did her brother have to be so bossy, always thinking he had to protect her?

Forcing a calm she didn't feel, she spoke into the phone. "I'm right here, Daddy. It's going to be okay."

"I dunno ... I dunno." A slurping sound came across the line, then a loud gulp and a sputter.

"Daddy. Please put the whiskey down." She'd memorized the different drinking noises he made, depending on his choice of alcohol. When he guzzled beer, a chest-rattling belch usually followed. Tequila led to more of a fire-breathing gasp. A mellow sigh accompanied slow sips of wine.

Then another sound snapped her to attention—the unmistakable click of Granddad's old revolver being cocked. Dad loved that gun, but usually he kept it locked in its case in the gun cabinet. If he'd taken it with him—

"Daddy?" Her heart hammered. She pressed the phone to her ear. "What are you doing?"

"Can't, baby ... can't keep doin' this to you."

"Doing what, Daddy? Please!" Anika scoured her brain for anything she could say to keep her father from going through with this unspeakable act. "I love you, Daddy. You've got to come home to me. I need you!"

"Can't ..." The background static coming across the airwaves went silent.

Pulse racing, Anika shot Luke a text:

HURRY! He has Granddad's gun!!!

Then she hit speed dial for her dad's number. The phone rang six times before voicemail picked up. She disconnected and tried again—then twice more, with the same results.

Fletch whined and pushed his nose beneath her arm.

Tears streaming down her face, she stroked the dog's head. "There's nothing I can do now but pray."

Chapter Fourteen

"Are we almost there, Mommy?"

Startled, Shannon blinked. How long had her thoughts distracted her? She should be paying attention to her driving, not replaying every moment she'd spent with Luke this afternoon ... and every confusing emotion those moments evoked.

"Getting close." She smiled at Tate through the rearview mirror. "Grampy's cabin is coming up around the next curve. Help me watch for it, okay?"

Seconds later, he shouted, "I see it!"

Shannon slowed as her dad's green metal ranch gate came into view. Dad waved from the door of his wood-working shop before loping over to swing open the gate.

She drove through and parked at the cabin. By the time she got Tate and Rowena out of the back seat, her father had caught up.

"So this is the cute little car I've been hearing about." He ran his hand over the shiny yellow roof. "Nice."

"It's fun to drive, and I got a great deal." She'd tacked

on that last part in hopes of fending off more offers of financial assistance.

Excited yipping reached them from the deck above. Julia's twin dachshunds raced down the steps to greet Rowena, then pranced around and through her legs.

Tate laughed and called Daisy and Dash to follow him upstairs. "Grammy, we're here!"

Looking relieved, Rowena rolled her big brown eyes toward Shannon as if to say, *Somebody needs to give those twerps a chill pill.*

Shannon could use one, too—except for the past several months, her doctor had been tapering her off the antidepressants. Eyes squeezed shut, she released a long sigh. Might be worth reconsidering that decision.

"Rough day, huh?" Her father slid his arm around her shoulders. "It's been tough on Julia, too. She's taking it out on the lump of bread dough she's attempting to pound into submission."

Shannon's brows shot up. "Julia's baking bread now?"

"It's her latest hobby. But don't expect much. Her first three loaves could have been boat anchors."

Picturing her stepmother doing anything in the kitchen besides heating frozen dinners in the microwave required a huge stretch of the imagination. "How long has she been at this?"

"A week. Maybe two." Dad shrugged. "I don't think she's handling semiretirement very well."

"Apparently." They could both testify to how long Julia had lasted at crocheting, candle making, and learning Italian. "She's a career veterinarian. I hate to say this, Dad, but maybe she needs to spend more time at the clinic, not less. Maybe living on the mountain is too ..."

"Isolating?" Jaw clenched, her father pulled her close

and kissed her forehead. "Believe me, sweetie, I learned my lesson with you. I've told Julia again and again that she should do what makes her happy, even if it means we aren't together as much."

Shannon frowned at her father. "Ever think maybe *you've* stayed too long up here on the mountain?"

A self-conscious laugh rumbled in his throat. "I've been better since I married Julia, haven't I? We come down to Elk Valley every Sunday for church. And I get into Missoula way more often than I used to, now that you're living there."

"It's progress." Shannon patted his chest, then started up the deck steps. "We should go inside and make sure Julia can't blame Tate if her bread doesn't turn out."

Either Julia had gotten her loaves into the oven before Tate interrupted, or she'd given up entirely. Shannon smiled at the sight of them snuggled together in the rocking chair Dad had made for Julia before they married.

Tate beamed at his mother. "I'm telling Grammy how we played pretend sheep for Luke and Fletch."

Ruffling Tate's hair, Julia cast Shannon a curious grin. "Sounds like a fun afternoon."

"It was." Shannon's face warmed, a mixture of pleasure and uncertainty swirling in her belly. She should change the subject before Julia or her father read anything more into how much time she'd already spent with Luke after having met him only last weekend.

She plopped onto the sofa. "So. Dad says you've been baking bread."

After eating entirely too much of Anika's delicious lasagna, Shannon appreciated the light late-evening meal of home-made vegetable soup, courtesy of Dad's neighbor, Lila Vernon. While Dad and Julia washed dishes afterward, Shannon took Tate upstairs for a bath, then read him a story and tucked him into the new twin bed Dad had added to her childhood room.

When she returned downstairs, Dad had a cozy fire going in the potbelly stove. Julia patted the space beside her on the sofa. "Come sit with us, honey. Now that the little guy's asleep, we can have a nice grown-up conversation."

Shannon curled her legs under her at one end of the sofa and offered an enigmatic smile. "I told you about my new job already."

Sprawled in his easy chair, Dad laid aside his sudoku puzzle book. "It does sound like a good fit for you."

She'd worried both he and Julia would try to dissuade her from the proofreading job, but when the subject arose as they talked over their bowls of soup, they'd surprised her with their words of support. "I think I'm going to like it," she said. "And thanks for agreeing to entertain Tate tomorrow while I finish my first assignment. I still can't believe I left my laptop at home."

Julia waved a hand in dismissal. "We'd never pass up a chance to spend time with our grandson."

Dad agreed, casting Shannon a meaningful grin. "Plus, when we bring him home, it'll get us off this *lonely ol' mountain*."

"Daddy ..." She couldn't suppress a chuckle.

Julia straightened. Eyes a little too bright, she said, "I'd love to hear more about your new friend Luke."

Shannon's throat tightened. "Not today, okay?"

Julia offered an understanding smile as she patted Shannon's foot. "I think today's the perfect day."

"I'd really rather not." She gnawed her lower lip. "Mind if we change the subject?"

Dad rose from his easy chair. Propping himself on the arm of the sofa behind her, he massaged her shoulders. "You've overcome so much, sweetie. Don't you think it's about time you opened your heart again?"

"I will ... eventually." She drew a shaky breath. "When I'm ready."

"But you have to let yourself *be* ready," Julia insisted. "You have to give yourself permission, just like I did when I met your dad. I didn't think I was ready, either."

"And I definitely wasn't." Dad's tone mellowed with the sweetness of true love. "But God knew better than both of us."

It warmed Shannon's heart to witness how, after all the years of pushing God away, Dad had found his faith. Not to mention the happiness he shared with Julia was indisputable.

Unbidden, her thoughts returned to those moments on the terrace when Luke had taken her in his arms. She'd been awash in memories of Steven, drowning in fresh grief. And yet, something else had been happening, too. She'd felt connected to Luke in a way she never expected to experience again after losing her husband.

Hard as she'd tried to stifle them, those feelings had only intensified as the afternoon progressed. She liked Luke. Very much. As she and Tate were leaving, he'd all but asked her on a date. *What's wrong with you, Shannon? Would it have cost you so much to say yes?*

She stretched across the sofa cushions to give Julia a hug, then stood and shared one with her father. "If you two don't mind, I'm going to step outside and make a quick phone call."

Her dad caught her hand as she started for the front door. "You know we don't have decent cell service up here."

"Then I'll send a text." Even better. It would be a turnabout on Luke's intention to text her now and then with a friendly *How are you doing?*

Out on the deck, she braced herself against the rail and stared at her phone. The butterflies in her stomach felt like they were doing the salsa on rollerblades, but she couldn't chicken out now. Opening the messaging app, she composed a short but friendly text, then hit send and held her breath.

Don't do it. Don't do it. Don't do it.

The phrase thrummed through Luke's brain like the rhythmic *chug-chug* of a freight train as he sped toward the general store. If Anika was right, if Dad had Granddad's revolver and intended to use it on himself—

God, please don't let him do it!

It was the closest Luke had come to praying since the wreck that had nearly killed both his father and his sister. How dare the man wreak havoc on their emotions like this? Did he have no concept—no pity—for how taking his own life would destroy Anika?

Luke's cell phone signaled an incoming text. Hoping it was Anika reporting that she'd reached Dad and all was well, he instructed the phone's digital assistant to read the message aloud.

Text from Shannon Halsey. Hi. Thanks
again for a fun afternoon. It helped more
than you know. If your dinner and a
movie offer is still good, maybe we can
plan something for next weekend?

His stomach plummeted. Half an hour ago, those words would have sent his heart soaring. Now, all he could think about was keeping his father from doing something stupid. And irreversible.

But he couldn't leave Shannon hanging. If he didn't give some kind of response, she could take his silence the wrong way.

After navigating a hairpin curve, he dictated a reply: "Sorry, things got complicated after you left. Can't explain. I'll be in touch."

Siri repeated back his words in her affectedly cheery AI voice and waited for his approval. If he weren't in such a hurry, he'd delete and start over. Maybe try to sound a little less negative, more like he truly wanted to see Shannon again. Because he did.

The general store came into view around the next bend. He told Siri to send the text.

He spied Dad's truck beneath a floodlight on the far edge of the parking area and skidded to a stop next to the passenger door. When he glimpsed his father's unmoving form slumped over the steering wheel, his breath caught in his throat. He leapt out and tried to pull open the door, but it was locked. Granddad's revolver lay on the seat next to an empty bottle of whiskey. A quick scan of the area around his father didn't reveal any signs of blood.

Luke pounded on the window. "Dad? Dad! Can you hear me?" He raced around to the driver's side and yanked on the door handle to no avail. "Dad! Wake up!"

His shouts must have alerted someone inside the store. A big, bearded man wearing camo pants and a red-checked flannel shirt marched over. "What's going on? You need some help?"

"My father's passed out in his truck. I can't get to him."

The big guy peered in the window, then gave a disgusted snort. "Some folks can't hold their liquor—or shouldn't be drinking at all. Be right back."

Seconds later, the man returned with a long, skinny gadget that he slid between the window and the door frame. He wiggled it until a telltale click sounded. Moving aside, he nodded for Luke to try the handle.

This time, the door swung open, releasing the fetid odors of vomit, sweat, and spilled liquor. Luke swallowed his revulsion long enough to press two fingers to his father's carotid. The pulse was slow and irregular, but at least he had one.

Turning away, Luke hauled in a few cleansing breaths of pine-scented mountain air, then turned to the man from the store. "Can you help me move him into my truck? I need to get him to a hospital."

Chapter Fifteen

L uke handed his sister a Styrofoam cup of strong hospital coffee. "You're not doing yourself or Dad any good by staying here. Why don't you go home and get some rest?"

Anika took a careful sip of the steaming brew, then returned her gaze to their father's sleeping form. The egg-and-ham croissant Luke had picked up for her on his way to the hospital sat untouched on the tray table. "I'm fine," she insisted. "You didn't need to come. Don't you have ranch stuff to handle?"

After spending the past thirty-six hours at their father's bedside, she didn't look anywhere near fine. She winced and massaged her temple, a clear sign of an impending migraine.

"You heard what the doctor said. It'll take a few days to clear the alcohol from his system and get him stabilized. They'll call us if anything changes." Luke gave her shoulder a gentle squeeze. "If it'll convince you to go home, I'll stay with Dad. Tobias can handle things at the ranch."

As if she hadn't heard him, she murmured, "This is my fault."

"What? No. Why would you say that?"

"Because I've been an enabler. If I'd stood up to him about his drinking instead of—instead of—" Her voice broke on a stifled sob.

Luke pulled a chair over and sat facing his sister. Before she spilled her coffee, he took it from her and set it on the tray table, then cradled her hands. "Look at me, Ani." When she lifted her eyes to his, he went on, "Nobody is to blame except Dad. He did this to himself. All you've done is love him the best you know how."

"Which obviously wasn't enough. I just don't understand." She cast their father a helpless glance. "*Why*, Luke? Why is he like this?"

There was a lot he wished he understood better about their father, but he'd given up trying. "Maybe this episode will finally be his rock bottom. We have to hope he'll wake up and realize he needs to get off the booze and into rehab. It's either that, or ..." He finished the thought with a rough sigh. They both knew how this could have ended.

And still might, if Dad didn't pull through. The doctor on duty in the ER Saturday night hadn't minced words. If Luke hadn't found him and brought him straight to the hospital, Dad would likely have died right there in the truck.

Granddad's revolver was superfluous.

"We can't just *hope*, Luke." Sitting a little straighter, Anika gave a loud sniff. "I need you to pray with me."

He flinched. "You know I'm not very good with prayer."

"God doesn't care. Please?"

"If I do, then will you go home?"

With a sharp sigh, she nodded, then bowed her head. "Oh, Father, we're desperate for Your help." The words were soft and shaky at first, but her voice picked up strength as she continued. "Our daddy needs You. Not just to heal his body, but to restore his heart and mind. He needs to realize how desperately he needs the forgiveness and grace You offer through Your precious Son, Jesus. Please, God, wake him up to that truth. Make him a new creation in Christ."

Luke sat in silent awe of his sister's eloquence. Even more, her unwavering faith considering everything she'd been through. Not just her near-fatal accident and the aftermath, but how she'd loved, supported, and defended their father, even after Luke had all but shut the man out of his life.

Anika tugged a tissue from the box on the tray table, dried her eyes, and blew her nose. Rising, she bent to give her father a gentle kiss on the forehead, then gathered up her things.

Luke walked her to the door. "You're exhausted. Maybe I should drive you."

"No, I'll be okay. Stay with Dad. And call me right away if there's any news."

"I promise." He tilted her chin upward and locked eyes with her. "And you'd better promise me you'll eat something and get some rest."

He watched until she entered the elevator to make sure she didn't change her mind at the last minute. Not that he was all that keen on staying—he'd spent too many hours pacing hospital corridors, hovering at bedsides, and waiting for answers from doctors and nurses who never seemed to have anything good to report.

And here he was again. With a muted groan, he trudged to the vinyl recliner Anika had vacated. After giving his father's motionless form a cursory glance, he settled in for another marathon of waiting and wondering.

Remembering something he wanted Tobias to do, he took out his phone and called. "I nearly forgot it's payday for the ranch hands. The checks are all signed and locked in the barn office, middle drawer of the desk."

"On it," Tobias said. "How's it going with your dad?"

"No change. I just sent Anika home. Pretty sure she's got a migraine coming on. Would you check on her later?"

"Of course. You gonna stay awhile?"

"It was the only way I could talk Anika into leaving." Luke switched gears to cover a few other items of ranch business.

"Don't worry about stuff here," Tobias replied. "And maybe use the downtime to take care of yourself."

"Downtime. Right." Luke snorted. He could hardly remember what that felt like.

He ended the call, then scooted deeper into the recliner and raised the footrest. Might as well get comfortable since he was here for the long haul. Out of sheer boredom, he scrolled through email on his phone. There were three new dog-training queries and a reminder about an upcoming herding dog trial. He couldn't think about those until he had some answers about his dad.

Next, he opened the messaging app. And there, staring him in the face, was his terse reply to Shannon on Saturday.

Monday mornings at the clinic were typically busy, and today was no exception. At the first sign of a lull, Shannon escaped to the break room for a much-needed coffee refill.

It was a blessing that Dad and Julia had insisted on

keeping Tate at the cabin until today. Nervous about making a mistake on her first official proofreading assignment, Shannon had stayed up entirely too late last night, second-guessing every minor correction she'd made. Once she'd built up her confidence with a few successful edits, these assignments shouldn't take as long. Otherwise, her goal of not letting a second job steal quality time from her son would end in defeat.

With Dylan covering the reception desk, she decided she could relax for a few minutes. After pulling out a second chair to rest her feet on, she leaned back and took a calming sip of coffee.

When her phone buzzed, she pulled it from her pocket to find a message from Tate's great-grandmother. Dorothy had sent a photo of Tate attempting a headstand against a wall. Shannon laughed at the cockeyed angle of his legs and the way his bare belly pooched out above his drooping shirttail. She replied with several rolling-on-the-floor-laughing emojis and a heart.

She was about to close the messaging app when she glimpsed Luke's last message from Saturday.

> Sorry, things got complicated after you left. Can't explain. I'll be in touch.

I'll be in touch implied *Don't call me, I'll call you.* So she hadn't responded, leaving it to him to let her know what was going on when—*if*—he wanted to.

The problem was, her imagination could conjure up all kinds of "complications" Luke could be dealing with. Had there been a ranch problem? Maybe Fletch had gotten injured. Did Anika come down with another severe headache?

Or—worst case—Luke had decided Shannon herself

came with too many complications. In which case, he'd chosen to end things with a vaguely worded text before either of them had a chance to see what could develop.

Oh, well, it was for the best. What business did she have considering a new relationship at this point in her crazy, uncertain life? She laid her phone face down and determined to enjoy the remaining few minutes of her coffee break.

Her phone buzzed again. Probably Dorothy sending another cute photo of Tate.

Only it wasn't. It was an actual phone call.

From Luke.

She lowered her feet and inhaled a steadying breath before answering. "Hello?"

"Hi, Shannon." He sounded tired. More than tired—completely wiped out. "I hope you didn't give up on hearing from me."

Well, she pretty much had. Which didn't explain why her heart was racing. "Your last message had me a little concerned."

"When you texted me Saturday, I was on my way to find my dad. He's in the hospital."

"Oh, no! I hope it's nothing too serious."

"He's in pretty bad shape, actually." Luke huffed. "This isn't something I like talking about, but my father is an alcoholic. He nearly drank himself to death."

Her heart swelled with sympathy. "Oh, Luke, this must be terribly hard for you. For Anika, too. Is there anything I can do?"

"There's nothing to do but wait. Anika stayed at the hospital with him all weekend. I just sent her home to rest."

"You're there now? Which hospital?"

"St. Pat's."

Shannon had taken Tate to the St. Patrick's ER last winter when he caught a virus and she couldn't get his fever down. The hardest part had been the waiting. Just getting her little boy into an exam room seemed to take forever. Then the wait for answers from the doctor. Until Dad and Julia finally arrived, she'd felt frightened, helpless, and utterly alone.

Now Luke was alone, bearing the burden of his father's alcoholism and its horrible consequences. His overprotectiveness of Anika made much more sense now. "I'm not that far away," she said. "If you need anything—anything at all—you only have to ask."

"Thank you," he murmured. "This hospital stuff doesn't get any easier with experience."

"And you've had more than your share." She glanced at the wall clock. Dylan would wonder why she hadn't returned to the reception desk. "I could come over on my lunch break. I'll pick up something for you. Any preferences?"

"You don't have to do that."

"Please, let me. I know what it's like to wait and worry." Brightening her tone, she went on, "If you think of something you're hungry for, you can text me. But if I don't hear from you by noon, you'll just have to be surprised."

Without giving him the chance to argue, she ended with a cheery goodbye.

Between clients and other front-desk duties, Shannon pictured the various fast-food restaurants between the clinic and St. Pat's. If she took Reserve over to Broadway, there'd be plenty of options—burgers, Asian, Indian, Mexican. She hadn't known Luke long enough to glean much about his food preferences. Hopefully, he'd text her with a clue before twelve noon rolled around.

So long as he didn't instruct her not to bother coming at all. He had every right to his privacy, of course, but the rejection would sting.

His text came at eleven fifty.

> I decided I like being surprised by you.
> I'll eat anything. And by the way,
> breakfast was hours ago. I'm starved.

When her burst of laughter drew glances from clients in the waiting area, heat raced up her cheeks. She bit her lip and tried to look busy until Dylan came to relieve her. With a quick thank you, she hurried out to the little yellow Bug.

Turning onto Reserve, she kept her eyes open for an interesting place to order takeout. Her ham sandwich would keep in the break room fridge until tomorrow.

Chipotle Mexican Grill caught her eye. She pulled into a parking spot, then darted inside and joined the queue. Shortly, she returned to her car with a beef barbacoa burrito for Luke and a carnitas salad for herself, plus guac, chips, and two iced teas.

Fifteen minutes later, she texted Luke from the hospital lobby.

> Here with your surprise lunch. Tell me
> how to find you.

> Need to get out of this room for a bit. I'll
> come down.

She found a spot near the elevators to watch for him. When the doors opened and he stepped out, the combination of fatigue and relief in his posture evoked a sudden urge to drop the food and envelop him in a hug.

Which would be reckless and highly inappropriate.

Heart thudding, she held up the Chipotle bags and smiled. "Hope this is okay."

"More than okay." He came toward her, and for a moment, she thought *he* might move in for a hug. His fingers grazed her arm as he relieved her of the heavier bag. She tried not to shiver when he rested his free hand on the small of her back. "Let's head to the cafeteria and see if we can commandeer a table in a quiet corner somewhere."

She nodded and willed her feet not to stumble. She hadn't been this skittish since her college roommate first introduced her to Steven. They'd run into him and one of his friends at an off-campus coffee shop—supposedly by accident, which turned out not to be coincidental after all. Seemed their friends had been scheming for a while to get them together. Even as a confirmed introvert, Shannon had never felt so tongue-tied in all her life. It had taken Steven less than half an hour to break through her shell and make her feel as comfortable as if they'd known each other forever.

Luke must have sensed the slight hesitation in her step. "You okay?"

"Just having a flashback to another time and place."

"Not a disturbing hospital memory, I hope?"

"No, I was remembering the first time I met my husband. He was wonderful at making me feel at ease ..." Almost under her breath, she added, "Just like you always seem to do."

Luke hoped he'd heard her correctly, because if she felt at ease with him—comfortable enough to insist on driving all the way to St. Pat's to bring him lunch—then maybe something lasting could develop from this spark of interest between them.

True, she seemed a little jumpy at the moment, but no more so than he'd felt when the elevator doors opened and he saw her standing there. Her tender smile had banished all traces of his fatigue, and if she hadn't had both hands full of takeout bags, he might not have been able to resist hugging her.

The cafeteria was busier—and noisier—than he'd hoped, which he should have expected at this time of day. Not much chance for the quiet conversation he'd envisioned sharing with Shannon over lunch. Glancing around, he saw three women in scrubs clearing their cups and plates from a corner table. It would have to do.

He hurried over to claim the table and pulled out a chair for Shannon. "I guess we could have looked for a bench outside, but it looks kind of breezy out there."

"Yes, the wind's picking up." Smoothing her tousled hair off her face, she slid onto the seat. "I heard a weather report earlier saying a cold front's expected overnight."

"Well, it is September. Hot one day, chilly the next." Great, they'd already devolved into talking about the weather. Smothering a sigh, Luke helped Shannon empty the Chipotle bags. "Are these drinks both the same?"

"Iced tea. I hope that's okay." A worried look crossed her face. "But I forgot to ask for sweetener."

"No prob. Don't use it." He peeled the wrapper off a straw and poked it through the lid.

She passed him a foil-wrapped burrito and a handful of napkins, then pried the lid off her salad. "Wow, this is huge. I can save half of it for another meal."

The salad didn't look that big to Luke. Of course, he was a guy who could chow down with the best of them, but he suspected she was more concerned about economizing. Spying the receipt that had fallen out of a bag, he drew it closer and glanced at the total. "Let me pay you back for this. It's the least I can do to thank you for making a special trip on your lunch hour."

"Absolutely not." She snatched the receipt and stuffed it into her purse. "You've been a good friend to me. I wanted to do this."

He could see arguing would get him nowhere. Besides, the savory aroma coming from his burrito was making his stomach growl. He peeled back the foil, bit off a mouthful, and released a contented moan. "Haven't had one of these in a while. I forgot how good they are."

Shannon's pleased smile warmed his heart. "You said you liked just about anything, so I took a chance." After a few bites of salad, she grew serious. "I'm sorry about your father. Is his drinking a longstanding problem?"

"Dad's kept alcohol in the house for as long as I can remember. He and Mom enjoyed an occasional glass of wine with dinner, and Dad's always liked an ice-cold beer on a hot day. Sometimes when Mom's lupus symptoms flared, he'd drink a little more than usual. Then five or six years ago, I noticed the binges were getting more frequent."

"Do you think your mother's illness was the trigger?"

Luke thought about it while he took a swallow of iced tea. "Most likely. Dad's empathy gene is pretty much nonexistent. He's more into denial and avoidance."

"That must have made things even harder for you and Anika." Shannon's hand crept across the table to briefly touch his.

He offered a shaky smile and picked up his burrito.

They ate in thoughtful silence for the next few minutes. Then Shannon laid aside her fork and replaced the lid on her leftover salad. She glanced at her watch. "It's later than I thought. I wish I could stay longer and keep you company, but I should get back to the clinic."

He helped her stuff used napkins and food wrappings into the bags. On their way out, he deposited the trash into a waste receptacle. In the lobby, he paused and faced her. "This ... this was nice."

"If it helped to get your mind off things for a bit, I'm glad."

"It did. Believe me, it did."

She glanced up with an apologetic expression. "Even though I brought up those painful memories about your mother?"

"I didn't mind ... with you." He took Shannon's hand. "The truth is, I've rarely opened up about that time of my life with anyone. Not even Anika." He released a harsh laugh. "Maybe I'm as much into denial and avoidance as my dad."

Mouth firm, Shannon shook her head. "His abdication left you feeling responsible for both your mother's and your sister's wellbeing. You aren't in denial. You're just trying to move forward and focus on what matters most."

Her words nearly undid him. For the first time in years, he felt understood.

Before he embarrassed himself by getting choked up, he nudged Shannon toward the door. "You don't want to be late for work."

"You're right. As much time as I've taken off lately, my bosses wouldn't be happy." She paused on the threshold. "I'll be praying for your father. And for you. Call me later?"

"As long as you promise we won't talk about me and my family issues the whole time. I'd rather hear more about you."

Color rose in her cheeks, and she smiled. "If you call after eight, Tate will be in bed and it'll be easier to talk uninterrupted."

He gave her a thumbs-up. "Later, then. Be safe, and thanks again for lunch."

He watched through the glass until he lost sight of her in the parking lot, then trudged to the elevator. The last place he wanted to be right now was his father's hospital room. All he felt for the man was simmering anger for how he continually disrupted their lives—either by disappearing into a bottle when they most needed him or by scaring them half to death with a stunt like this.

Anika might blame herself for being an enabler, but Luke carried his share of guilt, too. By turning his back on their father, he'd left his sister to shoulder the burden of trying to rein in Dad's drinking—a battle she could never win.

Again and again, Luke's thoughts returned to the night of the wreck. If Dad hadn't gotten hammered at the cattle auction, he'd have been driving instead of Anika. Dad knew good and well she'd never felt comfortable driving his massive Ford F-450 crew cab. If he'd been behind the wheel —sober, of course—maybe they could have avoided the collision.

So many *what ifs* and *if onlys*. And nothing Luke or anyone else could do to change the outcome.

Chapter Sixteen

Anika made it home with just enough time to force down a slice of toast, swallow her meds, and then crawl into bed before the blinding headache turned into a full-blown migraine.

Four hours later, she startled herself awake with a scream.

"Anika?" Tobias's voice, then heavy footfalls on the staircase. He burst into her bedroom. "Ani, what's wrong?"

She sat upright and fought to catch her breath. "I ... I think I was dreaming."

"Here, take a sip." Tobias handed her the glass of water she'd left on the nightstand, then eased onto the bed and massaged between her shoulder blades. "Musta been a pretty scary dream."

She tried to remember, but the images were fuzzy. Or else her mind didn't want to remember. When Fletch whimpered and pushed his snout beneath her hand, she eased her feet to the floor and caressed the dog's head. "How'd you two get up here so fast? Were you already in the house?"

"Luke asked me to keep an eye on you. I brought my laptop to work on some ranch business, and Fletch was keeping me company in the kitchen."

Anika rolled her eyes. "Honestly. How will I ever convince him I don't need a babysitter?" Giving Fletch a pointed stare, she added, "Either one of you."

Stiffening, Tobias inched away. "The last thing I want to be is your babysitter. Can't you just think of me as a friend?"

"Of course you're my friend." Sorry she'd offended him, Anika tucked her hand in the crook of his elbow. "You're way more than a friend. You're—you're—"

She didn't know how to describe what Tobias meant to her. At least, not in a way she could easily say out loud. To him, she'd always be Luke's pesky little sister.

He slanted her an inscrutable frown before shoving up from the bed. "If you're doin' all right, I'll head back downstairs. It ain't exactly proper for a gentleman to be alone with a young lady in her boudoir."

His choice of words made her chuckle, as did many of the turns of phrase Tobias came out with. "Thank you for checking on me—*both* of you." She gave the dog another pat.

"You're welcome." He motioned for Fletch to follow him. "If you're hungry, there's some soup left on the stove. I heated up a can of chicken noodle for lunch."

"I'd love some soup. I'll be down in a few minutes."

After spending most of the weekend at the hospital, she could use a shower, but the mention of soup set her stomach to growling. She settled for washing her face and running a brush through her hair. As an afterthought, she applied a touch of mascara and pale pink lip gloss—just so she wouldn't look like death warmed over, she told herself.

As she entered the kitchen, Tobias glanced her way from where he stood at the stove. "I'll have this warmed up again in another minute or two. Saltines and cheese slices are on the table."

She helped herself to a cracker and offered one to Fletch, then took a lemon-lime soda from the fridge and sat down opposite Tobias's computer. A few sips of the chilled drink soothed the ache in her throat, a reminder of the scream that woke her. Fragments of the dream, nothing solid enough to make sense of, haunted her thoughts.

Tobias brought over a bowl of soup and placed it before her. "Careful. Don't burn your tongue."

"Yes, sir." She cast him a withering stare.

"Feelin' good enough to find your sarcasm, I see." He snorted and pulled out his chair.

After a few spoonfuls of soup, she asked, "What are you working on?"

"The vaccination and deworming schedule."

"What fun," she deadpanned. She made a cracker sandwich with a square of cheese, but when she brought it to her mouth, a wave of nausea hit. She laid the crackers on her napkin.

Tobias looked up from his computer with a frown. "Something wrong?"

"I, um ..." The queasiness didn't seem to have anything to do with the food or the last remnants of her headache. "I just suddenly feel ... scared."

He stood and came around to the chair catercorner from hers. "Scared? Of what?"

"I think it's about my nightmare." Her voice faded to a mere whisper as she met his gaze. "Except it feels more like a memory."

Scooting closer, Tobias took her hand. "A memory? Of your accident?"

Eyes squeezed shut, she struggled to coalesce the images into something intelligible. *The livestock auction. Two burly cowboys helping them out of the arena. Then tires screeching. The truck rolling and rolling and rolling. The sound of her own screams ... and then nothing.*

"Anika." Tobias tugged on her arm. "You're shaking. Look at me."

Her breath came in sharp gasps. She stared at him, her thoughts still riveted on what she'd seen in the dream. "That can't be right. It *can't* be."

"What, Ani? Talk to me."

Grounded in the present once more, she said, "This is going to sound crazy, but I keep seeing Daddy driving the truck that night. But it was me ... wasn't it?" She sought Tobias's face for confirmation. "That's what everybody told me. Daddy, Luke, the accident investigators—they all said I wouldn't let Daddy drive because he was too drunk."

Jaw working, Tobias sat back. His silence—and the fact that he wouldn't make eye contact—only added to her confusion.

"It was just a dream, right?" She clutched his arm. "Tobias?"

"Yeah, yeah. It must have been a dream." He bolted upright, then closed his laptop and tucked it under his arm. "If you're gonna be okay for a while, I got some stuff to do in the barn." The back door banged shut behind him.

As Anika puzzled over his mood shift and sudden departure, Fletch rested his chin on her thigh. His soulful eyes spoke the comfort and reassurance she hungered for.

"Sweet boy." Cradling his furry cheeks, she bent low to kiss the top of his head. "Even though you don't use actual words, sometimes it feels like you're the only one on this ranch who's one hundred percent honest with me."

But the dog's calming presence wasn't enough to ward off the return of a dull ache at the base of her skull. Zigzagging flashes of light preceded its slow but relentless crawl up the right side of her head and into her temple. She made it to the downstairs bathroom before losing the contents of her stomach, then collapsed on the cold tile floor.

Chapter Seventeen

hree days passed with no word from Luke. When Shannon left the hospital Monday after their lunch together, she'd believed her gesture had meant something to him.

She believed she might even be on the verge of opening her heart to something more.

Maybe the timing was all wrong. Luke had plenty of family issues to deal with, and Shannon's second job demanded more time and brainpower than she'd anticipated. The last couple of nights, she'd worked past midnight to meet her next deadline, and now she was making up for it by doubling her coffee intake and paying for *that* with caffeine jitters.

Julia was in the clinic today to fill in for Dr. Kruger, who had a family emergency. She caught Shannon staring at the empty coffeemaker. "Normally, you have to add water and grounds and then push Start."

Coming out of her daze, Shannon huffed a self-conscious laugh. "You mean I can't just wish a steaming mug of coffee into existence?"

"If you figure out a way to do that, let me know." Julia took the carafe and filled it at the sink. As she poured the water into the reservoir, she cast Shannon a concerned look. "You look exhausted, honey."

"Just a bit sleep-deprived." She scooped fresh grounds into the filter basket. "I'll catch up this weekend."

"Need us to take Tate for a few nights while you get some rest?"

"No," she replied, a bit too forcefully. "I mean, I already promised we'd take Rowena to the dog park on Saturday afternoon."

Julia turned on the coffeemaker, then slipped her arm around Shannon's shoulder. "You know your dad and I fully support you, but we don't want you burning yourself out. If this second job is proving too much—"

"I'm still adjusting. That's all." She clutched her mug and willed the coffeemaker to hurry and finish.

"If you say so." Stepping away, Julia wet a dishcloth and wiped a spill on the counter. "Just know we're here for you if you need us."

Shannon heaved a sigh. "I know, and I appreciate it. Sorry if I sounded snippy."

"You didn't." Julia smirked. "Well, not much, anyway."

The coffeemaker burbled, hissed, and went silent. Shannon filled her mug, then blew across the surface before taking a cautious sip. "Can I talk to you about something else?"

"Of course. Anything." Julia motioned toward the table.

After they sat down, Shannon briefly described taking lunch to Luke at the hospital. "I haven't heard from him since then, and I'm getting a little concerned."

"And you haven't tried contacting him again?"

She shook her head. "I don't want to intrude. He has enough to worry about already."

"Is it that, or ..." Julia tilted her head and smiled. "Is it possible you're letting something else hold you back?"

"Steven's memory? No, I don't think so." Lips flattened, Shannon studied the light swirl of foam on the surface of her coffee. "Sometimes I can almost hear him telling me it's okay to move on. And I think he'd like Luke a lot."

"Then what do you suppose the real problem is?"

"I think I'm scared. Scared of putting myself out there and risking another loss."

"I remember that feeling all too well." Smiling tenderly, Julia covered Shannon's hand with her own. "After what we've each gone through, fear is normal. But you don't have to let it win. Take the risk. Follow your heart, trust God, and leave the results to Him."

Julia's advice played through Shannon's mind in odd moments during the remainder of the workday. By the time she picked up Tate from his great-grandparents' and warmed leftover beef stew for their supper, she'd decided to reach out to Luke. What was the worst that could happen, after all?

Well, the worst would be if his father had experienced a drastic setback, perhaps even died. Shannon prayed not, but even if that were the case, she could offer a sympathetic ear or whatever else he and Anika may need.

With Tate parked on the den sofa watching a kids' Christian video on Shannon's iPad, she slipped around the corner to the kitchen. After taking a few minutes to frame her thoughts, she sent a text:

> Hi, it's me. Just wanted you to know I've been keeping you in my prayers. If there's anything I can do, please call.

Barely a minute passed before her phone rang. Seeing Luke's name, she inhaled a quick breath and answered. Her "Hi" came out in a high-pitched whisper. "I've been worried."

"It's been a rough few days." He sounded tired and distracted.

"Your father. Is he ..."

"He's going to make it—although he doesn't deserve to." Bitterness laced his tone.

Sensing he needed to talk, she gathered her courage and pressed on. "I understand how angry you must be. Alcoholism is a dreadful disease that hurts everyone it touches, especially the people we love most."

An ugly laugh sounded through the phone. "You don't know the half of it."

"Then would you tell me? Because I care, Luke, and I'd like to help."

He hesitated, then lowered his voice. "I can't. Not over the phone." Another pause. "Are you at home?"

"Yes."

"I'm at the hospital. I can be there in twenty minutes."

Not what she expected at all. She stepped around the corner and glanced into the den. Tate's video was almost over. In twenty minutes, she could have him tucked into bed—which was when she'd planned to settle in with her laptop and get started on some proofreading.

But friends were more important. What did it matter if she burned the midnight oil for one more night? This weekend was her Saturday off, and she'd already planned to sleep in—with Tate's cooperation, of course. At worst, she'd nap after lunch with her son before they went to the dog park.

"Okay," she said. "I'll be waiting."

Luke dimmed the lights over his sister's hospital bed. The sedative a nurse had injected into her IV had taken effect, and she'd drifted into another fitful sleep.

"I won't be gone long, kiddo." He smoothed aside a sweat-dampened brunette strand before dropping a kiss on her forehead. "Hang in there, okay? We'll get through this."

It had been a long time since one of Anika's migraines had put her in the hospital. Long enough to make them complacent and hope the worst of her headaches were behind them.

They may well have been, if not for what Tobias pieced together a few days ago. The news had sent Luke scrambling for confirmation of a truth too cruel to accept. In some ways, it meant good news for Anika, relieving her of any blame for the accident that had nearly destroyed her life … and taken someone else's.

But in other ways? Luke hadn't thought he could hate his father more than he already did. This news changed everything.

Unburdening himself to Shannon felt selfish, considering her personal struggles. But if he didn't talk to someone—a friend he could trust to be more objective than he was capable of at the moment—he'd drive himself mad. Tobias, too close to both Luke and Anika, couldn't be that person this time.

He arrived at Shannon's a few minutes after eight.

When she answered the door, her gaze swept him from head to toe and back again before she pulled him into a hug. He wished he could melt into her arms and stay there forever.

"Come inside," she murmured, drawing him through the doorway. "I just got Tate to sleep. I'll make some tea and we can talk in the kitchen."

He gave a halfhearted chuckle as she led him through the small house. "You women and your tea."

"Tea is comforting for both body and soul." She filled the kettle at the sink, then set it on a stove burner. "Are you hungry?"

"I had something at the hospital earlier." A sandwich he choked down only out of necessity. He collapsed into the nearest chair, only then realizing the big Irish wolfhound wasn't anywhere to be seen. "Where's Rowena?"

"With Tate." Shannon smirked. "She's supposed to sleep on her doggy bed, but knowing those two, they're probably snuggled together in Tate's bed."

Since Fletch ended up sleeping with Luke most nights, he couldn't pass judgment. He doubted Tobias had been as accommodating as a pet sitter these past few nights.

When the kettle whistled, Shannon poured hot water over tea bags in two aqua ceramic mugs. She placed one in front of Luke. "It's chamomile and lavender. Very soothing."

"Soothing. Exactly what I need right now."

She eased into a chair near his. "Whenever you're ready to talk, I'm listening."

He'd managed to put the whole thing out of his mind for the few minutes since she'd invited him in. Now the tidal wave of emotion came flooding back. Ignoring the aromatic mug of tea that beckoned, he bent forward and pressed both hands to his face to stifle an anguished howl.

"Luke." A gentle hand touched his shoulder. "Please, tell me what's happened."

Gathering what composure he could muster, he sat erect. He stalled another moment by attempting a sip of tea, but his hands shook so badly that he had to set the cup down. "I'm almost angry enough to kill him myself." The admission sliced through his throat like a rusty blade. "How could he? *How could he?*"

Shannon steadied his hands between her own. "Who? Your father? Luke, what did he do?"

"*He* was driving that night. Not Anika. *He* caused the accident that nearly killed both of them." More clear-eyed than he'd been since the discovery, he met her gaze. "He lied, Shannon. In the hospital after the wreck, while his own daughter lay in a coma, he told the cops *she'd* been driving. But it was him. He was totally wasted, but he got behind the wheel anyway."

Shannon slowly shook her head. "You know this for a fact?"

"There's no proof, never was. But I found out Anika's been having dreams. Only not dreams, but fragments of memories. She remembers now that she argued with Dad that night, pleaded with him to let her drive. But he kept insisting he was fine, that she didn't know how to handle a big truck like his anyway, and if she didn't want to ride with him, she could find her own way home."

He paused, imagining the scene. Dad had been in denial about his worsening drinking binges ever since Mom's lupus diagnosis, and nobody got away with telling him what to do. Luke pictured Anika walking Dad out to the truck, arguing with him the whole time about who should drive. But with him twice her size and refusing to give her the keys, she'd been powerless to keep him from scrambling behind the wheel.

"When Anika couldn't reason with him," he went on, "she climbed in the passenger seat. But the snow was getting heavier, and with road conditions becoming more treacherous by the minute, she was terrified. She grabbed the wheel more than once to keep the truck in their lane and begged him to pull over. Then a stalled car appeared on the shoulder at the same moment an eighteen-wheeler was passing on their left. Dad jerked the wheel and they spun out of control, and then—"

He squeezed his eyes shut against the fiery aftermath playing out in his mind. Shannon rose and stood behind him, her firm touch reassuring as she silently kneaded his shoulders.

Once his muscles relaxed, she sat in front of him again and cradled his hands in her own.

He inhaled deeply. "I was in Anika's hospital room when you texted earlier. The shock of remembering hit her hard, and the headaches got so bad that she had to be admitted."

"Oh, Luke, how awful. But surely there's a sense of relief that she wasn't responsible. That she did everything she could."

"I hope she'll get to that point, eventually." He chewed the inside of his lip. "All this time, I've been shielding her from the fact that another driver died in the accident. At least now, she'll never have to carry that blame."

"I didn't realize there'd been a fatality."

"It was a guy returning home from a business trip. He left a wife and three kids."

He wasn't so consumed by his wretched thoughts that

he didn't notice the subtle shift in Shannon's expression. Eyes lowered, she stiffened and turned away.

He scooted closer and cradled her cheek. "I never meant for all this to bring up bad memories for you."

Her smile was brief but sincere. "It's not your fault. Those memories are never far from the surface, but with God's help, I'm slowly coming to terms with them."

Disbelief narrowed his eyes. "How? How can you still trust in God after all He's taken from you?"

"What choice do I have?" She shrugged. "Like Job said, 'Though he slay me, yet will I hope in him.'"

Her faith, simple and deep, brought a sharp ache to his chest. Was it skepticism ... or longing? Because if both she and his sister could find such peace by trusting in God, why couldn't he?

Even Anika's last muttered words this evening before the meds took hold were a prayer, and not only for herself, but for their father: *"Jesus, help him. And please, help me forgive him."*

What am I missing, God? He'd tried prayer, of a sort. More than ever these last several days. But what had it gotten him? No answers—at least, not the ones he needed. And certainly not peace.

He stood. "I'd better get back to the hospital."

"I don't think that's a good idea." Shannon spoke with disconcerting calm.

Confused, he stared at her. "What?"

"I mean, I don't think that's where you should be right now."

"But Anika could wake up. She'll need me."

"No, not this version of you." Shannon rose, her penetrating gaze freezing him to the spot. "You can't help your sister while you're still so shaken. Angry. Lost."

"But—"

"Believe me, I know. After Steven was killed, I gave in to those same emotions and let them slide into crippling depression. I became absolutely useless, even to my son. It was better for me not even to be around him until I got myself together." Her voice trailed off as tears sprang into her eyes. "Until I allowed the Lord to do His healing work and make me whole again."

He fisted his hips. "And you think you're *whole* now? You forget it wasn't even a week ago that I witnessed you totally break down. I held you in my arms. I—"

Head tilted, she cast him a look that implied his utter folly. "After all your family has been through, surely you realize that getting over heartbreak and loss is never a one-and-done. It's a process, and it takes time. Yes, I still grieve, and some days are far worse than others. But with each milestone that passes, I get a little stronger, and the really bad days are fewer and farther between."

There went that ache in his chest again, the nagging feeling that Shannon and Anika—and even Mom when she was alive—all shared a secret he hadn't yet caught on to.

"Okay," he said, jaw clenched, "if I shouldn't be with Anika right now, what do you suggest? Because I don't want her to deal with this alone."

Arms crossed, lips skewed, Shannon studied him. "How would you feel about staying here overnight with Tate?"

His knees nearly buckled. "Wh-what?"

"I'm offering to stay with Anika at the hospital tonight, but obviously, I can't leave Tate home alone."

Luke couldn't believe what she was suggesting. "I know zero about babysitting a kid."

"You helped look after Anika when she was little,

right?" Shannon flicked a hand. "Besides, Tate's easy. He can dress himself in the morning, and he'll show you where everything is for breakfast. He'll feed Rowena, too. Anyway, I'll need to be home by seven to get ready for work."

Another reason he couldn't let her do this. "But you'll be exhausted. I can't do that to you."

"I'll sleep—don't worry. And if you're concerned I won't hear Anika if she wakens, don't forget I'm a mom. Alerting to every little sound is part of my job description." She brushed past him. "You can camp out on the den sofa. I'll get you a pillow and blanket."

"Wait." He reached for her arm. He'd planned simply to thank her, but when his glance fell to her lips, softly parted in a questioning look, words fled. Pulse racing, he drew her closer. "Shannon ..."

They stood inches apart, his mouth hovering over hers. He could see in her eyes that she knew his intention, and he hesitated just long enough that she could have stopped him if she wanted to. Instead, she moved toward him, her lips brushing his in a tentative kiss that only inflamed his longing.

He kissed her again, slowly this time, purposefully, his deep yearning undisguised. When she pressed against him, her arms sliding around his torso, he felt the rapid flutter of her heart in sync with his own.

It seemed they each came to their senses at the same moment. Shannon lowered her head to Luke's chest, her hands slipping between them to rest on his collarbones. "It's been so long," she murmured, breathing hard. "So long."

"If I overstepped—"

"No. I wanted this, too." She backed away and cleared her throat. "I should get to the hospital."

"Right."

"Extra pillows and blankets are in the hall closet. Can you—"

"Of course."

She snatched a jacket and her purse from a row of hooks by the back door. A minute later, she was gone.

Chapter Eighteen

You kissed him!

Traffic was light as Shannon drove to the hospital, which was a blessing. Lost in her scattered thoughts, she could only thank God for getting her safely to her destination.

Finding Anika's room, she tiptoed in to find a nurse checking the young woman's vitals.

"I'm a family friend," Shannon whispered. *Friend? After that kiss?* With difficulty, she pushed aside the memory. "How is she?"

"She's comfortable, not as restless as she was earlier." The nurse typed something into the bedside computer terminal, then adjusted Anika's pillow and pulled the blanket up around her shoulders. Turning to Shannon, she cocked her head and smiled. "Didn't I see you having lunch with Luke the other day?"

"In the cafeteria? Yes, that was me. I'm Shannon. Shannon Halsey." She moved closer, her heart aching at the sight of her vibrant new friend in a hospital bed.

"I feel terrible for her," the nurse said. "My name's

Darla, by the way. I've known Anika since high school. I was two years ahead of her, but we hung out with a lot of the same kids." When Anika stirred, Darla spoke soothing words and stroked her arm until she quieted.

Shannon slipped off her jacket and set her things on a nearby chair. "Then you know about the accident."

"Oh, yes. That was a terrible time. Heartbreaking." Brow furrowed, Darla studied Shannon. "I don't remember you from back then."

"I only just met Anika and Luke a couple of weeks ago." Hearing herself say it aloud, she sucked in a breath. More to herself, she muttered, "How can it feel like I've known them forever?"

Darla laughed softly. "When you really click with someone, that's how it works sometimes."

"I guess so." Of their own accord, Shannon's fingertips went to her lips.

"Well, they're good people. Especially Anika. Their father, though? He's another story." Darla grimaced. "Sorry, I shouldn't speak out of turn."

"Luke told me some of their ... struggles." Glancing around the room, Shannon spied the vinyl recliner near the window. "I'll be staying with Anika tonight while Luke gets some rest. Is there anything I should know?"

"Hopefully, she'll sleep for several hours. And that's really sweet of you. I have the night shift, but I'll try not to disturb you too much. You can ask for me at the nurses' station if you need anything."

Shannon gestured toward the recliner. "Um, maybe a pillow and blanket?"

"Of course. Be right back."

Before long, Shannon had made herself a comfy nest. She dimmed the lights just enough that she could peek at

Anika during the night and then settled in to try to get some sleep.

She roused each time Darla stepped into the room for a quick check but soon dozed off again. Then around three a.m., Anika's soft moans awakened her.

"It's okay, honey." With the blanket wrapped around her against the chill in the room, Shannon sat next to Anika and took her hand. "It's me. Shannon. I'm with you."

Anika squinted up at her, a sleepy smile forming. "Hi."

"Hi, yourself. Do you want me to call the nurse?"

"No, I ... I just need to ..." She glanced around as if getting her bearings. "Did Luke leave?"

"He's at my house with Tate. He's been very worried about you, but he desperately needed some sleep. I offered to stay with you tonight."

Heaving a sigh, Anika pushed herself higher in the bed. "Thank you." She glanced away. "He's been through so much."

"You both have. I hope it's okay that Luke told me about ... everything."

"I'm glad you know." A coarse laugh vibrated in Anika's throat. "It saves me having to repeat the whole sordid story."

"We don't have to talk at all if you don't want to. Just know I'm here for you." On the bedside table, Shannon spotted a plastic container with a straw sticking out. She checked to see if it contained ice water and then offered it to Anika.

After a few sips, Anika set the tumbler aside and rested her head on the pillow. "Who knew plain water could taste this good?"

"How's your headache? Better?"

"Gone for now, praise the Lord." Anika shoved the

fingers of both hands through her hair. "What time is it? What *day* is it?"

Shannon glanced at her watch. "Coming up on three thirty on Friday morning."

"It's Friday already? Wow. I must really have been out of it."

The nurse peeked in just then. "Oh, you're awake. How are you feeling, Anika?"

"Darla? Is that you?"

"In the flesh." Darla raised the lights slightly before striding over to Anika's bedside. "Wow, you look a ton better than when you were admitted three days ago."

"Gee, thanks. Except I'm a little loopy from whatever you've got running through my veins." Anika paused while Darla ran a thermometer across her forehead, then checked her pulse. "Have you been my nurse the whole time? Sorry, I don't remember much about the last few days."

"Just for the night shifts." Darla made some adjustments to the IV drip. "Your head should start clearing up soon, but if the pain returns, let me know right away."

"I'm praying that won't be necessary."

"Me, too." Darla patted Anika's arm. "Gotta check on my other patients. I'll see you in a bit."

When the nurse had gone, Shannon said, "She seems very sweet."

"Yes, she's a good friend. I used to think she and Luke might—" She cut herself off abruptly, lower lip pulled between her teeth.

Striving for a disinterested tone, Shannon asked, "They dated?"

"They went out a few times. Total fiasco. It was *not* meant to be." Anika's eyes looked a little too bright, her tone too animated, most likely the effects of the drugs in her system. Gaze lowered, she concentrated on taking another sip from the water tumbler.

Shannon covered a yawn. What with all the interruptions, she'd gotten perhaps four hours of decent sleep. At this rate, she'd need several cups of strong coffee to make it through the workday. She wouldn't let herself think about the proofreading job she hadn't even touched last night.

As for the kiss ...

Oh, Luke, you have turned my life upside down in more ways than one!

❧

"Hey. Hey!" The strident voice pierced Luke's brain. Somebody was punching his arm. Hard. "What are you doing in my house, and where's my mommy?"

He sat up and rubbed the back of his head to dispel the cobwebs. "'Mornin', Tate." Absently, he patted the head of the big dog at Tate's side. "Your mom's at the hospital."

The boy's brows shot up, his eyes wide with worry. "She's not sick again, is she?"

"No. No, she's fine." Luke pulled Tate onto the sofa next to him and gave the kid's knee a reassuring pat. "But Anika got sick, and your mom wanted to be with her last night, so she asked me to stay with you."

"Oh. Is Anika gonna be okay?"

Luke sighed. "I sure hope so."

"Did you pray for her?"

"Best I could, yeah." Leave it to the kid to rub it in. "Want some breakfast?"

"Okay. Is Mommy coming back soon?" Tate was already jogging toward the kitchen.

"Think so." Still groggy, Luke traipsed after the boy and dog. "What shall we—"

The back door swung open, and Shannon stepped into the kitchen. Tate raced over to give her a hug. "Mommy! You forgot to tell me Luke would be here when I woke up."

"I'm sorry, sweetie, but you were already asleep when I left." Her ponytail was lopsided, and smudges of mascara darkened her lower lids. Even so, she'd never looked prettier. When she planted a kiss on Tate's head, the memory of last night's kiss filled Luke's thoughts, and he experienced a moment of envy.

When Shannon straightened to shrug off her jacket, Luke hurried over. "Let me get that for you." He draped the jacket over a hook while she did the same with her purse. Their shoulders brushed, and it seemed as if they both repressed a shiver. Putting space between them, Luke murmured, "Rough night?"

"Not too bad. Anika awakened in the wee hours, and we talked for a while before we both dozed off again. She's doing much better."

"That's good news. Really good news." To keep from pulling her into a hug, Luke jammed his fingers into his jeans pockets. "Guess I should head over there."

"She's going to be okay, Luke." Shannon's tender smile brought a pleasant ache to his chest. "She's much stronger than you give her credit for."

"I know you're right. And you ..." This time, he couldn't stop himself from moving close enough to caress her cheek. "You're strong, too. Next to my mom, you and Ani are possibly the strongest women I've ever known."

Shannon glanced down shyly. "That's quite a compliment."

"It's true." He looked across the kitchen to make sure

Tate was otherwise occupied, then drew Shannon toward the living room. Alone with her, he searched her face for some sign that their kiss had meant as much to her as it did to him. "About what happened last night ..."

"Luke, I ... I should get changed for work." The glimmer of longing in those gorgeous brown eyes belied her words.

He wouldn't let her go until he said what was in his heart. "Look, we've both been going through a lot, and I realize we haven't known each other very long. But for the first time in ages, I'm feeling like I could actually be happy again. With you."

Her throat worked as she forced down a swallow. "I'm starting to feel that way, too." She peered up at him. "But I'm scared, you know? I've already lost so much, and I can't bear going through that again. I can't bear doing it to my son."

"No pressure. I'm willing to take it slow." He slid his thumb along the back of her hand. "Just two people getting to know each other while we see where this leads."

Shannon gave a slow nod. "I guess I could do that."

He tempered his burst of elation by breathing in and out. "Okay, then. You need to get ready for work, and I need to head to the hospital. What if I call you later, maybe over your lunch hour?"

"That would be nice."

"Okay, then," he repeated. "Later." *Way to impress her with your stunning vocabulary, goofball.*

She walked him to the door, and he waved as he walked backward toward his truck. When he almost tripped over a tree root, he decided he'd better quit acting like a lovesick calf and pay attention to his footing.

Lovesick? How had indifference turned to *like* in a

matter of days, only to quickly lead to dreams of something more?

Anika's doctor released her that afternoon, and Luke brought her home. Now that the truth had come to light, she claimed she only wanted to put the accident behind her, but Luke suspected she had plenty of healing left to do.

He most certainly did. He doubted he could ever forgive their father for the lies.

"Good news only," Anika said as Luke settled her in the den with chai tea in one of her favorite china cups. "Tell me what's going on between you and Shannon. I heard you sweet-talking her over the phone while I was having lunch."

"I *wasn't* sweet-talking." Avoiding his sister's pointed stare, he straightened a pile of ranching magazines on the coffee table. "There's nothing more to tell."

"Right. Because it's perfectly normal for you to go gaga over any attractive single woman you just met."

Heat singed Luke's ears. "I haven't gone *gaga*." Well, not much, anyway. "And for the record, Shannon isn't just *any woman* to me. I honestly can't say where this is headed, but we both agreed we wanted to find out."

"Thank You, Jesus. My prayers are at last being answered." A self-satisfied smile narrowing her eyes, Anika sipped her tea.

Before he said something he'd regret, Luke announced he had work to catch up on. "I've let things go around here long enough."

Anika seized his wrist as he brushed past. Her expression softened as she gazed up at him. "Hey, big brother, have I told you lately how much I love you?"

Swallowing, he dipped his chin. "I love you, too, little sister."

"Sit with me five more minutes? Please. The ranch isn't going to implode if you don't hurry right out there."

Luke stifled an eye roll as he pulled an ottoman closer. He sat facing his sister. "Okay. Five minutes."

She leaned forward and clasped his hand. "I know how you worry. About me. About the ranch. If you'd only trust God instead of feeling like you have to do it all yourself—"

"Stop." He firmly shook his head. "Give it up, Ani. I'll never have as much faith as you do. As Mom did. I've tried. I just don't."

"See, that's just it. You don't *try* to have faith. It's God's gift to us. All you have to do is open your heart, let it in, and let it grow."

That made no sense. "How am I supposed to open my heart to faith in God when I'm not even sure I believe He's real?"

Anika pressed one finger against the corner of her skewed lips. "Hmm, two weeks ago, I'm pretty sure you didn't believe your heart was capable of falling in love." Her grin widened. "But now ..."

"I'm not there yet." Except he sort of was, and the thought made his pulse skitter. "Anyway, that's a whole different subject."

"Is it? Really? Because love is God's gift, too."

He pointedly looked at his watch. "Your five minutes are up. I'll be back later to make us some supper."

"It's only been *two* minutes, cheater," she hollered after him. "And I'm not an invalid, you know. *I'll* do the cooking."

Fine with him. At any rate, arguing with his sister reassured him she'd soon be back to her usual spunky self.

As he neared the barn, Fletch ran out to greet him and danced around his feet until he picked up a stick and threw it.

Tobias watched from the open barn door. "Saw y'all drive up earlier. How's our girl?"

"Taking it easy. Headache's gone—for now." Fletch returned with the stick, and Luke tossed it again, this time a little farther. "How are things here?" he asked Tobias.

"Humming along. Another truckload of hay got delivered this morning. Also got the first batch of pregnancy tests ready to send in."

"Good. I'm hoping for a bunch of healthy calves from those new heifers next spring." Luke signaled for Fletch to follow him to the barn office.

Passing the bulletin board, he glimpsed the flyer for the herding dog trial coming up at the end of the month. The entry deadline had passed two days ago. Fletch's practice was at a standstill anyway, no thanks to the troubles Luke's father continually brought into their lives. He ripped the flyer down, wadded it into a ball, and dropped it in the wastebasket.

Tobias huffed. "Sorry, man."

"There'll be other opportunities." Luke sank into the leather desk chair and began sorting through a stack of mail.

Tobias plopped down in a chair on the other side of the desk. "Afraid you're just gonna find bills and more bills."

"Figures." As big a spread as Fox Pass Ranch was, people assumed the family must be rolling in dough. They had no concept of the planning and effort it took to maintain profitability.

After a few minutes, Tobias asked, "What's the latest on your dad? Have you talked to him since ... everything?"

"I can't even bring myself to look at the man." Luke

rolled the chair back and covered his eyes. "Last time I talked to his doctor, he recommended a full psych eval and a month or two in rehab for substance abuse. I told him to do whatever he thinks best."

"You're basically giving up on your dad?"

"He gave up on us a long time ago, and I'm sick and tired of cleaning up behind him. Anyway, he brought all this upon himself, so good riddance." Luke ripped open another envelope, then glared at his friend. "Don't you have something else to do?"

Tobias rose stiffly and walked out without a word.

Realizing Fletch was staring at him, Luke harrumphed. "Don't look at me like that. Yes, I was rude, okay? I'll apologize later."

The dog went to his bed and lay down with his face turned away.

Judgment from all sides. Great.

Luke picked up another piece of mail and tried to concentrate, to no avail. After kissing Shannon last night, and then her agreement this morning to be open to what might develop between them, he'd practically been walking on air. Then the reality of his dysfunctional family—every bit traceable to the sins of his father—had to slap him in the face.

Wasn't there something to that effect somewhere in the Bible? Even more reason not to trust a God who, generation after generation, made children pay for their parents' mistakes. Luke felt like he was in a hole he could never climb out of, and it kept getting deeper.

And you want to bring a sweet, kind, caring woman like Shannon into your life?

What was he thinking?

Chapter Nineteen

I t wasn't working.

Anika tried all day to put her reclaimed memories of the accident out of her mind, but with the sedating migraine drugs out of her system, the images kept flooding back.

The fight with her dad to keep him out of the driver's seat. Then the struggle to keep him steering between the lane lines instead of weaving all over the highway. Dad slapping her hands away, shoving her against the passenger door.

His curses, then maniacal laughter mixed with tears. And something about being done with the guilt, and maybe he'd crash the truck on purpose just to be free of it all.

Brakes squealing, sparks flying as metal ground against metal. The truck tumbling over and over and over. Her door bursting open and the eerie, slow-motion sense of escaping gravity for those blissful but terrifying moments until she slammed into the snow-covered ground and all went black.

Now that her brain had delivered most of the truth, perhaps the time had come to face the memories head-on. With Luke working in the barn, Anika determined to do the one thing she'd promised both her brother and herself that she'd never do. She opened her laptop and searched online for news reports about the accident.

The first item to pop up in a Google search was the recording of a live newscast from a TV station in Butte. While the anchorman spoke from behind his desk, an inset above his left shoulder played videos shot at the scene of the accident.

"Earlier this morning, at approximately 1:00 a.m., a semi hauling a fully loaded trailer collided with a late-model Ford F-450 truck on westbound Interstate 90 about halfway between Racetrack and Deer Lodge. Low visibility and deteriorating road conditions due to snow were contributing factors, according to authorities. A man and a woman were ejected from the truck before it burst into flames. A medevac transported them to St. James Hospital in Butte, where both are listed in critical condition, names being withheld pending notification of the family. The semi driver was uninjured, but a three-car pileup resulted as other vehicles braked and swerved to avoid the accident. At least one of those drivers died at the scene."

Someone had *died*?

Anika's stomach plummeted. Believing not only that she'd been driving but then to learn someone had died— how could she have borne the guilt?

But she *hadn't* been driving. This was all on her father.

She needed to see him, but not today. Not until she felt a little stronger and took some time to pray about what she'd say. And she didn't need Luke trying to stop her, either, because he surely would.

Yes, maybe on Sunday, she'd go to see her father after church.

Maybe by then she'd be ready.

●

Larchwood Glen Fellowship, established by early settlers in the area, had been Anika's church home since her mother first enrolled her and Luke in Sunday school twenty-plus years ago. The white-steepled sanctuary, located off Mullan Road between Missoula and Frenchtown, was almost a century old. A more modern fellowship hall and Sunday school building sat adjacent.

Anika was fairly certain her father had accepted Christ during his teen years, but as an adult he'd never been much of a churchgoer, no matter how often Mom tried to persuade him. Like Luke, he seemed to have forgotten how much he needed the Lord, but that hadn't stopped Mom from praying for them both. And it wouldn't stop Anika.

Today, kneecaps pressing into the upholstery of the old-fashioned kneeler at her pew, Anika prayed for her father's healing in both body and spirit. She prayed for the strength to forgive him for the lie he'd burdened her with for nearly four years. And she prayed for the Holy Spirit's wisdom and guidance when she finally confronted her father.

As the congregation stood for the closing song, Anika slipped out. She didn't have the emotional energy for small talk with acquaintances, and though Pastor Keegan's counsel might have served her well, she felt an urgency to go straight to the hospital and get this encounter over with.

Arriving at St. Patrick's, she took the elevator to her father's floor, only to find his room occupied by a complete stranger. Embarrassed, she apologized for the intrusion and hurried out.

At the nurses' station, she got the attention of an RN who'd been on duty when her father was first admitted. "I'm Victor Daniels's daughter. Can you tell me where they've moved him?"

The tall, silver-haired woman cast Anika a confused look. Tone clipped, she replied, "He transferred out last Wednesday. You didn't know?"

"No. I was hospitalized last week myself." Why else would Luke not have told her? Except he'd had plenty of opportunities since she'd been home. Forcing a smile into her voice, she asked, "You said transferred? To where?"

After confirming Anika was authorized to access her father's medical records, the nurse told her he had voluntarily committed himself to a private facility for substance abuse rehabilitation. "Your father is now at Mercy Cottage. I'll jot down the address and phone number."

Anika thanked the nurse and tucked the slip of paper into her shoulder bag. She contained her fury until she reached her car, then pounded the steering wheel and released a guttural moan. *Luke Daniels, how could you not tell me this?*

After several calming breaths, she took out her phone and called her brother.

"Hey, Ani. Everything okay?"

"No. Everything is *not* okay. I just learned Dad checked himself into a rehab facility. *Last Wednesday.*"

Tense silence stretched between them. "I knew it was coming, just didn't know how soon." Another pause. "Did they say where?"

Anika ground her teeth together in stunned disbelief. "You don't even know *that*?"

"Dad's an adult," he said defensively. "I left it to him and his doctor to work out the arrangements. Besides, I was more concerned with taking care of you."

"Well, he's at Mercy Cottage, and I'm headed there right now."

"Ani, don't. He's not worth it."

"You may not think so, but it doesn't matter. I'm going to face my father because *I'm* worth it." She pressed the End button and tossed the phone onto the passenger seat.

Twenty minutes later, she parked outside Mercy Cottage. It took another ten minutes of pleading with God for strength before she gathered the nerve to walk through the door.

At the reception desk, Anika introduced herself as Victor Daniels's daughter and asked if she could see him.

"I'm sorry," the woman said with a regretful tilt of her head, "but Mr. Daniels isn't allowed visitors during his first week in treatment. After that, it will be up to his doctor to authorize family visitation."

"But—but I really need to talk to him." Hands clasped, Anika leaned across the counter. "I'm his daughter, and I didn't get to see him before he was admitted. Can't you make an exception?"

"I'm afraid not. However, if you leave your name and number, I can have his doctor contact you. He'll be back in his office tomorrow morning." The receptionist handed her a ballpoint pen and a message pad.

She tried to keep her hand from shaking with frustration as she printed her name and cell phone number. As an afterthought, she wrote URGENT in large block letters and underlined it twice.

There was nothing left to do for now but leave and wait

for Dad's doctor to call—and pray she could stave off another stress-induced migraine until then.

Chapter Twenty

O ver the weekend, Shannon tried to make up for lost time with Tate. They spent a fun Saturday afternoon with Rowena at the dog park, where Tate practiced the commands Luke had taught them the day they'd visited the ranch. Rowena soon mastered "sit" and "shake," but with her massive size and stiff rear leg, "roll over" proved anything but graceful.

On Sunday, they attended worship with Tate's great-grandparents. Afterward, the Frasiers took Tate to their house while Shannon went home to work on a proof-reading job. She gave herself a two-hour limit and then returned to the Frasiers' for pizza and whatever football game Martin was watching on TV. Shannon couldn't care less what was happening on the field, but Tate and Rowena kept her and Dorothy entertained with their antics.

The time had been restorative, a much-needed distraction from Shannon's confusing mix of feelings for Luke. She couldn't stop thinking about Anika, though. How many new struggles would she face now that her memories had returned? Would she succumb to the same bitterness toward her father that Luke harbored?

Somehow, Shannon doubted it.

Once Tate drifted off to sleep Sunday evening, she opened her laptop and gave the corporate restructure document a final review before forwarding it to Ravi. His high praise for her first few assignments had given her confidence an enormous boost. The work was also reawakening a long-suppressed dream of writing. Maybe not anything as all-consuming as a novel, but perhaps a weekly blog or a column for a local newspaper.

The ideal topic arose—pithy essays on the trials and joys of being a single working mom. She could write from experience!

Why not start now? Just for fun, of course. She could try her hand at a few practice pieces. She opened a blank Word doc, took a deep breath, and then ...

Nothing. Her brain completely shut down.

Writer's block? Before she'd even written her first word? Drumming her fingers on the table, she glared at the blinking cursor for a frustrating few minutes before closing the computer and shoving it to the side.

Her cell phone lay a few inches away. She itched to snatch it up and call Luke, her heart beating faster with the longing to hear his voice. Even better if she could see his smile on a FaceTime call.

Besides, she longed to know how he and Anika were coping after the ordeal of this past week. She took a chance and pressed the FaceTime icon next to Luke's name in her contacts.

Five rings later, his image appeared on her phone screen. "Hi, Shannon." His voice didn't carry its usual resonance, and the worry lines around his eyes and mouth added ten years to his appearance. "How are you?"

"I'm okay. But I've been concerned about you. Anika, too. Is she home from the hospital?"

"Yeah, they released her Thursday afternoon. I should have let you know, but things have been ..."

"No need to explain. I'm glad she's better." She paused. "And your dad? Is he improving?"

Lips flattening, he looked away for a moment. "He's at a rehab hospital now. Mercy Cottage."

"Oh." Shannon's breath sharpened. "I spent six months there myself. I told you about my clinical depression. If not for the care I received at Mercy Cottage, I may not have survived."

Luke moved closer to the phone, his gaze softening. "I didn't realize you'd been that sick. It must have been a rough time for you. And for Tate."

"It was. But my time there helped me get my life back." She ran a finger along the screen as if stroking Luke's cheek. "If your dad will open his mind and heart to the process, it can do the same for him."

"Don't count on it." Luke lowered the phone and shook his head. In the background, Shannon glimpsed honey-gold log cabin–style walls and a leather sofa. Fletch lay stretched out at one end. Raising the phone again, Luke grimaced. "I don't mean to trivialize what your treatment did for you. But you obviously *wanted* to get well. I'm not sure my dad's there yet, or ever will be."

"I wasn't, either, at first. Like I said, it takes time."

"Well, I'm not holding my breath."

Shannon decided to change the subject. "Does Anika seem to be handling her memories any better?"

"Not sure. We haven't talked much." His frown deepened.

"Is that your choice ... or hers?"

"Both, I guess. Talking about Dad always leads to an argument."

Shannon and Steven had often disagreed about how to deal with parent problems. He'd sympathized with her feelings about growing up in isolation on the mountain but had urged her many times to mend the rift between her and her father. It had taken Steven's death and Shannon's breakdown—and a lot of faith and prayer—but she thanked God every day for the healing He'd brought about and the closeness she and Dad now shared.

Luke heaved a sharp sigh. "Shannon, I never meant to involve you in our family drama." His Adam's apple worked. "I'm starting to care for you. A lot. The last thing I want is for the issues with my father to come between us. He has a way of ruining everything."

"I care for you, too," she murmured, dipping her chin. "But I'm not sure anything can come of ... us ... when there's still so much you need to deal with. And not only concerning your father," she added gently, "but your relationship with God."

Way to hit him where it hurt. Luke eyed the End button while he considered whether to hang up on Shannon without another word. He wouldn't even have to explain himself, just go on his merry way. Since they traveled in different circles, likely their paths would never cross again.

Unless Anika did another arts and crafts fair where Maddie Wittenbauer recruited Shannon as her assistant.

Another problem—Anika really liked Shannon. Their friendship would likely continue, which meant Luke's chances of avoiding her became slim to none.

Who are you kidding, Daniels? He no more wanted to avoid Shannon Halsey than cut off his right arm.

She'd gone silent, brows slanted and lips pressed together as if she feared exactly what he'd been thinking.

"I know you're right," he hedged. "I get that from Anika all the time. Truth is, we disagree about God and prayer almost more than we do about Dad. It isn't the way I want things. But I can't get past all the ways God has let my family down."

"Maybe if you counted your blessings instead?" At his involuntary eye roll, she hurried on. "I know it sounds corny, but it works. And once you acknowledge all the good things God has brought into your life, you'll see how much He truly loves you. You'll realize He's always been there with you, through the good times and the bad. Lifting you up. Opening the exact right door at the exact right time. And I know from experience that the doors He closes turn out to be for your own good, even if you can't see it right away."

All the while she spoke, Luke slowly shook his head. But inside, he felt something crack. Eyes closed, he massaged the ache in his chest. "I hear you. I heard every word. But I can't talk about this anymore."

"Luke?" Her face filled the screen, her gaze pleading. "Whatever happens, wherever your thoughts and feelings take you, just know I'm praying for you."

With one last look into those tender brown eyes, he ended the call.

Fletch crept closer and laid his head on Luke's thigh, another brown-eyed gaze accusing him.

"What should I have said?" he asked the dog. "We're miles apart on the subject of God. The conversation was going nowhere."

Fletch stared a moment longer, then jumped down and pranced from the room. Seconds later, Luke heard him scratching at the front door.

"Now you want to go outside?" Luke heaved himself off the sofa and grabbed a windbreaker. A walk in the night air could benefit them both.

As soon as Luke opened the door, the dog shot off toward the main house, apparently seeking more pleasant company than his master. A light shone in the kitchen window, which meant Anika must be baking. If Fletch had caught the aroma of freshly made dog treats, no wonder he was in such a hurry.

Well, Luke wouldn't be joining him. He'd had quite enough God talk for one evening and didn't need Anika piling on.

If his sister was even speaking to him yet. Would she ever let him off the hook for distancing himself even further from Dad after this latest debacle? The man didn't deserve all the second chances Anika had given him, much less her forgiveness and compassion. He was bound to hurt her again. Why didn't she learn her lesson?

Nickers from the horse barn drew his attention, and he wandered inside. Tobias stood at Socks's stall gate, stroking the bay mare's ears while feeding her a carrot.

Luke ambled over. "Thought you'd be twirling ladies around the dance floor at Rattlesnake Jack's tonight."

"Nah. Not in the mood." Did Tobias just cast a surreptitious glance toward the main house? He pulled another carrot from his back pocket and let Socks bite off the end.

When Zorro whinnied from his stall, Luke nudged Tobias's arm. "Got an extra carrot?"

Tobias handed him one, and for a few moments, the horses' crunching filled the gap in their conversation.

"Look, I, uh ..." Giving his horse another pat, Luke cleared his throat. "I owe you an apology for the other day."

"Yeah, you do." Tobias cocked a brow and looked at him.

"Are you accepting my apology or not?"

"You said you owed me one. So far, I haven't heard it."

"Okay. I'm sorry. I shouldn't have spoken to you like I did." A sigh raked through Luke's chest. "I guess I assumed a friend would understand what I've been going through."

"This friend does understand." Tobias fed the last of a carrot to Socks and then faced Luke. "But this friend also isn't gonna let you off the hook. Man, you gotta get your act together and your head on straight, or you're gonna lose every last person you care about. And that includes Shannon."

"If you mean I have to get right with my father, you're asking the impossible." Weariness seeped into Luke's bones. He crossed his arms and leaned against the upright between the horses' stalls. "Guess I'm doomed to a life of loneliness."

"See it like that if you want to. Or do something about it." Tobias wiggled his brows as if Luke should know what he meant. When Luke didn't respond, he changed the subject and reminded him they needed to get an early start in the morning. It was time to move the remaining cattle from the high pastures down to more protected grazing land. "I told the crew to be saddled and ready by six a.m."

"Yeah, yeah. I'll be there." Luke gave a halfhearted wave as Tobias strode out of the barn.

The trip would mean staying overnight near Dad's

hunting cabin. With a propane cookstove and cots to sleep four, plus space to pitch tents in the surrounding area, the cabin served as base camp on these treks.

Depending on the condition Dad had left it in, Luke might just decide to stay awhile and, in Tobias's words, get his head on straight.

Shannon regretted pressing the issue of Luke's relationship with God. She'd only wanted to persuade him that he shouldn't give up hope, even for a man as deeply troubled as his father.

But he hadn't wanted to hear it, and their parting words on the phone had sounded too much like a last goodbye.

Is this relationship over before it even began?

The thought made her heart ache with a sorrow she hadn't thought possible. Since losing Steven, she'd never imagined letting someone new into her life. Never dreamed of another man's tender embrace. Never imagined another man's lips upon hers.

Never imagined she could fall so hard for someone she was only just getting to know.

"It's for the best," she said aloud, as if hearing the words echo in the silent house would convince her. "We're too different. It would never have worked anyway."

If nothing else, the time spent with Luke had proven she did have the capacity to love again. Her thoughts drifted to the tall, blond guy who often sat near her at church. When they exchanged handshakes during the sharing of the peace, there was a look in his eyes that she now realized expressed interest. With her attention often diverted to picking up the crayon Tate had dropped or admonishing her son to quit squirming, she'd done little more than smile in return. Sadly, she didn't even know the man's name.

But if she wanted to meet an upstanding man who shared her Christian faith and values, church would be a much more likely place to do so. Thus far, she'd avoided the Young Singles adult Sunday school class, going instead with Dorothy and Martin to their Bible study. Maybe the time had come for a change.

Chapter Twenty-One

Wrapped in an old quilt, Luke sat in a rickety rocking chair on the cabin porch. A pale sun cast orange and gold streaks into the purple sky as it disappeared beyond the horizon. The silhouette of an owl passed overhead. Somewhere in the distance, a coyote howled.

As the sky darkened, the quilt did little to ward off the chill. Yet Luke stayed where he was. Making himself endure the frigid evening outdoors felt like part penance, part preparation. If he had any hope of making sense of his life, he needed cold objectivity.

On Monday, the crew had ridden on horseback to the cabin and unloaded their camping gear. They'd spent the afternoon rounding up the herd to prepare for moving them down from the highlands. The next morning, Luke helped drive the cattle as far as a midrange pasture, then cut back up a mountain trail to the cabin, where he'd left enough supplies for several days. Tobias told him to make good use of this time away and promised to look after things at the ranch, including Anika.

Luke released a wry chuckle. Why hadn't he seen it before, the special interest his ranch foreman had taken in his sister? Of course, Luke knew all about Anika's teenage crush on Tobias. She used to follow the guy around like a besotted kitten. But with Tobias a good ten years older and way too flirtatious with the single ladies at Rattlesnake Jack's, Luke hadn't figured he had any reason to be concerned.

He'd better re-evaluate the situation pronto, because no way would he allow the womanizing cowboy to put another crack in his sister's already fragile heart.

If only he could get Anika away from the ranch. Away from their father. How could he convince her to focus on building a life for herself instead of pouring all her energy into coddling a hopeless alcoholic?

Fletch whimpered and pawed at Luke's knee, then sat facing the cabin door and wagged his tail.

"Sorry, fella, didn't realize how late it was getting." Luke heaved himself out of the creaking rocker and wadded up the quilt. "I'm getting hungry, too."

If not for his furry alarm clock to alert him to mealtimes, bedtime, and other urgent needs, up here so far from civilization, Luke could easily forget his own name. Without a schedule to keep, and surrounded by the quiet beauty of nature, he could understand why Dad escaped to the cabin every chance he got.

Shuddering, Luke quashed the comparison. This getaway had nothing to do with hiding from his problems. He'd come seeking peace and perspective. That's all.

This would be his third night alone on the mountain. For the first couple of days, he'd tried *not* to think. Each day, he checked the game cameras and noted elk, deer, and bighorn sheep in the area. A black bear showed up in one clip, a bobcat in another.

Fishing in the stream the first day, Luke caught a good-size brown trout and fried it up for supper. Earlier today, he'd reeled in two whitefish. While not as flavorful as trout, with proper seasoning, they'd make a decent meal. A can of green beans and a roasted sweet potato would round out tonight's menu.

After supper, with Fletch sound asleep after downing a bowl of kibble and some leftover sweet potato, Luke added another log to the stove. As the cabin warmed, he sank deep into an easy chair and put his feet up on the sagging ottoman. Stuffing peeked through a few worn spots in the ancient leather upholstery, but the flaws detracted little from the comfort.

A full stomach and the flickering firelight soon set Luke adrift in a haze of semiconsciousness. He saw Shannon walking toward him, her silky blond hair lifted by a light breeze and her smile entrancing. But when he reached out to her, something unseen pulled her farther and farther away, and no matter how hard he tried, he could never catch up.

"Don't leave, Shannon. I care for you," he shouted.

"I care for you, too," she called, her voice growing fainter. Sadness and something else—pity?—filled her eyes. "But there can never be anything between us until you mend your relationship with your father … and with God."

"Please, wait! I need you!" He tried to run faster, but thick, sticky mud sucked at his feet. "Shannon!"

"Shannon!" Luke sat up with a gasp, the sound of his own voice ringing in his ears.

He cast his gaze around the small sitting area, scraped his hands along the worn leather of the chair arms, heard the creak of the floorboards beneath his feet. Yes, he was still at the cabin.

And Shannon had never been here at all.

Ears pricked, Fletch looked up from his bed near the stove and whimpered.

"I'm okay, boy. Just a dream." Luke pulled both hands down his face. What a wasted trip. He'd made no progress at all toward getting a grip on his life.

One thing the dream had confirmed, though—he still had feelings for Shannon. And if he failed to get his act together, she would remain lost to him forever.

During the passing of the peace at Sunday worship, Shannon decided to be bold and introduce herself to the blond guy. His name was Jeff Bowman, and it turned out he knew Dylan, the vet tech from Frasier Veterinary Clinic. In fact, they were cousins.

Jeff grinned as he clasped her hand. "Small world, huh?"

"Yes, isn't it?" She wondered if he ever intended to let go.

"I noticed you in the Young Singles class this morning. A few of us made plans to grab lunch after church. Any chance you'd like to join us?"

Freeing her hand, she cast a pointed glance at Tate, who was busy running a miniature stuffed horse along the back of the pew. "I shouldn't."

Dorothy turned from greeting someone behind her. "We can take Tate home with us. Go ahead, Shannon," she added with a wink. "Enjoy yourself."

Left with no excuse, she shrugged. "Okay, I guess. Thanks."

The introductory chords of a praise song ended conversations. Shannon tried to turn her attention to worship, but her mind refused to cooperate. Second, third, and fourth thoughts intruded about this impromptu lunch date. The people she'd met in the Sunday school class were friendly enough, and she found their current study more relatable than the class she'd been attending with Tate's great-grandparents.

But did she really want to pour time and emotional energy into another new relationship? Late Friday afternoon, Ravi had forwarded a proofreading assignment with a hard deadline of 5:00 p.m. Tuesday. She'd gotten a good start, and though the document wasn't long, unfamiliar terminology required extra research to confirm spelling and usage.

She heaved a mental sigh. None of this would even be a question if Steven had lived.

But he was gone. Forever. And nothing she could do would change the fact.

As the praise music swelled, she closed her eyes and lifted her hands in supplication. *Oh, God, this isn't the life I imagined. Help me. Guide me. Show me how to find joy again.*

She certainly wouldn't find it by juggling two jobs and shortchanging her son—and herself. Yet what was she supposed to do? A widowed mom who had never completed her college degree didn't have a lot of choices.

"You have a support system, babe." Steven's voice whispered through her thoughts. *"Why won't you use it? You could go back to school and get that journalism degree. You could follow your dreams, just like we planned."*

Like they'd planned until her husband's life was cut short and all their dreams came to nothing.

The music ended, and the pastor announced the scripture passage he'd be preaching on. As Shannon opened her Bible, it seemed the sanctuary lights had dimmed. Unable to make out the words on the page, she looked around to see if anyone else was having difficulty, but those near her didn't seem bothered. Even Tate was happily coloring his children's bulletin.

The darkness closed in, like the narrowing of a tunnel. Her breath grew shallow. Her hands shook.

Dear God, please, not another panic attack. Not here. Not now!

Trying not to betray her distress, she got Dorothy's attention. "Can you watch Tate?" she whispered. "I need to step out for a minute."

"Of course. Honey, are you feeling all right?"

"Just a little warm." She fanned her face with one hand. "I'm going to get a drink of water and some fresh air."

Controlling her pace until she reached the sanctuary doors, she nodded to the usher before exiting to the lobby. Once there, she broke into a jog and didn't stop until she burst through a side door to the parking lot.

A crisp breeze whipped at her hair. She brushed strands out of her eyes and slid her arms into the fleece jacket she'd had sense enough to grab along with her purse on the way out.

Breathe, Shannon, breathe. Hand to her chest, she repeated the *in-hold-out-hold* pattern Dr. Yoshida had taught her. After several repetitions, her breath rate slowed to something closer to normal. She tilted her face to the sun and filled her lungs once more before exhaling slowly.

As clarity returned, she took her phone from her purse.

Dr. Yoshida had often reminded her she could call anytime, day or night. She hadn't needed to—at least, not with this urgency—since the first few months following her release from Mercy Cottage.

She found the doctor's name in her contacts and prayed she wouldn't interrupt something important.

Two rings later, Dr. Yoshida answered. "Hello, Shannon. How can I help?"

Tears sprang to her eyes as she explained about the panic attack. "I thought I was going to die right there in the church pew."

"But you didn't." The doctor gave a gentle laugh. "You remembered your breathing, right?"

"I did. It helped. But I'm so embarrassed." She sniffled. "And confused. I thought I was past all this."

Dr. Yoshida paused a moment. "As I recall, your last follow-up visit was over four months ago. We should schedule an appointment and talk through any concerns that may have brought on your anxiety."

"Yes, I'd like that."

"You're sounding much calmer now. I can be available tomorrow afternoon, if that's all right."

"With my job, it would have to be as late as possible."

"I'll be in my office until seven. Come as soon as you get off work."

"I will. Thank you." Ending the call, she hurried back inside and scooted in beside Tate.

The closing prayer had just ended. As the praise band began the last song, Dorothy looked over with concern. Shannon assured her she was okay.

After the pastor's blessing and dismissal, she stepped into the aisle and pulled Jeff aside. "Thanks for the lunch invitation, but I won't be able to join you after all."

Disappointment furrowed his brow. "Sorry to hear that. Maybe next week, then?"

She hated to get his hopes up when she didn't see the point in pursuing their acquaintance. Lips pursed, she left it with a polite "We'll see."

❧

"Please, Luke. I don't want to do this alone."

Tired and saddlesore, he'd arrived home less than an hour ago, and already his sister was on his case. Jaw clenched, he concentrated on currying Zorro, but his gaze drifted toward the tack room, where he'd stashed a battered shoebox beneath a pile of horse blankets. He'd come across the box while sweeping out the cabin this morning, and until he made sense of what he'd found inside, the *last* thing he wanted was to accompany Anika to a family counseling session with their father's shrink.

"I can't see how it'd help," he hedged. "Besides, I've got plenty to catch up on around here."

"Only because you spent an entire week moping at the cabin. Explain to me how *that* helped, will you? Because from what I can tell, you're just as moody and disagreeable as you were before you left."

"I am not!" he snapped, then winced, because *moody and disagreeable* described him perfectly.

How he'd been acting. How he *felt*.

"I'm sorry, Ani." A long, ragged sigh seeped out. Leaving Zorro secured in the crossties, he clasped his sister's shoulders. "I get how committed you are to Dad's recovery, but I can't justify wasting my time trying when I'm not convinced it's possible."

"Not *possible*?" Anika shrugged out of his hold and

locked her arms across her abdomen. "Good thing what's possible isn't up to you. Because all things are possible with God, and I choose to trust Him."

Jaw firm, he turned to finish grooming his horse.

"Okay, be that way." Anika's voice trembled. Marching out of the barn, she called back to him, "But just so you know, I'm still believing God can heal your wounded heart, too."

"My heart's—" Before he could finish with *not wounded*, she was out of earshot.

Besides, it was a lie, because his heart hadn't been right since Mom got sick. From the onset, he'd blamed God for the gradually worsening illness that stole their sweet, devoted, self-sacrificing mother from their lives. After the wreck that almost killed Anika and their father, then Mom's death, Luke's faith plummeted to almost nonexistent. And then to find out Dad had lied about not being behind the wheel—

The guttural sound that came from his throat made Zorro shy. Fletch slinked away as well, eyeing Luke from inside an empty horse stall.

"Sorry, boys." He stroked the horse's neck.

Face it—your heart's so messed up that even a woman as compassionate as Shannon Halsey is shutting you out.

They hadn't communicated in over a week, and he missed her. It surprised him how much. But she'd made her feelings clear, both in person and in that hauntingly vivid dream.

After picking Zorro's hooves and feeding him a peppermint, he released the horse into a pasture with three other geldings. Zorro spun away and kicked up his heels like a colt, as if happy to be done with his work for the day.

Watching from outside the fence, Luke couldn't

remember when he'd last experienced such joyous freedom. It seemed to him as if he'd borne the responsibility for his family and the ranch for his entire adult life.

Not alone, though. Not alone.

The words emanated from somewhere at the center of his being. Not a human voice. More like an impression.

Frowning, he cast his gaze skyward. "If that's You, God, You've got a lot of explaining to do."

Nothing.

Figured.

"Let's go clean up and unpack," he said to Fletch and started for the cabin.

The dog didn't follow. Instead, he pranced halfway up the driveway to the main house, then plopped onto his belly and rested his chin on his forepaws.

Why did Luke continually get the feeling his dog was smarter than he was?

"Okay. Okay!" He threw up his hands. "But I still need to clean up first. You can either wait there or come with me. What's it gonna be?"

The dog hopped up and trotted over, apparently satisfied with his human's change of heart.

Looked like Anika would get her wish about dragging Luke along to the family counseling session. Which meant poring over the confusing contents of that shoebox would have to wait.

Chapter Twenty-Two

Anika paced to the window and stared unseeing toward the Mercy Cottage parking area. She'd expected to feel anxious about seeing her dad again, the first time since he'd committed himself to rehab. But the knot in her stomach came close to doubling her over.

She'd prayed every day for the ability to forgive her father. Part of her wanted to believe the simple answer that he'd been too drunk to remember his actions that night. But another, much larger part suspected he'd known all along what he'd done and had lied to protect himself. A DUI conviction could have stripped him of his driver's license and landed him in jail. If the family of the man killed in the wreck chose to file a wrongful death suit, they might even have lost the ranch.

Anika glanced at Luke from the corner of her eye. One ankle resting on the opposite knee, he paged through a magazine. His façade of nonchalance didn't fool her for a minute, especially when she noted the magazine's title, *Quick & Easy Quilts*.

Honestly, she never thought he'd change his mind about coming along. If only she could believe he truly cared about helping with Dad's recovery. More likely, his only reason for being here was to protect his baby sister. Why did he refuse to see her as a capable, self-reliant adult?

She plopped down beside him on the sofa and perused the magazine page. Tapping the color photo of a quilt draped over a chair, she said, "That's a pretty one. Thinking of trying a new hobby?"

"Huh? No." Luke tossed the periodical onto the coffee table then crossed his arms. "Just passing time."

"A new hobby might be good for you." Mimicking his posture, she went on, "Maybe not quilting—I've seen your clumsy attempts at sewing on a button. But something artistic to engage the creative part of your brain. Like an adult coloring book. That could be fun."

One eye narrowed, he leaned sideways and frowned. "You're kidding, right? Please tell me you're kidding."

"Not entirely." She poked him with her elbow. "Although teasing you is a whole lot more fun than arguing." Or letting her thoughts linger on why they were here.

His frown mellowed. "Yeah. Sorry about that. I—"

Before he could complete the thought, the inner door opened. A young man in a baby-blue polo and khaki slacks stepped through. His attire matched that of the receptionist at the front desk. "Are you the Daniels family?"

Pulse thrumming, Anika stood. "Yes, we're here to see our dad, Victor Daniels."

The man nodded. "Dr. Ingalls will speak to you privately first. I'll show you to his office."

Shortly, they were seated on a loveseat across from a pencil-thin man with steel-gray hair and a neatly trimmed beard. The angle of his knees suggested he must be well over six feet tall. He reached across to shake hands with Anika, then with Luke. "Glad you could both be here. I'm sure you have a lot of questions, but let me start by explaining that your father's treatment is protected by privacy laws. Without his written consent, I can't share specifics."

Anika laced her fingers into a tight knot. "What *can* you tell us?"

"Your father is currently in both individual counseling and group therapy, and he's being treated by a multidisciplinary team that includes an addiction specialist. In addition, we believe that healing isn't just about physical or emotional recovery—it's also about spiritual renewal and seeking God's help in restoring relationships."

Stiffening, Luke said, "I'd feel better if you could convince me he's actually taking this seriously. He's put our family through enough already, and if he isn't—"

"What my brother is saying," Anika interrupted, "is that we want to believe our father will get better and *stay* better."

Dr. Ingalls nodded. "Family support can make a big difference in recovery, which is why you're both here today."

"So, fine, he's getting counseling." Luke sat forward and rubbed his palms together. "But he can leave whenever he wants, right? We can't keep playing this game."

"I understand what you're saying," the doctor replied. "Rest assured, we strongly encourage our patients to complete the program to give themselves the best chance at recovery. If your father expresses concerns or struggles, we'll address those with him directly."

Beneath Anika's forced composure, one enormous question simmered. Unable to hold back another second, she spoke through tight lips. "I guess all these privacy issues mean you can't tell me if my father has expressed remorse about the lie he let me live with for the past four years."

After a telling pause, the doctor said, "I'm sorry, I cannot. I can see how much this is weighing on you, Anika," he continued, his tone calm but firm. "Addressing past mistakes is an essential part of recovery. But it has to come from him."

Luke braced his hands on his thighs. "I truly doubt the man is capable of admitting the damage he's done." He shoved to his feet. "I don't even know why I came. He's never going to change."

"I hear your hurt, Luke, and it's valid." Dr. Ingalls offered a kind smile. "Let me assure you that your father is here because he wants to be, and he's on a path toward seeking accountability—for himself and before God. My prayer is that your visit with him today can help all of you take even a small step toward the healing God offers."

Anika tugged on her brother's wrist. "Please, Luke, we have to give this a chance—for the sake of our own recovery, if not for Dad's. If I can find the courage to try, can't you?"

When Luke's shoulders sagged and he dropped onto the cushion beside her, she released a silent sigh of gratitude. Until the moment she'd walked through the door of Dr. Ingalls's office, she hadn't been sure she could go through with this. And she absolutely couldn't do it without her brother's support.

Hands shaking, she wove her fingers through Luke's and held on tight. She looked at the doctor and hiked her chin. "Okay, what happens next?"

Chapter Twenty-Three

By four fifteen, Shannon was on her way to Mercy Cottage. Once again, Brad had been more understanding than she deserved about letting her leave work early. Dorothy hadn't minded keeping Tate a little longer and told Shannon to plan on having supper with them after her appointment.

She could only hope to be in a more positive state of mind by then.

As always, Dr. Yoshida greeted Shannon with a warm hug. "You look well. And I like your longer hairstyle. Very becoming."

"Thank you." When she'd first come to Mercy Cottage as a patient, she'd given little thought to her appearance. Wearing her hair whacked off just below her chin, she'd tucked it haphazardly behind her ears.

They took chairs in the cozy seating area at one end of Dr. Yoshida's office. After offering a brief prayer, the doctor invited Shannon to share what was on her mind.

Exhaling thoughtfully, she gazed out the window and

watched the slow descent of a falling leaf. "I feel kind of like that," she said. "Like I'm drifting. Lost. Stuck."

The doctor gave a soft laugh. "*Drifting* and *stuck* are a bit contradictory. Can you elaborate?"

"I guess I'm drifting because I don't feel like I have a real purpose in life." Shannon shrugged. "That isn't entirely true. Taking care of my son is pretty much my *only* purpose."

"And you feel stuck because ..."

"Because nothing ever changes. Everything I do revolves around making a loving and secure home for Tate."

"Being a working mother isn't easy under the best of circumstances." Dr. Yoshida shifted and folded her hands. "Let's talk about your anxiety attack yesterday. Was there a specific trigger?"

Shannon grimaced at the memory. She described visiting the Young Singles class at church, introducing herself to Jeff, and accepting his lunch invitation. "I thought I wanted to go. That it would be good for me to ..." She shrugged. "I don't know—expand my horizons. But then it all hit me, and I panicked. I ran outside and called you."

The doctor smiled and reached across to pat Shannon's arm. "Expanding one's horizons can be both challenging and rewarding."

"Which is what made me want to try." After a brief pause, she lowered her gaze and added, "Actually, what happened yesterday isn't the first time recently that I ventured out of my comfort zone. I ... I met someone."

She confided in Dr. Yoshida about meeting Luke while assisting Maddie at the arts and crafts fair, then how he'd helped her find a replacement for her broken-down car. She told about taking Tate out to Luke's ranch on the Saturday that happened to be the anniversary of Steven's death, how she'd fallen apart and Luke had held and comforted her. She described the rapid progression from casual friendship to the possibility of something more.

"Except I think we may have moved *too* fast." Shannon brushed away a tear. "We're both too broken—Luke with his family issues, and me just trying to make it day by day. Then there's the fact that Luke is so far away from God right now. I need someone who will encourage and support me in my walk of faith. I don't have the strength to be someone else's crutch."

"Those are wise observations," Dr. Yoshida said with a nod. "However, I sense you still have powerful feelings for this man. Perhaps that's why accepting the invitation from your new acquaintance at church was unnerving."

As Shannon let the possibility sink in, she knew it to be true. She plucked a tissue from the dispenser on the end table and dabbed her cheeks. "But what if these feelings are only because Luke is the first man I've let into my heart since Steven died? If I don't give someone else a chance, how will I know when it's right?"

"How did you know when it was right with Steven?"

"Because ... because of how he made me feel. Cherished. Valued. Seen."

"And how do you feel when you're with Luke?"

A tiny tremor began deep in Shannon's chest. Unable to speak for a moment, she pressed a hand to her heart. "The same," she whispered. "The same."

Waiting for Dr. Ingalls to return with Dad, Luke couldn't sit still. Hands stuffed into his jeans pockets, he crossed the room and rocked on his heels. He would have to work extra hard not to lash out with a barrage of choice words the moment he set eyes on the man.

He'd have to work even harder not to seize Dad by the collar and punch him in the face.

When the door eased open, Luke cast a worried glance at his sister. She perched on the loveseat, hands curled into fists and resting on her knees. Her chin trembled, but her wide-eyed gaze held steady as she looked toward the door.

Dr. Ingalls entered first, then stepped aside and motioned their father through. "Vic, please take a seat."

Eyes lowered as he leaned on his cane, Dad slunk into the room and lowered himself into the chair at Anika's right. His cane resting on the armrest was a harsh reminder of the accident and how he'd lied about it.

The doctor returned to his chair, then smiled up at Luke. "Will you sit down and join us?"

"I'm okay over here." Safer for all concerned if he stayed put.

"Very well," the doctor said. "Vic, I believe you have something to say to your children?"

"I, uh—" He cleared his throat. "I just wanted to say I'm sorry. For ... for everything."

Rage exploded inside Luke. "You're *sorry*," he blurted. "Sure, that makes everything all right, doesn't it?"

"Luke, please," Anika murmured, one hand lifted. She shifted to face their father, her voice tight. "Daddy, we're just trying to understand."

"Yeah? Well, so am I." A belligerent tone entered the man's voice. At a look from Dr. Ingalls, Dad inhaled deeply and closed his eyes. "What I mean is, I have a lot to work through. I'm taking it one day at a time."

Those sounded like words someone had coached him to say. Which meant they were meaningless. Luke turned to the side and gave his head a quick shake. If not for deserting Anika, he'd walk out right now.

"Luke," Dr. Ingalls began, his frown mildly condescending. "Your insistence on standing apart from the rest of us isn't conducive to open, honest communication. I'll ask you again to please sit down."

He almost refused until he glimpsed the tear sliding down Anika's cheek. All this tension risked triggering another migraine, and Luke couldn't let that happen.

Smothering a groan, he returned to the loveseat and edged onto the cushion. When Anika clutched his hand, he felt the tremors coursing through her. "It's okay," he whispered, giving her fingers an encouraging squeeze. "Hang in there."

How they made it through the next half hour, he'd never know. He could hardly make himself listen to what his father was saying—most of it still sounding scripted. Something about working the Twelve Steps. Knowing he needed to make amends. Hoping his kids would someday find it in their hearts to forgive him.

After Dad seemed to run out of words, Dr. Ingalls invited Luke and Anika to be honest with their father about what they were thinking and feeling.

Luke didn't trust himself to speak. He nodded at Anika to go first.

Lips pressed together, she scooted forward and angled her body toward their father. "Daddy, I want nothing more than for you to get better. But you have to know how devastated and angry I am. All this time, you let me believe the accident was my fault. And when I found out a man died—" Her voice broke.

Luke tucked her trembling body beneath his arm. She buried her face against his chest, the sounds of her suppressed sobs ripping a hole in his heart.

Dad's face paled. He wouldn't look at either of them. His claw-like fingers dug into the chair arms, while his heels beat a dull staccato rhythm on the carpeted floor.

"We should end for today," the doctor stated. "Vic, let me—"

"Wait," Luke interrupted. "I need to have my say." Continuing to comfort his sister, he looked squarely at his father. "You're right, Dad. You have a lot to make up for and even more explaining to do. But don't expect to see Anika or me again until you're ready to be honest—and I mean *completely* honest—with your doctor, your therapy groups, and most of all, with yourself. Because I won't let you hurt us, especially Ani, any more than you already have."

Ignoring his father's blank stare, he helped Anika to her feet and slipped her jacket around her shoulders. "Let's get out of here."

Dr. Ingalls followed them into the corridor. "Please don't give up hope," he urged. "Today may have felt like a failure, but we are still in the earliest phase of your father's recovery. As he progresses, it's important that you don't shut him out. He needs to believe his family wants him to succeed."

"What I *want*," Luke stated, "is to have him out of our lives. Permanently."

"Luke, don't." Chagrin filling her expression, Anika pushed against his chest. "Don't say things like that."

The doctor's scowl conveyed his displeasure with

Luke's attitude. He reached out with both hands to touch their arms. "I recommend you give yourselves time to put today's visit in perspective and bring your concerns to God in prayer. I'll be praying for you as well."

"We will. Thank you," Anika murmured. She grabbed Luke's arm and pulled him along the corridor as if she couldn't escape fast enough.

They hadn't gone twenty feet when another office door opened. Luke skidded to a halt before tripping over the woman who stepped into their path.

"Shannon?" He nearly choked on her name.

She spun around, honey-blond waves sweeping across her shoulders. "Luke."

Before he could form a reply, Anika swept Shannon into a hug. "It's good to see you again."

"You, too, honey." Shannon wore a stunned expression as she looked past Anika into Luke's eyes. "I've been worried about you. How are you?"

"Terrible." Straightening, Anika swiped at her cheeks. "We just came from seeing our dad."

"Luke told me he'd been admitted here. I promise, he's in good hands."

Luke flinched beneath the cool smile she cast him. He caught Anika's jacket before it slipped off her shoulders. "We should be going. It's getting late."

Anika ignored him. "Wait—Shannon, are *you* okay?"

"Yes, fine. I was just here for a follow-up appointment." Her gaze shifted briefly toward the office she'd just come from.

Luke read the nameplate: *Irene Yoshida, MD*. The last conversation he'd had with Shannon slammed into his thoughts—the things she'd confided about her emotional struggle after losing her husband.

The things she'd said about faith and prayer and how her treatment here at Mercy Cottage had given her back her life.

If only someone could give him back *his* life—all the years that mourning his mother, despising his father, and fretting over his sister had stolen from him.

Anika gave Shannon another brief hug. "I hope we can get together and talk soon. I could really use a friend like you right now."

"You can call me anytime." Shannon's sympathetic gaze shifted to Luke. "You, too."

Luke jutted his chin. "I thought after the other night you didn't want to talk to me anymore."

A sad smile forming, she tilted her head. "I'm not the one who ended the call."

Anika passed a confused look between them, but the truth stung, and Luke wasn't in the mood to explain.

Shannon checked her watch. "I have to go. Tate's great-grandparents are expecting me. But I'll be praying for both of you."

"Thanks, we need all the prayers we can get." Anika linked arms with Shannon. "We're just leaving, too. We can walk out together."

Luke held back, an ache forming in his chest. Holding God at arm's length while desperately needing Shannon in his life—it felt like an unwinnable war. And the cost would be his heart.

⚬

Shannon had given no thought to the possibility that Luke and his sister might also be at Mercy Cottage that afternoon. Perhaps it was God's perfect timing, though.

With the quaver in Anika's voice and the sense of desperation in her embrace, it seemed as if she barely held it together.

As for Luke, his Mr. Tough Guy act didn't fool Shannon for a moment. Clearly, he was hurting more than he could even admit to himself.

They'd reached the parking lot and said a polite goodbye before turning in opposite directions toward their vehicles. Shannon had just unlocked her yellow Beetle when she felt Luke's hand on her arm.

"Wait," he said. "I can't let you leave before I apologize."

A shiver worked its way up her spine. She forced a smile. "It's not necessary, Luke. I understand what a difficult time this is for you."

"But that night on the phone ..." The lines at the corners of his eyes betrayed his struggle to get the words out. "It's not how I wanted things to end for us. The truth is, I don't want things to end. If you—" He faltered, hauling in a shaky breath. "If you shut me out, I'm not sure how I'll ever get through this."

A lump rose in her throat. "I never meant to shut you out."

"That's what it felt like, though." His tone hardened. "You implied I had too many issues."

"*Issues*? You're looking at the queen of issues." Giving a sardonic laugh, she tipped her head toward the building behind them. "Did you forget where we both just came from?"

"Then what are you saying? You're going to have to tell me straight, Shannon. Are you in my life or not?"

"I—I want to be." She took his hand, her thumb caressing each knuckle, her fingertips memorizing every work-worn callus on his palm. "But I need a promise from you."

His eyes narrowed. "What kind of promise? Because if this has anything to do with God—"

"All I ask is that you keep your heart open to Him." She tucked his hand against her chest. "Because if you can do that much, I'll know you have room in your heart for me."

"You are one persuasive woman, Shannon Halsey."

Her glance fell to his lips, and she suppressed a shiver. Would he kiss her again? It surprised her how much she wanted him to. A tremor in her voice, she asked, "Is that a yes?"

"Is it enough if I promise to try?"

All she could do was nod. Glimpsing Anika standing near Luke's truck, she heaved a reluctant sigh. "Your sister's waiting, and I'm sure she's exhausted. You should get her home."

Stepping back, he roughly cleared his throat. "Can I call you later?"

"You'd better."

Pulse racing, she held herself rigid as he slid his hand from hers and strode away. *Please, Lord, don't let this be a mistake.*

After tucking Tate into bed and putting in three solid hours on the proofreading job due the next day, Shannon began to wonder if Luke had already changed his mind. She'd thought *later* meant he'd call tonight, not tomorrow or next week.

And she needed to hear his voice. She needed to believe

he truly intended to try—and not just with her, but with God.

Her phone rang a few minutes past eleven. She'd been working in bed and had just closed the document file. Moving her computer off her lap, she grabbed the phone from the nightstand. When Luke's name flashed across the display, she took a moment to slow her breathing before she answered.

"Hi," Luke said, a weariness in his voice. "Sorry I couldn't call earlier. Did I wake you?"

"Hadn't turned out the lights yet." Even though it wasn't a video call this time, she gave her messy topknot a self-conscious pat.

"Working late again? Shannon, I hope you don't burn yourself out."

Face warming, she tried not to let resentment bleed into her tone. "I don't have much choice. I need the extra income."

Luke huffed. "There I go, micromanaging everyone else's life while making a mess of my own."

Had Anika raked him over the coals again? No doubt, after they'd seen their father this afternoon, his overprotectiveness had come out in full force. "I know you mean well."

"Which is no excuse." Another explosive sigh. "I wish I didn't live an hour away, or I'd be on your doorstep right now. Being with you ... you have this firm but gentle way of redirecting me."

A smile formed as she pictured the afternoon she and Tate had pretended to be sheep while he worked with his dog. "Kind of like you do with Fletch?"

"Exactly." He released a wry chuckle. Growing serious, he went on, "Look, I know what I promised this afternoon, and I know it's important to you that I get right with God. But it's hard, Shannon. After everything my dad has put us through, it's really, really hard."

Fatigue was catching up with her, but the pain in his voice tugged at her heart. She stifled a yawn and nestled deeper into the pillows. "Do you want to talk about it?"

After a moment of silence, he replied, "Not yet. I need to get a handle on some things first. But it helps knowing you haven't given up on me."

"I haven't, and I won't. And God hasn't given up on you, either." An image rose in her thoughts. "When you were waiting to see your dad this afternoon, did you notice the plaque over the inner door?"

"Not that I recall." He snorted. "I was working too hard on not making a run for it."

"Well, here's what it says: *Mercy unto you, and peace, and love, be multiplied.* It's from the Book of Jude, and I'm praying those words over you right now."

Silence, and then a shuddering breath.

"Luke? Are you okay?"

His voice an unsteady murmur, he said, "You should get some sleep. Good night, Shannon."

The line went dead.

The minute Luke hung up on Shannon—again—he regretted it. He should be grateful someone cared enough to pray for him. And not only Shannon, but his sister, too. With those two determined women storming heaven on his behalf, not to mention the countless times Mom had prayed for him while she was alive, it was a wonder that God hadn't breached Luke's walls long ago.

It isn't that I don't want to let You in, God.

Because a part of him did. And not merely because Shannon had made it a condition of their relationship. But after all the heartache his family had endured, he had a hard time trusting that God even cared.

Restless, he dropped a decaf pod into the coffeemaker. After it finished brewing, he carried his mug to the living room and stood before the wide picture window. The ranch lay bathed in moonlight, and without the competition of city lights, the stars gleamed like diamonds scattered across black velvet.

Mom had always loved gazing up at the stars. On a clear night like tonight, she'd often set up her telescope on an upstairs balcony and help Luke and Anika pick out the constellations and planets.

"Isn't it beautiful, kids? Just think, our heavenly Father created every single one of those lights in the sky, each one special in its own way. He made you special, too, and He loves you so much. Even if you could count all the stars in the universe, God loves you a billion times more."

Luke's eyes welled at the memory, and he missed his mom more than ever. He'd asked her that night how she could be certain of God's love when He seemed so far away.

"I know His love is real," Mom had answered, "because He gave us such an amazing sky to enjoy—the stars and moon by night, the sun and clouds by day. He gave us the changing seasons, the animals, the plants and trees and myriad flowers. But most of all, I know He loves me because He gave me my precious family." Stretching her arms around Luke and Anika, Mom kissed their heads.

Luke, not quite fourteen then, ducked out of her reach. "I don't like God very much."

"That's not nice," Anika retorted. "Say you're sorry, Luke."

Mom patted Anika's shoulder. "Feelings are feelings, honey. We don't argue with them."

"But you always say God's our heavenly Father. We have to love Him. Right?"

"A good father doesn't let bad stuff happen to his kids," Luke snapped.

"God gets sad, too, when bad things happen." Mom spoke tenderly, patiently. "But He promises to be with us and strengthen us, no matter what we face."

"Well, if He's all-powerful, why doesn't He just fix things? Why doesn't He make you better? Why doesn't He make Dad stop running off all the time?" Luke's throat ached, but he wouldn't let his mother see him cry. "Why couldn't God give us a dad who'd be here when we need him?"

Mom pulled Luke close until he gave in and melted into her hug. "Oh, my sweet boy. I know sometimes it seems like your daddy doesn't love us the way he should. But some people never really learned how to love, which means they need our love all the more." She sighed and looked skyward. "I suspect that's why God puts people like your dad into our lives, so we can fill their hurting souls with all the love God graciously showers upon us."

To this day, Luke couldn't fathom how to love a man who seemed determined to destroy himself—and take the whole family along with him. Mom and Anika had always been far better at it than Luke. He'd never understood how they could repeatedly give Dad the benefit of the doubt.

Mercy unto you, and peace, and love, be multiplied.

Mercy, Mom had taught them, was about not getting the punishment you deserved. But where did that leave justice? Shouldn't there be consequences for hurting other people—especially the ones you were supposed to love and care for?

"See, that's the problem, God," Luke said aloud. "Your rules don't make sense to me."

He stood at the window a few minutes longer, on the off chance God had anything to say in reply. Giving his head a resigned shake, he finished his cooling decaf, set the mug in the sink, and headed to bed.

Chapter Twenty-Four

With several pressing ranch tasks demanding Luke's attention that week, he had no choice but to shift his brain into full administrative mode. A top priority was making sure buildings and equipment were in working order before the winter snows set in and maintenance became difficult if not impossible.

On Wednesday, he rode the fence line and scouted for weakened or broken posts and overgrown vegetation. Fletch trotted along beside the horse until his short legs needed a rest. Then Luke would hoist him across his lap and let him ride for a while.

When they took a lunch break beneath the sparse canopy of a silver maple, Fletch sniffed out a gopher. The destructive burrowing rodents were the bane of Montana ranchers, and Luke dispatched the critter with his .22. When the sun dipped low, he turned Zorro around and headed toward the barn.

With still a mile to go, he heard Fletch yelp. Reining Zorro to a halt, he glanced back to see the dog favoring his left front leg.

"Stay put, boy. I'm coming." Luke dismounted and jogged back to where Fletch had plopped down in the grass. The dog winced as Luke palpated the leg and paw. "Pretty sore, huh? What'd you do, step in a gopher hole? Let's get you home."

Hefting the dog into the saddle with him, Luke continued on. By the time they arrived at the barn, Fletch's foreleg had become swollen and hot. Luke laid the dog on an old horse blanket, then clipped Zorro in the crossties.

Tobias appeared in the barn office doorway. "I was just about to send out a search party."

"Long day. Fletch got hurt on the way back. Not sure how bad it is."

Kneeling beside Fletch's blanket, Tobias stroked the dog while inspecting the injured leg. "Yep, looks like a sprain. Hope that's all it is."

"If he doesn't improve by morning, I'll get him to the vet."

"Good idea. Let me take care of your horse. You look like you need a long, hot shower and some food in your belly."

"Thanks. Everything okay here?"

Tobias filled him in on the maintenance tasks he'd been overseeing. "Might need an electrician to look at the fuse box in the calving barn, though."

"Do what needs doing." Luke scooped Fletch into his arms and started out.

"By the way," Tobias said, "your friend Witt called on the landline this morning. Figured your cell must be out of range. He wanted to confirm you'd be at the dog class on Saturday."

Luke had been so preoccupied with everything else that

he'd neglected his obedience class commitments. "I'll call him right away."

In the cabin, he made Fletch comfortable on the sofa, then grabbed an ice pack from the freezer and a soda from the fridge. With the ice pack wrapped in a towel, he eased down next to Fletch and applied it to the sore leg. Supper would be a little later tonight.

While they sat there, he called Witt. After extending his apologies, he promised he'd be at Hope House as scheduled on Saturday morning. "If it'll help, I can work in a week-night catch-up class. I'll make this right—you have my word."

"I know you will," Witt replied, kindness in his tone. "Everyone understands you're going through a rough time. We're all praying."

"Thanks." Not that Luke was happy about his family problems being aired far and wide. "What have you heard?"

"No details, really. Just that both your dad and sister had been in the hospital." The statement ended on a higher pitch that implied a question.

Which Luke didn't feel capable of answering. "We're getting by," was all he said. "I'd better go. Let the guys know I'll be there Saturday."

"I will. And Luke?"

"Yeah?"

"If you ever need to talk …"

"I appreciate the offer. I'll let you know."

❧

What with setting an alarm to check on Fletch and ice his leg every couple of hours through the night, neither Luke nor his dog got much rest. By morning, a trip to the vet seemed inevitable.

Luke could have taken the dog to the clinic he'd been using for the past several years—it was a few miles closer than Frasier Veterinary Clinic—but the chance to see Shannon again trumped distance. Besides, he owed her an apology for ending yet another conversation so abruptly.

Just after 8:00 a.m., he parked his truck outside the clinic. Through the front windows, he glimpsed Shannon taking a call at the front desk. He probably should have called for an appointment, but that would have delayed his arrival. One look at Fletch trembling in the passenger seat, his eyes dulled by pain, and Luke didn't waste another second. He hurried around to the other door, gently lifted the dog, and strode to the entrance.

A young guy in green scrubs pulled open the door for him. "Looks like somebody's not feeling too good. How can we help?"

"He hurt his leg yesterday. I—"

"Luke?" Shannon rushed forward. "Oh, no! What happened?"

"I think it's a sprain." He explained about Fletch getting injured on the way home last night.

The guy glanced between them. "You know each other?"

"This is Luke Daniels," Shannon said, a hint of color rising in her cheeks. "Remember I mentioned Tate and I pretended to be sheep to help him practice with his dog?"

"Ah, this must be the talented Fletch. Hi, Luke. I'm Dylan. Let's get your boy to an exam room." He started for the inner door. "Shannon, would you ask Dr. J to step in?"

"Of course." To Luke, she said, "Dr. J is Julia Frasier, my stepmom. She'll take great care of Fletch."

Luke had little time to process that information as he hurried after Dylan down a short corridor. In the exam room, he eased Fletch onto a shiny stainless-steel table. The dog whimpered and stretched out on his side, his ribcage rising and falling with each panting breath.

Seconds later, Shannon entered with a tall, dark-haired woman. She introduced Luke and his dog.

"I don't always recognize owners," Julia Frasier said, "but I rarely forget their pets. Fletch has been here before, hasn't he?"

"Yeah, I think it was two years ago. He landed hard after catching a Frisbee."

"Oh, yes, I remember." Dr. Frasier spoke soothing words to the dog as she examined his leg. "Sorry, boy, I know this hurts." She nodded to the vet tech. "We should do some X-rays."

"On it." Dylan slipped out.

"This is going to take some time," the veterinarian said. "Shannon, ask Brad to cover the front. You go sit with Luke in the break room. Amy just brewed fresh coffee, and I picked up a dozen bagels on my way in this morning."

Luke hated leaving Fletch, but the dog seemed in capable, caring hands. He waited while Shannon said something to a man in the office across the hall, then followed her to a kitchenette near the back.

She invited him to sit at the table while she poured him some coffee. "I can toast a bagel if you're hungry. There's cream cheese, too."

He was about to refuse, but his stomach reminded him he hadn't had breakfast. "Sounds good. Thanks."

A few minutes later, Shannon brought over a toasted cinnamon-raisin bagel on a paper plate. While he spread cream cheese across the halves, she took the chair across from him. "I'm sorry this had to happen on top of everything else. How are you doing?"

"I've been better, that's for sure. Keeping busy helps." He started to take a bite of bagel, then set it back down. "That thing you said on the phone the other night, the quote about mercy? It's been on my mind a lot."

"Has it?"

"My mom tried hard to pass on her faith to her kids. It took with Anika. With me? Not so much." Luke snorted. "Especially the mercy part. Guess I'm more into judgment and condemnation."

"Then ... you want to be in the place of God?"

Uncomfortable beneath Shannon's frown, he devoured a huge chunk of bagel. Once he could swallow, he washed it down with several sips of coffee. "All right, maybe I do want the right to condemn and punish. At least where my dad is concerned. I know it's wrong, but I can't help how I feel."

Shannon glanced toward the window. "Oh, believe me, I understand."

"My mom always told us feelings are feelings, and we can't argue with them." Luke flattened his lips. "But I'm sure she'd be as disappointed in my attitude as you are."

"I'm not disappointed, Luke." She sat forward and took his hand. "Not in the way you think."

One brow dipped. "What way, then?"

"I'm sad that you're not letting God walk with you through these trials."

Letting her words penetrate, he studied her fingers. His gaze lingered on the simple gold wedding band she still wore. "I'm not sure I even know how."

She tucked her hands into her lap and sat straighter.

"Well, you could try simply asking Him. Like you'd ask help from any friend."

"That easy, huh?" Luke released a humorless laugh. "Even a friend you've been ignoring for too long to count?"

She peered up at him with a hopeful smile. "Or you could ask a current friend to reintroduce you and smooth the way."

His throat tightened. His heart thumped with unexpected urgency. "Would ... would you ..."

She reached again for his hands, then bowed her head. "Dear Lord, Your son Luke needs You like never before. He's feeling lost and helpless and angry—feelings I know all too well. You loved and carried me through my darkest days, and I know You're still with me no matter what my circumstances look like. Let Luke know how much You want to be there for him. Soften his heart. Heal his woundedness. Show him Your deep love in a mighty way. For we ask all this in the power of Jesus' name."

The prayer faded into silence. Luke couldn't move, couldn't speak. A buzzing sensation circled his chest and swept down his limbs. Any second now, he'd shatter into a million pieces. And the weird part? He didn't care.

Something had changed. Shannon wasn't sure what, but she sensed it in the way Luke gripped her hands as if he couldn't let go. Tilting her head for a better look at his face, she whispered, "Are you okay?"

He gave a jerky nod. "I think I need a minute."

"Would you rather be alone?"

"No. Please don't go." Releasing a shuddering breath,

he peered into her eyes. "Your prayer—how do you know the words to say? How do you know God hears?"

She shrugged, her smile tilted. "I just picture Jesus sitting across from me with this welcoming, caring look on His face, and I tell Him what's on my heart. As for how I know He hears, it's faith, pure and simple. Plus, He's already shown His love for me in a thousand different ways. I know I can trust every part of my life to Him."

Luke's throat worked. "I want to trust God again. If only—"

She silenced him with a finger to his lips. "No *if onlys*. Just do it."

The squeak of sneaker soles drew her attention as Dylan appeared in the doorway. "Fletch is waiting for you in the exam room."

Luke clutched Shannon's hand as he burst up from his chair. "Is he okay?"

"Dr. J will fill you in."

Before Luke could rush out, Shannon pulled him to a halt. "This would be a good time to exercise those faith muscles."

He drew a breath and released it slowly. "I'm working on it."

"All right, then. Let's go see your dog."

Julia stood next to Fletch as he lay on the exam table. Head up and eyes alert, he sported a red brace around his leg and seemed in much less discomfort. He gave a joyful bark as Luke strode over.

"Hey, boy." Luke ruffled the dog's fur. "You sure look better than you did when I brought you in."

"I gave him a mild pain reliever before we did the X-rays," Julia said. "Nothing's broken, but he sprained his wrist pretty badly. Plus, he's got some arthritis, which exacerbated the injury."

"Arthritis?" Luke's brows bunched. "But he's not quite seven years old."

"As active as Fletch is, wear and tear alone can weaken cartilage. Anti-inflammatories can help, along with joint supplements. I'll send some home with you today." Julia gave a few more instructions for Fletch's care and said he could pick up a detailed printout at the front desk, along with the prescriptions.

Luke thanked her as he gingerly lowered Fletch to the floor. Shannon led the way to the front.

Three clients and their pets now occupied the waiting room, so she took over for Brad behind the counter and reverted to professional mode. She brought up Fletch's records from his previous visit, then swiveled the computer screen for Luke to see it. "Please make sure all the info is current."

He gave it a quick once-over. "Looks good. What do I owe you?"

"It'll be a few minutes while everything's finalized. Dylan will bring up your scripts shortly." Shannon already missed the closeness they'd shared in the privacy of the break room. She took a dog treat from the canister on the counter and went around to offer it to Fletch. "Here's something for our very patient patient. I hope your leg gets all better soon."

The dog yipped his gratitude and crunched away.

Rising, Shannon faced Luke. "Will you call and let me know how you're—how he's doing?"

"I will." His fingers grazed the back of her hand, and she shivered.

Behind the counter, the printer came to life. "That'll be your discharge instructions. Your bill should be ready, too."

While Shannon checked Luke out, Dylan came to the front with a small white bag containing Fletch's prescriptions. "You'll find dosage information on the discharge sheet."

"I appreciate you getting us seen so quickly," Luke said, shaking Dylan's hand. "If it's okay, I'd like to get Fletch's records transferred here permanently."

Glancing at Shannon, Dylan wiggled his brows and grinned. "I'm sure that can be arranged."

Shannon hoped the warmth spreading up her face wasn't obvious. She took charge of Luke's paperwork and the prescription bag. "I'll help you get everything out to your truck."

Once they settled Fletch in the truck, Luke drew Shannon into his arms and pressed his cheek to her temple. "Thank you. For everything."

"If I helped at all, I'm glad." She'd come outside without grabbing a jacket, and the chilly air nipped at her exposed skin. She leaned just far enough away from his warmth to look into his eyes. "I guess we won't be playing 'pretend sheep' again anytime soon. Tate had tons of fun that day. He misses you, too."

"You could bring him to my place this weekend. We'll find something else fun to do." He brushed his lips across her forehead. "I need to see you again, Shannon. Please."

The urgency in his tone squeezed her heart. "I'll probably have a proofreading job."

"Bring your laptop. I can keep Tate occupied. I don't care what we do, as long as we can spend time together."

She longed to say yes, but something held her back, and too many times she'd learned the hard way what could happen if she ignored the Holy Spirit's promptings. Easing from his embrace, she focused on smoothing his jacket collar. "I'll think about it. Let's see how things go."

He nodded, then glanced toward the building. "Any reason I can't kiss you goodbye?"

"I can't think of any." Her breath quickened with anticipation.

He pulled her close again, one hand at the small of her back, the other weaving through the strands of her hair. Her arms slid beneath his jacket as his lips closed over hers. Melting into him, she could have stayed like this forever.

Only Fletch's sharp bark brought the kiss to an end.

"Okay, okay, we're going home." Luke reached into the truck to give the dog a pat, then touched his forehead to Shannon's. "To be continued."

"I certainly hope so."

Hugging herself, she watched from the sidewalk as Luke drove away. Had he reached a turning point in his faith today? She prayed it was true, but only time would tell.

Recent events had drained him, but the hope of seeing Shannon this weekend—of holding and kissing her again—gave Luke the motivation to keep plugging away. And not just on the unavoidable ranch chores, but on his relationship with God.

On Friday morning, Anika came looking for him in the barn office. She knelt before Fletch's plush dog bed and gave him a scratch behind the ears. "How's our boy doing?"

Luke rolled back from the desk and stretched his legs

out. "He had a good night. I did, too. Best in weeks, actually."

"Oh, really?" Head tilted, Anika squinted hard in his direction. "Yep, that *is* a smile."

Face warming, he waved away her remark and returned his attention to the computer spreadsheet he'd been working on.

"No, seriously. Something's different about you." Anika stood and massaged her hip as she leaned against the desk. Brows shooting up, she blurted, "It's Shannon, isn't it? Something happened when you saw her at the vet clinic yesterday."

He finished entering a line of data, then huffed. "Yes. Something happened."

Anika scooted closer. "Well? Tell me. Because I could use some positive news right now."

Groaning, he leaned back and scraped his hands down his face. "I don't know how."

"Oh, Luke." Both her tone and her expression shifted toward concern. "You know you can talk to me about anything."

Not entirely true. For a troubled moment, his thoughts returned to the shoebox he'd brought home from the cabin. He hoped it remained well hidden in the tack room.

He slanted a look her way, then lowered his voice. "It started with her praying for me."

Anika pressed her lips together, her silence compelling him to say more.

"I promised her I'd try to quit shutting God out."

Eyes widening, his sister released a muted "Wow."

"And then she walked Fletch and me out to the truck, and I told her how much I wanted to keep seeing her, and ... we kissed."

A tear slid down Anika's cheek. She bent over to wrap Luke in a hug. "Thank You, Lord. Oh, thank You, thank You, Jesus!"

He didn't have to ask what she was most thankful for. Hadn't she been praying for years that he'd find his way back to God?

"Just so you understand," he said when she finally released her hold. "The Lord and I still have a few things to work out. Mostly where Dad is concerned."

"Yes, but it's a start." She used a knuckle to dab beneath her eyes. "And now that you've cracked open the door, God's going to keep inching His way in."

That was how it felt to Luke, too, like the crack in his heart kept expanding. He began to understand what Shannon had meant that night on the phone about keeping his heart open to God, because *"then I'll know you have room in your heart for me."*

After blowing her nose, Anika dropped the tissue in the trash and moved toward the door. "I should let you get back to whatever you were working on."

"No hurry. What are your plans today?"

"There's a Christmas arts and crafts fair at the end of November that I might sign up for. I thought I'd design some new bandannas and bows and start building my inventory." She gave a meaningful roll of her eyes. "Sure don't want a repeat of last time."

"Me, neither." Luke stood to give his sister a hug. "Let me know how I can help."

He watched with a sense of relief as she strode to the house. Though until now, he'd considered it more of a *hope* than a *prayer* that Anika would detach herself from their father, maybe she was finally moving in that direction.

God, if that's Your doing, then thanks.

Even so, he doubted his sister would ever lose hope that Dad could be redeemed. Her heart—and her faith—didn't allow giving up on anyone.

Maybe because God didn't give up on anyone?

A point Luke would have to struggle with a bit longer.

As he turned back toward the office, his glance shifted to the tack room door. He should move that problematic shoebox somewhere safe, where Anika wouldn't be as likely to find it. Checking to make sure he was alone in the barn, he slipped into the tack room.

The box was right where he'd left it. He scooped it up in a dusty horse blanket and tucked the bundle under his arm.

Fletch eyed him from the office doorway, head tilted and ears cocked.

"Nothing you need to concern yourself with," he told the dog. "Ready to head to the cabin?"

With Fletch hobbling along beside him, he tried to look nonchalant in case anyone was watching. At the cabin, he went straight to his study and removed the blanket, then set the shoebox on his desk. He backed away and stared at it like it was a rattler coiled to strike.

Why he continued to avoid a closer examination, he wasn't sure. Maybe because the first few items he'd glimpsed concerned him enough that he was afraid to look deeper?

Seemed his dad had collected news clippings covering his and Anika's wreck—the accident *he'd* caused. Had Dad been scouring reports for any suspicion of his culpability? Or was he so guilt-ridden that rereading the accounts became a form of self-flagellation?

Before Luke examined the contents more closely, he needed some objectivity. If he could bring himself to open up to anyone about all the stuff he was dealing with, it'd be Witt Wittenbauer.

He pulled out his phone and made the call. After assuring his friend that he wasn't calling to back out of another training session, he went on, "I'd like to take you up on your offer to talk. Any chance we could meet somewhere? Maybe later this afternoon?"

"How about Elk Valley Community of Faith, say around four? We can talk privately in one of the Sunday school rooms."

"I'll be there."

Chapter Twenty-Five

Luke—finding his way back to the Lord? Anika couldn't stop humming "How Great Thou Art" as she set up her laptop on the kitchen table. Opening a browser window, she began an online search for cute new dog accessory ideas. She'd like to expand into coats and booties and even holiday costumes. Since this would be a Christmas-themed fair, how about Santa and elf suits that could be adjusted to fit a variety of sizes? She chose a pattern from an online craft shop and placed the order. Tomorrow, she'd drive into Missoula and pick out fabric.

Having something positive to look forward to was a welcome change—although she almost felt guilty for hardly giving Dad a thought all morning. She'd been mentally storing away advice from the pamphlets Dr. Ingalls had given them, and one crucial reminder was that she couldn't "fix" her father. She could only support and encourage. And, above all, pray.

She also needed to take care of herself—physically, emotionally, and spiritually. Luke wasn't completely out of line in prodding her to build a life that didn't revolve around taking care of their father. But honestly, she couldn't fathom the idea of striking out on her own in the city.

Besides, selling doggy treats and accessories at arts-and-craft fairs wouldn't cover living expenses, even if she branched out with an online store. More importantly, she wouldn't allow what had begun as an enjoyable creative outlet to turn into an exhausting, all-consuming chore. She'd learned with her first booth experience what happened when she pushed herself beyond her limits.

As she sat pondering the current direction of her life—or lack thereof—a rider in the distance caught her eye. She swiveled toward the window and rested her forearms on the sill. Oh, yes, she'd recognize this cowboy by his posture alone. Upright but relaxed in the saddle, shoulders back and arms loose, his body following the horse's motion as if they were one.

Tobias.

A wistful sigh escaped. Would she ever mean anything more to him than the annoying adolescent who used to make up any excuse to hang out wherever he was working? Even worse, his boss's fragile sister who always seemed to need looking after?

It was a paradox, really. Luke repeatedly pressed her to get away from Dad and live her own life. Yet he also insisted on treating her like a china doll to be kept safely on the shelf or she'd break.

You can't have it both ways, brother of mine.

Her life choices had to be hers and no one else's. And one thing she knew for certain: She loved the ranch. Since her teen years, she'd often wished Dad and Luke would include her more in the day-to-day operations. Not that Dad stayed much involved anymore. After the accident,

Luke had taken on the bulk of responsibility, with a lot of help from Tobias.

Jerking upright, Anika closed her laptop. Why had the answer never occurred to her before? She grabbed a jacket on her way out the back door and strode across to the barn. Finding the office dark and empty, she continued to Luke's cabin.

She rapped on the door, then eased it open. "Luke? Anybody home?"

Rustling sounds came from the direction of his study. "Back here, Ani. Hang on a sec."

"I was hoping we could talk." She rounded the corner as he stuffed something into a desk drawer. "Sorry if I interrupted something."

"Just tidying up." Luke motioned her back toward the living room. "What's on your mind?"

They took seats at opposite ends of the distressed-leather sofa, and Luke helped Fletch get settled on a blanket spread out between them.

Anika gave the dog a scratch under the chin. "You're getting around pretty good, fella."

"He's a trouper," Luke said. "I hope he doesn't get too spoiled with all this pampering."

Her brother couldn't have given her a better lead-in. "Yeah, pampering is nice ... until it isn't."

Frowning, Luke crossed his arms. "We're not talking about Fletch anymore, are we?"

"I shouldn't have to spell it out for you, but I will." She curled one leg under her and faced him. "I need to feel needed. Useful. Competent."

"Come on, Ani. You're all those things."

"And yet you insist on protecting me from anything and everything."

He gave his head a hard shake. "Not true. I just—"

"Stop denying it, Luke. Anyway, it doesn't matter anymore. Because I came to a decision today. I know what I want to do with my life."

His eyes narrowed. "You do?"

"That's right. I want to learn everything there is to know about running the ranch. I want to be part of the team."

"No." Luke abruptly pushed off the sofa, startling Fletch. "No, Ani, you don't know what you're asking. You're not—this isn't—" An exasperated huff exploded from his throat.

"Are you trying to say I'm not capable? Okay, I get that I'll never be able to ride as well as you, or toss around a hay bale like it's a loaf of bread, or wrestle a steer to the ground." She crossed the room and stood toe-to-toe with her brother. "But I'm smart, and I'm a fast learner. You and Tobias both despise the desk work anyway, so let me do the things I *can* do—that I could be really good at, if you'd teach me. If you'd just give me a chance."

He gaped at her like she'd sprouted another eye in the center of her forehead. "You're serious."

"I am!" Regaining control of her voice and her emotions, she repeated calmly, "I am very serious."

Angling away, Luke rubbed his jaw. He looked back at her. "Guess I always assumed you'd rather do something else. *Anything* else."

"No, you decided I *should* want to do something besides live and work here on the ranch. The ranch that's been in the Daniels family for four generations. Going on five, if you'd ever get married and have a few kids of your own." A cajoling smile formed. "Even better, go for a ready-made family with Shannon and Tate."

Her normally self-controlled older brother actually blushed. Hands upraised, he backed up a step. "Okay, you've made your point. And you're right, desk work is my least favorite part of ranch management. It'd be my pleasure to hand that part over to you."

"You mean it? Oh, Luke, thank you!" She threw her arms around him and squeezed until he gasped for air. "Can we start right now?"

Grabbing her shoulders, he put some space between them and gave a nervous chuckle. "You've kinda caught me off guard, sis. Anyway, I ..." He checked his watch. "I have somewhere I need to be later this afternoon."

After everything he'd confided in her already today, she chose to ignore his evasive tone. He deserved a little privacy in his personal life. "Tomorrow morning, then?"

"Sure. We can put in an hour before I have to leave for my obedience class, then pick up after I get back."

She gave him another quick hug before hurrying to the house. The basket beside Dad's recliner in the den held at least a year's worth of ranching magazines. Until now, she'd had little reason to take an interest in them.

It was long past time.

Chapter Twenty-Six

As Shannon restocked the counter display with flea-and-tick prevention brochures, Dylan brought out a black-and-tan Min Pin after a toenail trim. The spunky little guy couldn't drag his owner out the door fast enough.

"Sorry, must run." Mrs. Gardner, a clinic regular, waved and promised to call later with a credit card number to pay her bill.

Shannon shared a laugh with Dylan. "No question who's the boss in that household."

"Like you've got room to talk. Rowena must outweigh you by at least ten pounds."

"Close, but at least she's docile. And usually more obedient than my son."

Chuckling, Dylan joined her behind the reception desk. He shifted the computer monitor to peruse the appointment calendar. "Wow. It isn't even four o'clock yet and we're all caught up."

"Unbelievable, huh?" For a change, the waiting room sat empty. "What's wrong with this picture?"

"Maybe everyone's getting an early start on weekend plans." Dylan plopped into the extra chair and folded his arms. "You've got tomorrow off. What fun stuff is on your agenda?"

She'd been trying not to dwell on the text from Ravi that had arrived a few minutes ago.

> Hope you don't have big plans this weekend. I need you for a rush job. Call ASAP for deets.

So much for any hopes of spending time with Luke.

Realizing Dylan was waiting for a reply, she shrugged and picked up a stack of patient folders ready to be filed. "No plans except going into hibernation with my latest proofreading assignment."

"Right, you're moonlighting for that tech writing company. How's it going?"

"*Moonlighting* pretty much describes it. Too many late nights." Pulling open a file drawer, Shannon smothered a yawn. "I'm sure you've made some fun weekend plans. Fill me in and make me jealous."

"Just me and some pals heading up to Flathead Lake for camping and fishing. Unless you're into chilly nights in a sleeping bag that smells like sweaty socks and dead fish, there's nothing to be jealous of."

She snorted. "You make finding typos and fixing punctuation errors sound more exciting by the minute."

If only that were true. Not that the job itself was unpleasant—she relished the challenge each new assignment brought. But working late into the evening and giving up big chunks of her weekends was wearing on her.

Dylan stood and said he needed to log some lab results

that had come in after lunch. At the doorway, he paused. "Say, I heard you met my cousin Jeff at church."

Shannon managed a neutral smile. "I did. He seems nice."

"He's a nice enough guy, that's true." Dylan hesitated. "But a word to the wise: When it comes to commitment and follow-through, he's a bit of a flake. You deserve better, Shannon. Lots better." The inner door closed behind him.

Dylan's words, spoken as the friend he'd become in the time she'd been working here, reminded her she was indeed worthy of being loved—and by someone who could commit fully to building a life together.

Steven had been that man, right up until the end. For the millionth time, she asked God why. *Our time had only just begun, Lord. Why did he have to die?*

She could imagine how Steven would fuss at her for clinging to his memory and all the might-have-beens. *"Come on, babe. You've got to live your life in the present, not the past. I want my girl to be happy again."*

Happy? Tate made her laugh a dozen times a day. Add Rowena into the mix, and they could have her howling and holding her sides. She had steady employment, a comfortable home, friends and family who looked out for her— blessings from God, every one of them.

But as a woman who'd also known the happiness only true love could bring, she yearned for more.

Luke's image filled her thoughts. She was falling for him, no doubt about it. There had to be some way to make room in her schedule so they could spend time together this weekend. She should call Ravi and ask the true scope of this job.

Not that she didn't desperately need the work—her cell

phone and utility bills would arrive any day now, and her bank balance hovered dangerously near the red zone. If only she could turn the assignment around quickly, without stealing too much quality time from the people she cared about most.

A few minutes on the phone with Ravi proved it would not be the quick turnaround she'd prayed for. The eighty-six-page business prospectus had to be in the hands of potential investors no later than 9:00 a.m. Monday. Unfortunately, the staff writers had taken longer to complete it than expected.

Since it was a rush job and the pay would be double the usual rate, how could Shannon refuse? Either her work continued to impress Ravi, or he figured she'd be the least likely to turn down the extra money. Maybe both? She told him to email the doc to her, and she'd start on it tonight.

She had no choice but to call Luke and let him know an urgent proofreading job had just upended their weekend plans.

The call went straight to voicemail. "Hi, Luke, it's me. I'm sorry, but tomorrow isn't going to work. I miss you already. I hope Fletch is doing better. Call me?"

A few minutes before four on Friday afternoon, Luke hauled in a bolstering breath and marched through the side door of Elk Valley Community of Faith. The church secretary directed him down the hall to Room 6, where he found Witt pouring coffee.

"Care for some decaf?" Witt took another mug from beneath the coffee stand. "Brought cinnamon rolls, too, fresh from the Smith Family Hometown Café."

He wasn't hungry until Witt mentioned cinnamon rolls. "Sure, thanks."

Witt brought the steaming mugs to one of the round tables spaced across the room, then frowned toward the shoebox tucked beneath Luke's arm. "That looks serious."

"It is." Luke placed the box on the table before taking the chair to Witt's right.

"So ... talk now, or gorge ourselves on carbs first?"

Luke gave a rueful snort. "I vote for carbs. I'm gonna need the fortification."

"My thoughts exactly. Just don't let word get back to Maddie. My cholesterol's been on the high side, and she's trying to keep me on a healthy diet."

"My lips are sealed." Luke helped himself to a cinnamon roll the size of a flattened softball and sank his teeth into the doughy sweetness.

When they'd each polished off two rolls and an equal number of coffee refills, Luke helped Witt clear the table. After a trip to the restroom to wash the frosting off their fingers, they returned to their chairs.

Witt sat forward, one elbow on the table. "Ready to talk about that box?"

Luke stared at it for a long moment, then gingerly lifted the lid. He laid out the top three items, newspaper clippings describing the crash. "This is all I've looked at so far. I haven't been able to bring myself to go deeper."

While Witt perused the articles, Luke braved a look at the next item in the box, a bill from a body shop in Great Falls. Apparently, Dad had gotten into a fender bender he'd never mentioned. The date on the bill was around the time they'd spread Mom's ashes, and Luke recalled now that Dad had disappeared afterward for nearly two weeks. Had he gotten drunk, then wrecked his truck while somehow avoiding a DUI citation?

And not once, but twice. Beneath the first bill was a similar receipt from an auto repair shop in Kalispell, this one dated two years ago for a blown tire and busted wheel rim. Except the repairs were for someone else's vehicle, not Dad's. Had he run somebody off the road and then promised to pay cash on the spot if they didn't report it?

When Witt looked up from reading the news articles, Luke tapped a finger on the nearest clipping. "These only tell half the story—and it's the wrong half. Until recently, everyone assumed my sister was behind the wheel. Then her memory started coming back, and it turns out my dad was driving. Driving *drunk*." He pushed the two repair bills toward Witt. "And then there's these."

Witt studied them, then raised his eyes to Luke's, grim comprehension darkening his expression. "I am so sorry."

"All these years, my dad's been a ticking time bomb, one drinking binge away from ruining—or taking—another life." Luke's voice shook with anger and dread. "I have to wonder what else he's been keeping from us."

Witt stroked his chin. "This isn't something you should wrestle with alone."

"I can't show these things to Anika, at least not yet. And I'd be ashamed for anyone else to know." He leaned closer, his gaze imploring. "You're the only one I trust right now. Would you go through the box and help me make sense of it all?"

After a moment's hesitation, Witt nodded. "If that's what you want, I can sure try."

Luke nudged the shoebox closer, then sat back, folded his arms, and closed his eyes.

Papers rustled. Witt's chair creaked. He cleared his

throat a couple of times but uttered only the occasional "Hmm" or "Aw, man."

Then all sounds ceased, and the silence was ominous. A sour taste filled Luke's mouth. He sat up and looked straight at Witt. "What is it? What'd you find?"

"Luke ..." Exhaling through tight lips, Witt slowly shook his head.

"Come on, I have to know." He snatched the yellowed newspaper clipping Witt held and read the headline, his eyes landing hard on each word. "No. ... No ..."

He didn't realize he was crying until a teardrop the size of a dime landed on the page. Sniffing hard, he flung the paper across the table and shoved to his feet.

"Luke, it may not be what you—"

Without letting Witt finish, he stormed from the room. He only knew he had to get as far away from that box—from the obituary he'd just read—as he possibly could.

Because every last hope he carried for a future with Shannon had vanished the moment he saw the name.

Steven Halsey.

After picking up Tate at his great-grandparents', Shannon splurged and took him to his favorite fast-food restaurant for burgers and fries. The kid's meal came with a miniature toy cowboy, complete with a hat, boots, and spurs.

Tate trotted the figurine on an imaginary horse across the restaurant table. "He looks kinda like Luke, doesn't he, Mommy?"

"Maybe a little, but the cowboy hat and boots make him look more like Tobias." She'd only ever seen Luke in "city" clothes—pullover, sneakers, baseball cap. But then, she hadn't seen him on a horse yet, either.

"Well, I'm gonna call him Luke anyway, 'cause he's the boss of the ranch."

More true than ever, and sadly so, with Luke's father in rehab. Random comments from Luke and Anika suggested their father had been stepping back from ranch duties for some time. With him out of the picture for now, Luke must be working harder than ever.

Envisioning the gigantic proofreading task ahead of her this weekend, Shannon could relate.

After wiping hamburger juice off her fingers, she snuck a peek at her phone in case she'd missed a call or text in response to her voicemail. The blank screen mocked her.

As she settled Tate into bed for the night, he asked again if they could go to the ranch this weekend.

"I don't think so, honey." Propped up on pillows beside her son, Shannon laid aside the book of bedtime stories she'd read from. "Remember, I have a big work assignment. Besides, Luke and Anika's daddy is sick, and now Fletch has a hurt paw. I'm sure Luke is very busy taking care of everybody."

"Then we should go see them tomorrow in case they need help."

"Even if I could get done with my work early, we shouldn't just show up."

"But Grammy and Grampy just show up whenever they think we need help."

That was a fact, and Shannon didn't always appreciate it. "I'll try calling again tomorrow to see how he's doing, okay?"

Tate skewed his lips. "Okay, but don't forget."

How could she, when growing concern gnawed at her

insides? She kissed her son goodnight, turned off the bedside lamp, and slipped from the room. Time to settle in at her computer and get to work.

But not before she brewed a pot of strong coffee. Hours of edits lay ahead, and she needed all her brain cells firing on full power.

The document was dry as dirt. Shannon wished she had free rein to do more than check for grammar, spelling, and punctuation. She found herself mentally adding hyperbole, substituting modern slang, tossing in a joke here and there, adding emojis, anything to give the prose some punch.

By midnight, she was halfway through a second pot of coffee and having to slap herself to stay awake. And still she had pages and pages to go.

Chapter Twenty-Seven

"Mommy, wake up! Why are you sleeping so long?"

Tate's piercing voice seemed to come from everywhere at once. Rowena was barking, too. Had someone broken into the house?

Shannon jerked upright, her neck and shoulders screaming. "Ouch."

Tate jostled her. "Are you awake now?"

"I ... I think so." She massaged her neck. And why did the side of her face hurt?

"Ew, Mommy." Poking her cheek with his index finger, Tate chortled. "You have little squares all smashed into you."

"Huh?" She knocked away his hand, then glanced around to get her bearings. Kitchen table ... laptop ... cold coffee.

Oh, great. She must have fallen asleep in the middle of proofreading. A few taps on her keyboard confirmed the battery had died sometime during the night. How far had she made it through the document before falling face-first onto her computer? No doubt that explained the indentations on her cheek.

Combing stiff fingers through her tangled hair, she cast Tate a drowsy smile. "How long have you been up?"

"Don't know. But me and Weena just finished watching that TV show I like with the nature guy. And we were hungry, so I gave Weena her food and made toast for me."

The moment he said it, Shannon caught a whiff of charred bread. Heart racing, she bolted to the counter where the toaster sat. A pile of blackened crumbs and a table knife lay next to a mauled stick of butter. How had she not heard all the commotion?

Because you're majorly sleep-deprived and you were out like a light.

"Honey," she began, trying hard not to alarm her son, "did you plug in the toaster all by yourself?" A stupid question, since there was no one else in the house.

"You said not to ever mess with 'lectricity. But you were sleeping, and I was very careful." His lower lip trembled. "Don't be mad, okay?"

"I'm more scared than mad. You could have gotten hurt very badly." *Or worse*. She could no longer disguise the tremor in her voice. Scooping her son into her arms, she held him close. "If anything had happened to you—oh, sweetie!"

"It's okay, Mommy." He tucked his cheek next to hers and gently patted her back. "It'll be okay."

Echoes from the past assailed her. Swallowing hard, she sidled over to a chair and sat Tate on her lap facing her. She clutched his pudgy hands. "I am very thankful I have such a sweet and thoughtful son," she began, her voice breaking. "But it's Mommy's job to take care of you, not the other way around. I'm sorry you had to make your own breakfast because I was asleep. I'll try hard not to let that ever happen again. But even if it does, you can always, always wake me up. Promise you will, okay?"

"Okay," he drawled. Eyes averted, he went on, "But when I'm bigger, I can get a job too. Then you don't have to work so hard."

His offer broke her completely. She clung to him while she stanched the flow of tears with her sleeve. When a measure of control returned, she cupped her son's cheeks and gave him her warmest smile. "Don't worry one minute more about how hard Mommy works. I do it because I love you. But I'll make you a promise, okay?"

"What do you promise, Mommy?"

"Ravi trusted me with an important rush job that he needs back by Monday morning. But I promise that after I turn it in, I'll tell him I need to work less for him because I want to be a better mom and have more time for you."

"And Weena, too."

"Weena, too." The faithful dog hovered near Tate, and Shannon reached over to scratch her furry neck. "So," she continued with a sharp sigh, "that means I need to spend today and tomorrow on this job so I can finish. What if we drive up to Grammy and Grampy's cabin? You can have fun with them while I work."

"Okay, I guess." Pouting, he plucked at the hem of his sweatshirt. "If we can't go to Luke's ranch."

"I thought you loved it up at the cabin with Grammy and Grampy."

"I do. But if I'm gonna be a cowboy someday like Luke and Tobias, I need to practice."

She looked at him askance. "When did you decide you wanted to be a cowboy?"

An eager grin stretched across Tate's face. "Since I saw real cows and horses at their ranch."

"Oh, you!" She tickled his belly until he squealed and jumped off her lap. She pretended to chase him through the house, then caught him as he sought refuge on the den sofa. Lifting his shirt, she gave him a raspberry on his bare belly.

"Mommy, stop!" He giggled and shoved her away. "Save me, Weena!"

When the dog let loose with one of her playful, deep-throated barks, Shannon raised both hands and straightened. "Okay, okay, I'm outnumbered. I need a shower anyway. See if you two can stay out of trouble until I'm done."

Later, as she pinned her freshly washed and dried hair into a topknot, her cell phone chimed. Rushing to grab the phone off the dresser, she hoped it was Luke calling.

Not Luke. Anika. "Hi," she answered hesitantly. "Everything okay?"

"I hope so," Anika said. "I just wondered ... is Luke with you?"

"What? No. I haven't seen him since he brought Fletch to the clinic the other day." Her heart clenched. "Has something happened?"

"That's what I don't know." Anika released a shaky breath. "We had plans this morning, but I can't find him anywhere, and his phone keeps going to voicemail. Even Tobias has no idea where he went. I thought—*hoped*—he'd gone to see you."

"There's no reason to panic," Shannon stated, as much for her own benefit as for Anika's. "When was the last time you saw him?"

"Yesterday, early afternoon. I went to his cabin to ask if he'd teach me more about managing the ranch, but he said he had to be somewhere. I saw him leave in his truck a little after three thirty."

"Did he return afterward?"

"I was baking dog treats and didn't notice. I'm not sure if he came home yesterday and left again early this morning or never made it home at all." Anika's voice cracked on the last word.

One hand pressed to her forehead, Shannon spun in a slow circle as she tried to think. "Wait—it's Saturday. Doesn't he have an obedience class somewhere?"

"That was my first thought. But the Hope House counselor called earlier wondering why Luke hasn't shown up. And he's getting annoyed because this is the second time in a month that Luke missed a class." Anika gave a loud sniff. "I'm used to Dad going MIA, but not Luke. He's always been my rock."

Shannon wished she could offer reassurance. "There has to be an explanation. Maybe Fletch's leg got worse and he took him to the vet clinic. I can call and check."

"Would you? I hadn't thought of that."

"Let me call you right back." Shannon disconnected, then phoned the clinic. Amy answered and confirmed that Luke hadn't been there. She received the same response from Luke's previous veterinarian as well as the after-hours emergency clinics in town.

Reluctant to call Anika back with the disappointing report, she sat on the bed and bowed her head.

Tate wandered in, interrupting her silent prayer. "Mommy, I heard you talking on your phone. You sounded sad."

She forced a smile. "I'm just a little worried. Anika doesn't know where Luke is, so I called some people to see if I could help her find him."

"Well, Pop-pop tells GiGi not to worry about him when he takes me for a walk with his roller-thingy, because God is always watching over us. Even if you don't know where Luke is, God does."

The *roller-thingy* was Martin's walker. "You're right, honey." Shannon smoothed a lock of dark hair off her son's forehead. "But even though we trust God, sometimes human beings can't help worrying about people we love."

Tate cocked his head. "Do you love Luke?"

Heart twisting, she sucked in a quick breath. "Yes. I ... I do."

It was no longer a case of *falling for* Luke. She'd already fallen hard and fast.

Dear Lord, help me. I'm in love with him.

I'm in love with her.

Then why was God doing this? Was it His way of punishing Luke for all the years he'd run from the Lord?

Once he'd calmed down yesterday, he'd thanked Witt, shoved everything back in the box, and headed home. Shut away in his study with the contents of the shoebox spread across the desk, he'd opened an internet browser to cross-reference locations and dates.

With each search result, the picture grew increasingly undeniable. For years, Luke's father had been covering up how deep into alcoholism he'd plummeted. If only the minor fender benders and secret repair bills were the worst of it. Not only had Dad lied about the accident that nearly killed Anika *and* caused the death of another driver, but his reckless driving while intoxicated on other occasions had put countless lives in danger.

And at least one more of those people had died.

Steven Halsey.

Shannon's late husband.

A bitter taste in his mouth, Luke made himself read the incriminating news article one more time.

COLLEGE STUDENT KILLED IN UNDERPASS COLLISION

COEUR D'ALENE — A motorcyclist lost his life Friday evening after crashing into the concrete wall of an underpass on US Highway 95 near Worley, approximately 25 miles south of Coeur d'Alene.

Steven Halsey, 22, of Missoula, MT, was pronounced dead at the scene.

According to a statement issued by the Idaho State Police, Mr. Halsey's motorcycle veered sharply toward the right side of the roadway as he entered the underpass at approximately 7:15 p.m. Authorities are investigating what may have caused him to lose control of the vehicle, including road conditions and whether another vehicle may have been involved.

A motorist discovered the accident and contacted emergency services. The witness reported being passed a few minutes earlier by a dark-colored truck traveling at high speed and weaving erratically but could not provide further details.

Anyone who may have been in the area between 6:45 and 7:15 p.m. is urged to contact the Idaho State Police, even if they don't believe they saw anything significant.

Halsey, a student at Washington State University, was wearing a helmet at the time of the incident. Family members told reporters that Halsey was an experienced rider who was returning home from school when the incident occurred.

The driver of the unidentified truck must have been Luke's father—why else would he have saved the clipping? Besides, Worley wasn't that far from Tekoa, where Dad regularly met up with a rancher acquaintance. Luke had long suspected they did more boozing than talking cattle business.

By midnight, he'd seen all he could stomach. He'd shut down the computer and crawled across his bed fully dressed, but sleep wouldn't come. Well before dawn, he packed up a few things for himself and Fletch, then helped the dog into the truck and headed west on I-90 with no destination in mind.

An hour and a half later, he crossed the border into Idaho and kept going, then stopped for gas and a stretch break at the Washington state line. They drove on for another hour or so, reaching Ritzville, Washington, shortly after nine o'clock. Spotting a McDonald's just off the highway, he got in line at the drive-through and ordered a sausage-and-egg breakfast sandwich and a large coffee. Order in hand, he pulled into a parking space across from the pickup window. He filled kibble and water bowls for Fletch and set them on the passenger-side floorboard, then climbed in behind the wheel with his own food.

Fletch took a few bites of kibble and lapped some water. Apparently not hungry, he hopped onto the seat and stared up at Luke.

The dejected look in his dog's eyes stole Luke's appetite. He folded the wrapper around the remains of his breakfast sandwich and dropped it into the white paper bag it had come in. He frowned at Fletch. "All right, I get it. Only cowards run away from their problems."

Cowards like his father, the last man on earth Luke wanted to emulate.

Highway signs at the intersection to his right offered three choices: I-90 West to Seattle, 395 South to Pasco, or I-90 East to Spokane ... and eventually all the way back to Elk Valley. He was literally at a crossroads, and though his brain knew which way he should go, his heart resisted.

Get a grip, Daniels. You're supposed to be the responsible one.

Heaving a groan, he popped open the glove compartment and retrieved his phone, which he'd switched off before stashing it there. No doubt Anika had missed him by now. Tobias, too. Once the phone powered on, he wasn't surprised to find a dozen voicemails waiting for him.

His guilt and self-loathing increased with each message he played. The first three were from Anika, wondering where he was and reminding him of his promise to teach her more about running the ranch.

Tobias's messages expressed frustration over Luke's ignoring the fact that he had people depending on him, and how could he just take off without letting anyone know?

Then Jordy, the counselor at Hope House, called twice, wanting to know if he'd forgotten about the obedience class. Witt's messages followed, the mix of disappointment and concern in his voice making Luke cringe.

A couple more from Anika, her pitch climbing with every word.

The last message was from Shannon, and Luke almost

couldn't bear to listen. *"Luke, people are worried about you, and we're all praying. Please, wherever you are, just let us know you're okay."*

Seconds after the playback ended, his phone rang. It was Anika. He swallowed hard before answering. "Hey, Ani."

"Luke, finally! The Friend Finder app just updated your location. What are you doing all the way over in Washington?"

"Not real sure," he said with a sigh. "Guess I needed some space."

Anika remained silent for a moment. When she spoke again, her tone hardened. "Does it have anything to do with that box of papers I found in your desk drawer?"

Luke bristled. "You snooped in my desk?"

"Only to look for something—*anything*—that might offer a clue about where you disappeared to. And don't you dare get angry with me about it. I've been half out of my mind with worry." She exhaled sharply. "Luke, how long have you had that box?"

"I found it while I was at the hunting cabin." He grimaced. "I didn't want you to know about it."

"Too late now." Her tone became a harsh whisper. "And I'm not the only one."

"What are you saying?" His heart pounded. "Did you show that stuff to someone else?"

"I had to, Luke. I didn't know." She was crying now. "I'm sorry."

"Anika. Tell me who else saw what's in the shoebox."

"Shannon." The name came out in a faint rasp.

No. *No, no, no!* He hunched over the steering wheel and tried to breathe. "Why?" he growled. "What was she even doing there?"

"When nobody could find you, she came to be with me. She was helping me look through the papers on your desk." A hiccuping swallow. "We went through the box together, and she saw the clippings about Steven."

His chest throbbed. He wondered if he might be having a heart attack. Fletch rested his good front paw on the console and stretched across the space to lick Luke's hand.

"Where is she now?" he managed.

"She left. I think she went home." Anika whimpered. "Luke? Please tell me it isn't what it looks like."

If only he could. *Dear God, if only I could!*

Shannon was thankful she'd had the foresight to drop Tate at his great-grandparents' with Rowena instead of taking them with her to the ranch. Tate had fussed about being left behind, but he'd be better off there until they had answers about Luke. Besides, once she'd seen the contents of that shoebox, how could she ever have explained to her son the sudden rush of tears—the overwhelming shock and anger and disbelief?

How long had Luke known his father had caused the accident that killed Steven? Had he ever planned on telling her?

Until this morning, she'd never read a single news article about that day. Never wanted to, never had the courage. She only knew that Steven's motorcycle appeared to have spun out of control before crashing into the concrete support of an overpass. The only blessing was that he'd likely died on impact.

As she reached Elk Valley's main intersection, she could hardly see the road through her falling tears. Not trusting herself to make it home safely, she turned in and parked at the grocery mart on the corner. Remembering Maddie Wittenbauer lived nearby, she found the number in her contacts and called.

"Hi, Maddie. It's Shannon." She choked back a sob. "Are you at home? Can I come over?"

"Of course, honey. What's wrong? Are you okay?"

"It'll be easier to tell you in person. I'm at the Elk Valley mini mall. Can you give me directions to your house?"

Ten minutes later, she wound her way toward Eventide Dog Sanctuary. A rambling white farmhouse came into view at the end of the lane. Across the way stood the barn and a long kennel building with an attached fenced yard.

Maddie strode out from the kennel and hurried over. When Shannon stepped from the car, Maddie wrapped her in a hug. "Let's go to the house. I'll put the kettle on and make us some tea."

"Thanks. I—I didn't know where else to go." A fresh spurt of tears erupted.

Maddie bustled her up the back steps and through the narrow mudroom. She guided her to a chair at the kitchen table and handed her a box of tissues. "Just breathe, honey. I'll be right back."

Shannon nodded and blew her nose.

While the electric teakettle burbled, Maddie pulled a chair close to Shannon's. "When you feel ready to talk, I'm here."

The back door creaked, and Witt's voice sounded from the mudroom. "Whose little yellow car—oh, hi, Shannon."

"She just got here." Rising, Maddie nudged Witt's dog, Ranger, out of the way while she gave her husband a quick kiss. "I didn't expect you home this early."

"I, uh, had some ruffled feathers to soothe." He cast

Shannon an uneasy glance. "Don't suppose you know where Luke is off to this morning?"

"No idea." She swiped at her cheeks. "But I'm pretty sure it has to do with why I landed on your doorstep on such short notice."

The teakettle clicked off. Maddie dropped tea bags into two ceramic mugs and filled them with hot water. She set one at Shannon's place and patted her shoulder. "Are you okay if Witt stays? He's a good listener and a pretty terrific spiritual guide. Something tells me that's what you need right now."

Nodding, she offered Witt a teary smile. "I think that's exactly what I need."

"If you're sure." Witt didn't look so certain himself, but he filled another mug from the coffeemaker that sat near the teakettle. He took the chair next to Maddie's, and Ranger stretched out on the floor nearby.

Drying her eyes once more, Shannon cleared her throat and met Witt's gaze. "I gather you've been looking for Luke today, too. Well, I think I know why he disappeared."

Witt's Adam's apple worked. "Go on."

His ominous tone sent a chill up her spine, but she made herself continue. She told about Anika's frantic call, trying to reach Luke herself, then driving out to support Anika while they waited for news.

She told about helping Anika look around Luke's cabin for any sign of where he could have gone. Going through the papers on his desk. Discovering the battered shoebox in a drawer.

Puzzling over random news clippings and receipts.

Finding Steven's obituary.

Reading the news article describing the accident.

"I took it with me," she said, reaching for her shoulder

bag. Her tears had dried now, her voice steady even though she felt hollow inside. She flattened the yellowed clipping on the table and slid it across to Witt and Maddie.

Grim-faced, Maddie read it first, then passed it to Witt and clutched Shannon's hand.

Ignoring the clipping, he closed his eyes and took a slow, tired breath.

Shannon studied him. "You knew already."

"It's true," he said, straightening. "Luke came to see me yesterday. We went through the box together and reached the same conclusion. Luke's father caused your husband's accident."

She shuddered and pressed a fist to her lips. "And then he just—what? Ran away because he couldn't face me with the truth?"

"He was stunned. Horrified. Heartbroken."

"And how do you think *I* feel?" She shoved away from the table hard enough that tea and coffee splashed from the mugs. "All along, I believed Steven's accident was just that —an unavoidable tragedy. Slippery roads. An animal running into his path. Some kind of engine malfunction. Now I know it was *entirely* preventable. If Victor Daniels hadn't been driving stone-cold drunk on the same highway as my husband that day, Steven would still be alive!"

Chapter Twenty-Eight

"Tobias?" Anika stood in the open door of the tack room. She'd found the ranch foreman perched on a stool as he rubbed Neatsfoot oil into a saddle. The musky smell hung heavy in the air.

His typical lazy smile morphed into concern. "You heard from Luke?"

"He's on his way home." She snorted. "All the way from Ritzville, Washington."

"Ritzville? What was he doing way over there?"

"Running away." Hands pressed to her temples, she heaved a sharp sigh before pouring out every detail of what she'd found in the shoebox. "And the worst part is, Shannon saw it all, too. How will she ever get over knowing our father is the reason her husband—her sweet little boy's daddy—is dead?"

"Aw, sugar, come here." Tobias wiped his hands on a rag before rising and drawing Anika into his arms.

She melted against his solid chest and inhaled the manly scents of cotton, leather, and a hint of woodsy aftershave. Being consoled over the misdeeds of her alcoholic father and runaway brother wasn't the kind of embrace she'd dreamed of sharing with her childhood crush. But right now, it was everything she needed.

Tobias eased back and crooked a finger under her chin until she looked up at him. "What's eating at you the most? Finding out your daddy's responsible for even more sorrow and heartache than you realized?" His mouth quirked into a knowing grin. "Or the likelihood you won't be getting Shannon for a sister-in-law anytime soon?"

"I'd say it's about fifty-fifty." She plopped onto the stool Tobias had vacated. "Yesterday, I was begging Luke to give me more ranch responsibilities. Today, I'm about ready to wash my hands of this ranch *and* my family."

Tobias sidled over to a rack of bridles and straightened one. Without looking at her, he said, "Well, I know of at least one cowhand who'd sure miss you if you weren't around."

Her heart stammered. "You'd really miss me?"

"I would." Head cocked, he cast her one of those endearing boyish smiles. "Ain't no other cowgirl in these parts whose pigtails I have so much fun tugging on."

She harrumphed and crossed her arms. "I haven't worn pigtails since I was twelve. And if *that's* the only reason you'd miss me—"

"Oh, don't kid yourself, sweet thing. There's plenty more ..." Looking away, he stiffened and cleared his throat. "You really asked Luke to give you more to do around here?"

"It sounded like a good idea at the time."

"Well, I think it's a mighty fine idea. I'll tell him so myself if he ever gets his sorry—uh, his sorry you-know-what back where it belongs."

Tobias rarely swore, but under the circumstances,

Anika wouldn't have minded if he had. Lately, choice words she refused to speak aloud had been slithering through her brain with increasing regularity.

She pulled her phone from her jeans pocket. "Let's see where that brother of mine has gotten to." The Friend Finder app showed him heading east on I-90. "Looks like he made it through Spokane and just crossed into Idaho."

"Another two or three hours, then." Tobias slapped his forehead. "What was that fool thinkin', taking off like this?"

No doubt *fool* was another mild substitution. "Surely you've noticed my brother hasn't been his normal self ever since Shannon came into his life. He's in love with her, Tobias. And now ..." She lifted her hands in a helpless gesture. "My heart breaks for both of them."

"They're both hurting. But you are, too. I say let's do something about that." Tobias pulled her to her feet.

One eye narrowed, Anika shot him a doubtful look. "Like what?"

"If you're serious about getting more involved in the workings of the ranch, there's plenty of prep work to do before winter. Since the crew's out doing health checks and your brother's made himself scarce, I could use some help checking feed stocks." He winked. "You up for the job?"

"Yes, sir." She grinned and saluted. "At your service."

Striding across to the massive feed barn behind the bunkhouse, Anika couldn't think of anywhere she'd rather be today than working alongside Tobias Flynn.

Chapter Twenty-Nine

L uke made it home around midafternoon. After getting little sleep the night before and then being on the road for eight hours, he was running on fumes. Strong roadside coffee and a couple of cans of Red Bull only went so far.

Fletch had had his fill of riding in the truck, too. Luke let him into the cabin, where he could stretch out in his own soft bed for a while.

Next, Luke went to the house to look for his sister. He owed her a big-time apology.

"Ani?" he called, letting himself in through the kitchen door. The lights were off. Two empty Coke cans sat on the counter. Used plates and utensils soaked in the sink. The only time his sister left the kitchen in a mess was when she got distracted baking dog treats or crafting new pet accessories at her sewing machine.

He went to the foot of the staircase. "Ani, it's me. I'm back."

Nothing.

If his self-absorbed nonsense had given her another

migraine, he'd never forgive himself. He willed his tired legs into motion and trudged up to Anika's room.

She wasn't there.

And now he was getting worried. *Really* worried.

Which, considering how he'd taken off early this morning without a word to his sister, he deserved.

The kitchen door banged shut, and laughter floated up the staircase. Two people, it sounded like. Anika and ... Tobias?

Relieved, Luke hurried down. "Ani, I was looking all over for you. Where have you been?"

Turning from the fridge with two water bottles, she shot Luke a wordless glare.

He cringed. "Sorry. Unfair question and totally out of line."

"*That's* the truth." Rolling her eyes, Anika handed one water bottle to Tobias. She'd twisted her hair into a messy braid, and Tobias bore a streak of dirt across his forehead. Both looked like they'd been rolling in dust.

"Glad you're back safe." Tobias uncapped his water bottle and took a long swig. "But next time you decide to take off for parts unknown, at least have the courtesy to give a heads-up to the folks who care about you."

Luke cast his friend a remorseful smile. "Does that still include you?"

Brows arched, Tobias shared a look with Anika. "What do you think? Should we give the guy a break?"

"Well, he's been pretty hard to live with lately. Making promises, breaking promises ..."

"Ani, I'm sorry." Luke extended both hands, palms up. "You have every right to be mad. I've got no excuse except —" Eyes closed briefly, he clenched his jaw. "Scratch that. There's no excuse at all for my recent behavior."

Anika's expression softened. She took another water bottle from the fridge and passed it to him. "Have you eaten anything today?"

"Not since a late breakfast at the McDonald's in Ritzville. And most of it went in the trash."

"We had chicken salad sandwiches earlier. I can fix you one."

"That would be great." While his sister excused herself to wash up, he took a seat at the table.

Tobias pulled out a chair and joined him. "Anika told me about your dad and Shannon's late husband. That's rough, man. Real rough."

"No kidding." Luke massaged his temple. "I'm scared she'll never want to speak to me again."

"You need to give her more credit than that." Tobias snorted. "Give *God* more credit than that."

"I've been trying harder to trust Him again. But after this ..." His shoulders lifted in a hopeless shrug.

Moments later, Anika set a sandwich and corn chips at his place, then patted him on the shoulder. "Tobias is right. We need to leave this in God's hands. Our anger with Dad, how Shannon's handling it, how we move on from here—all of it."

Covering his sister's hand with his own, he looked up at her. "You sound so much like Mom. Wish even a tenth of her lessons in faith had sunk in with me."

"It's never too late." She winked and settled into the chair on his other side. Arms folded on the edge of the table, she angled him a thoughtful frown. "You do need to talk to Shannon, though. In person."

He picked up a chip, then dropped it back into the pile. "I wouldn't even know where to begin."

"How about ..." Anika looked toward the ceiling, then at him. "'I love you and I'm sorry'?"

It sounded too simplistic, but it was the truth. "And then what—provided she hasn't already thrown me out?"

"Then you give her a chance to voice her feelings. No matter how ugly or hurt or angry, you stand there and you take it. Convince her you won't run away again. That you'll be there for her no matter what. That you aren't scared of a woman's deep emotion."

A tremor went through his belly. "Even if I am?"

Tobias poked Luke's ankle with the toe of his boot. "*Especially* if you are."

How could he argue when deep down, he knew they were right? Besides, the thought of a future that didn't include Shannon in his life had become unthinkable.

After a gulp from his water bottle, he stared at his sandwich. "Maybe you should have baked me some humble pie instead."

"Oh, just eat. You're going to need your strength." Anika gave his arm a backhanded slap. "And I'd strongly recommend a shower, because you're pretty rank."

Tobias leaned in with a meaningful look. "Here's another suggestion. Just like you, Shannon needs time to process. Pray about it tonight, then sleep on it. Go to church with us in the morning and fill up on God's Word. Pray for Him to heal Shannon's heart, and ask Him to show you what to do next."

Brow furrowed, Luke cast Anika a questioning glance. She smiled and nodded.

This faith business was going to take some getting used to. Good thing he had a sister and a friend willing to show him the way.

By the time Shannon started home from Maddie and Witt's, perspective had returned. Not a lot, but enough that she could give the situation over to God and trust that somehow, some way, He could bring good from it.

The big question they'd left her with was unnervingly simple: *Do you love him?*

Yes was the simple answer. The unnerving part was whether she could ever look at Luke without seeing his father's truck running Steven off the highway and to his death.

When she arrived at the Frasiers', Dorothy took one look at her and drew her into a hug. "They didn't find Luke?"

"They did. He's probably home by now." A brief text from Anika earlier had informed her that Luke had finally checked in and was on his way back.

Dorothy cupped Shannon's cheek. "Well, that should be good news, but it isn't what I see on your face."

Shannon's throat closed. "Sorry, I've been at Witt and Maddie's for the last few hours. I'm all talked out."

"I understand." Dorothy ushered her to a chair in the living room. "You don't have to say a word. But do stay for supper. I'll let Tate know you're here. He and Rowena are in the backyard with Martin enjoying the sunny afternoon."

She nodded her thanks as her body melted into the cushions. "I think I could fall asleep right here."

"Then that's what you should do." Dorothy lifted the hinged top of a nearby ottoman and took out a crocheted afghan. She spread it over Shannon, then moved the ottoman close enough for Shannon to rest her legs. "It'll be about an hour before supper's ready. I'll make sure you're not disturbed before then."

Shannon didn't know another thing—didn't even dream—until a small hand shook her awake.

"Mommy?" Tate's whisper was gentle but insistent. "GiGi said to wake you for supper. Are you through resting now?"

She scooted up in the chair and pulled her little boy onto her lap. "Rested enough to cuddle with my Tater-Tot. I missed you today."

"Did you find Luke? Is he okay?"

"I didn't stay long enough to see him, but I'm sure he's fine." Or not. The truth must have hit him almost as hard as it had Shannon.

"Then why do you look sad, Mommy?"

She couldn't begin to explain in words a four-year-old would comprehend. "I—I'm sad about Luke's Daddy. Remember me telling you he's in the same hospital where Mommy was when you lived with Grampy on the mountain?"

Tate nodded solemnly. "But he'll get better like you did, right?"

"Only if he listens to his doctor and trusts God. Like I had to. But it could take a long time, and I—" She smoothed Tate's hair while forcing down the lump in her throat. "I don't think we can see Luke and Anika for a while."

"But why?" Tate frowned. "'Cause I like Luke and Anika very, very much, and Weena misses playing with Fletch. And I miss the horses and cows, and someday if Luke gets real sheep, I wanna see 'em and pet 'em."

"Oh, honey." It was hard not to laugh at her son's reasoning. "When you're older, you'll understand." She cringed. How many times had she asked her father why she didn't have a mommy, only to hear the same evasive reply?

How many times had she promised herself she'd never use it on her own child?

"When will I be older, Mommy? When I'm five?"

Before she could reply, Dorothy peeked in. "Supper's on the table."

"Be right there." Shannon nudged Tate off her lap. "Let's go wash our hands."

Hopefully, the distraction of mealtime would forestall more questions and give Shannon time to come up with better answers.

If only God would provide answers to the maelstrom of uncertainty tearing her heart to shreds!

Chapter Thirty

After working all day Sunday and turning in the rush proofreading job barely on time, Shannon informed Ravi she had to scale back or risk burning out. He said he understood and would honor her time constraints as much as possible.

A busy day at the clinic got her through Monday, but by the time she picked up Tate and Rowena after work and made it through the usual evening routine of supper, bath time, reading a couple of storybooks, and tucking her son and his dog into bed, she felt numb with the exhaustion of holding herself together.

Ready for an early night, she changed into her pajamas and had just finished washing her face when the doorbell rang. She hoped Dad and Julia hadn't come to check on her. Leaving Dorothy's Saturday evening, she'd specifically asked her not to tell them anything about how upset she'd been.

On the way to the door, she slipped on her terry robe and finger-combed her hair. She'd been praying about how and when to tell Julia what she'd learned about Steven's death. *Please, Lord, if it's them—*

A glimpse through the peephole confirmed it wasn't.

Stomach in knots, she opened the door. "Luke."

He stood rigid beneath the amber porch light. "Can we talk?"

"I—I don't—"

"If you don't want to talk to me, I get it." He edged closer. "But I need you to listen to what I have to say. Afterward, if you never want to see me again, I won't blame you. It'll break my heart, but I'll understand."

Never want to see him again? Her heart already threatened to shatter into a million tiny fragments.

With a stiff nod, she stepped back and motioned him inside. The living room seemed more appropriate than the den for a conversation of this magnitude. Arms folded, she faced him from the far end of the coffee table. "Okay, I'm listening."

For a moment, he didn't seem to know what to do with his hands. He finally stuffed them into his jeans pockets and inhaled a shuddering breath. "Number one, I'm sorry. Sorrier than you can possibly imagine for what my father took from you."

A tiny whimper escaped Shannon's throat. She pressed one hand to her mouth but made no reply.

"Number two ..." He swallowed hard. "Look at me when I say this, Shannon."

Lips quivering, she slowly raised her eyes to his.

"Number two is I love you. More every day." His gaze held hers. "I ran off before, but that won't happen again. This is me telling you right now that I intend to fight for you. For *us*."

Tears slid down Shannon's cheeks. She mopped at them with her sleeve.

"Number three," he began, his tone mellowing into buttery warmth. He edged around the coffee table. "I know you're gonna need time, and I will never, ever rush you. But if you have feelings for me—any at all—I'm asking you to keep the door open. Being honest with each other is the only hope we have."

He'd reached her side and gently drew her hands into his. How silly to suddenly become aware of how she must look—wearing pajamas and her ratty old robe, hair in a tangle, eyes red and cheeks blotchy from crying.

"Luke ..." His name came out in a raspy whisper.

"Shh, you don't need to say anything now." He leaned forward and kissed her forehead, a kiss as soft and fleeting as the brush of a feather. "Just know I'll wait for you as long as it takes."

He released her hands and stepped back. Seconds later, the front door clicked shut behind him.

In the echoing silence, Shannon mentally replayed every word Luke had spoken. She knew he couldn't be blamed for his father's mistakes, but could she ever look at him without remembering?

"I intend to fight for us," he'd said.

If she really wanted a future with Luke, she must find the strength to fight as well.

A week went by, then another. Shannon continued working for Zootown Tech Writers but put in only an hour or two each evening after tucking Tate into bed. It meant less extra income and more belt-tightening, but her well-being took priority. As she felt more rested and less pressured, her scattered thoughts began to settle.

Best of all, she and Luke had begun talking again. He usually called on FaceTime after she'd shut down her computer for the night and was propped up in bed. Each time, he gently coaxed her to be truthful about her feelings, which meant their conversations often brought tears—both hers and his.

They talked about other things, too. Luke confided how hard he'd struggled with his mother's illness and death. Anika's long recovery after the wreck. The pressure to take over responsibility for both the ranch and his sister as their father disengaged and his drinking worsened.

Shannon described her loneliness growing up on the mountain with only her dad, then escaping to college, meeting Steven, and finding more happiness with him than she'd ever thought possible. Then his death, followed by her descent into clinical depression and wishing she could die, too. Her only reason to fight—to *live*—had been Tate.

Her talks with Luke—no matter how cathartic, no matter how her feelings for him had deepened—left her with one unspoken question: Did she dare risk her hard-fought recovery from loss, despair, and grief—*her very heart*—all over again?

And it wasn't only her own heart, but Tate's affections. With her son continually wanting to know when they could visit Luke at the ranch again, she knew he deserved a better explanation.

When another Saturday rolled around with Tate pestering her again about going to the ranch, she led him to the den sofa and sat down facing him.

Using the words she'd practiced in her head several times already, she began, "Sweetie, the reason we haven't gone to see Luke is because I found out something about his daddy that makes me very sad. Even angry." She paused for a steadying breath. "I'm praying every day that I'll be able to forgive Luke's daddy, but my heart just isn't ready. Luke and I have been talking on the phone, but for now, being with him in person seems just ... too hard."

Head tilted, Tate wrapped one arm around Rowena's furry neck. "What did Luke's daddy do, Mommy? Did he hurt somebody?"

After a painful swallow, she replied, "He hasn't been a very careful driver. He's responsible for accidents that ... that hurt people badly."

"People we know?"

"Yes. He hurt Anika, and ... others." She couldn't yet bring herself to say more.

"That's not nice." Brows meeting above the bridge of his nose, Tate frowned. "The police should arrest him and take him to jail."

A thought that had occurred to Shannon more than once. Though authorities may not have found physical evidence connecting Victor Daniels to Steven's death, Anika certainly had grounds for reporting her father as the driver at fault in their accident. But that was nearly four years ago. Was there a legal statute of limitations? Besides, there'd been no proof then either. It would be Anika's word against her father's.

As Shannon puzzled all this out, she caught her son's narrowed eyes. Snorting through his pug nose, he twisted his pursed lips from side to side.

He looked up suddenly, his face brightening. "Does Luke's daddy know Jesus? 'Cause if he does, he can just ask Jesus to forgive him, and then you can forgive him, too, and everybody can be happy again."

"I'm afraid it's a little more complicated than that." She sighed and looked away. More to herself, she murmured, "If only I could believe he was truly sorry."

"Well, can't you ask him?"

She stared at her son. Would Mr. Daniels's doctor even permit her to see him?

An idea formed. She grabbed the TV remote and found a Saturday-morning nature program Tate liked. "Honey, I need to make a phone call. Can you stay in here with Rowena and quietly watch your show?"

At his nod, she slipped out to her bedroom, closed the door, and left a voicemail for Dr. Yoshida. When the doctor returned her call five minutes later, she calmly but tearfully described Mr. Daniels's apparent connection to Steven's death.

"Oh, Shannon, that's heartbreaking." The doctor's voice grew tender with compassion. "You should have come to see me when you first found out."

"Probably, but while it all sank in, I needed some semblance of *normal*—for myself and for Tate. I haven't even found a good time to tell Steven's mother yet. Last week she was sick with a stomach bug for several days, and now she's filling in for one of the clinic doctors who's away on a family emergency. Even though I see her at work every day, it isn't the place for this kind of news."

"No, you're right. But you should tell her soon. She deserves to know."

"I will, I promise." She inhaled deeply. "In the meantime, is there any chance I could just *talk* to Mr. Daniels? Because I don't know how I'll ever get past this otherwise."

After a thoughtful silence, Dr. Yoshida said, "You must realize this involves major privacy issues. Ethically, I cannot discuss any information about another patient at Mercy

Cottage. And to set up a meeting? The only way that could happen is with the patient's formal consent. Even if we could arrange it, are you sure you're emotionally ready for such an encounter?"

"Please. His negligence killed my husband. I need to face him."

The doctor sighed. "Very well. Within ethical boundaries, I will convey your interest in meeting with the patient, but I can make no promises. Ultimately, it will be between him and his doctor."

"I understand."

"In any case, I'd very much like to see you for additional counseling. This could be a significant crossroads in your emotional and spiritual healing."

Shannon agreed, and they set up an appointment for late Monday afternoon.

That still left her to come up with something to keep Tate entertained and his mind off Luke and the ranch.

Before she could think of anything, her dad texted.

> Julia wants to take Daisy and Dash to the Elk Valley dog park. Nice day for an outing. Want to meet us there around 2:00?

Any other time, she'd jump at the chance for both Tate and Rowena to burn off some energy. But a public setting like the dog park definitely wasn't the best place for the talk she needed to have with Julia. Could Shannon keep her inner turmoil hidden?

With Tate soon to be bouncing off the walls, she'd have to. She shot her dad a thumbs-up emoji, then returned to the den to tell her son. "We can go early and have a picnic if you'd like."

"Yay!" He jumped up from the carpet. "I'll get Weena's leash and stuff ready."

Half an hour later, Shannon carried a soft-sided cooler and an old tablecloth out to the car. With Tate buckled in and Rowena perched like a giant furry vulture on the rear seat beside him, they headed to Elk Valley.

From a picnic table next to the fenced dog park, they watched the other dogs and their humans at play. Dad was right—the sunny fall weather made ideal conditions for enjoying the outdoors before winter's frigid temps set in with little respite until spring.

As they finished their sandwiches and chips, a white passenger van pulled into the parking lot. A gray-haired man with a scrawny ponytail climbed from behind the wheel. Four other men piled out, and all of them went around to the back. Happy barking erupted as, one by one, four dogs of various sizes and breeds jumped to the pavement.

The pony-tailed guy led them to a gathering spot beneath a tree shedding the last of its golden leaves. "Your dogs can stretch their legs around this area for a few minutes while we wait for Luke."

Luke? Shannon's stomach flipped. This must be the group from the transitional home where he'd been giving obedience classes.

On the one hand, as close as their phone conversations had brought them, she longed to see Luke again. But she dreaded how things could go if Dad and Julia showed up at the same time. What if questions arose that she wasn't yet prepared to answer?

She glanced across the table, where Tate offered Rowena a drink from her water bowl. If they left right now ...

Gathering up their picnic supplies, she stuffed everything into the cooler. On her way to deposit soiled napkins and wrappers in the trash barrel nearby, she glimpsed Luke's truck pull in next to the van. He couldn't have missed her bright yellow VW, parked only three spaces away.

Their gazes met through his windshield, and she froze.

"Mommy?" Leading Rowena, Tate came to Shannon's side and slid his hand into hers. "Did you know Luke was coming to the dog park, too?"

"No, honey, I didn't."

"Are you glad?"

"I—I'm not sure ..." Her heart hammered as Luke emerged from his truck. He hadn't taken his eyes off her.

And he was walking this way.

❧

Maybe it was a mistake to approach Shannon before she told him she was ready to see him again. But she was right there in front of him, and Luke couldn't make his feet turn in the opposite direction any more than he could tear his gaze from hers.

"Hi." He formed a hesitant smile as he drew near. "Nice day for the dog park, huh?"

"Yes. It is." Looking toward the men and dogs under the tree, she remarked, "I thought you usually held your classes in the morning."

"I had some missed lessons to make up for. After today's obedience class at Hope House, I suggested we meet here after lunch for some playtime combined with dog park etiquette."

"I'm sure you'll have fun." Shannon's smile flickered as

she adjusted the shoulder strap of the cooler she carried. "Looks like your students are ready to get started. We were just leaving."

"Not on my account, I hope. I've missed you." Mouth dry, he reached for Shannon's hand. "Missed ... this."

"Me, too," she murmured, glancing down. She gave his fingers a squeeze before pulling away.

"Mommy." Tate tugged on the sleeve of her hoodie. "Aren't we gonna wait for Grammy and Grampy?"

"I'll text them." With an uneasy glance past Luke, she pulled her phone from her pocket. "Maybe we can come back tomorrow."

Luke couldn't let her go yet. "Don't leave. Please."

Her shoulders rose and fell in a quick breath. She set down the cooler and knelt to speak to Tate. "Honey, can you walk Rowena around over there by the picnic table? Stay where I can see you, though."

As Tate led the dog away, Shannon stood and faced Luke. "I haven't found the right time to tell my dad and stepmom everything, and now I'm nervous about them showing up with you here."

"Ah. And complicating things even more."

"Exactly." A sad smile curled her lips as she peeked over her shoulder at Tate. "One of the hardest parts has been trying to explain to my son why we haven't been to see you again. He misses you almost as much as ..." Her words trailed off, and she ended with a shrug.

"So you do miss me?" He ventured a boyish grin. "A little?"

Toeing a pebble, she sighed. "A lot, actually."

His heart swelled, and he wanted to kiss her more than ever. Instead, he tucked his thumbs into his jeans pockets and murmured, "That's really good to know."

They both grew quiet for a moment. Then Shannon shrugged and asked, "No Fletch today?"

"He's taking it easy until his leg's fully healed."

"That's probably wise." Shannon matched his posture and skewed her lips. "We really should go. It'll be easier for everyone if—"

Before she finished the thought, something behind him caught her eye. She stiffened. "Oh, no. My dad and Julia just got here."

"Don't worry, I won't give anything away." He stepped closer and tucked a loose strand of hair behind her ear, letting his fingertips trace the curve of her neck.

She shivered beneath his touch. A sigh slipped between her parted lips as she gave her head an almost imperceptible shake. "Luke ..."

"It's okay," he murmured, giving her more space. "We agreed, no pressure."

At the sound of footsteps behind him, he turned as Dr. Frasier and a well-built gray-haired man strode over. Two dachshunds on leashes trotted along beside them.

"Luke, hi. How's Fletch doing?" Dr. Frasier's smile warmed with concern.

"Better every day, thanks."

Trying not to trip over the prancing dogs, the man extended his hand. "Lane Bromley, Shannon's dad. We haven't officially been introduced, but I've heard a lot about you from both Shannon and Tate."

"Glad to meet you, sir. You'll have to excuse me. My students are waiting. It's these guys' first experience taking their dogs on an outing like this."

With a tip of his head toward Shannon, he backed away and strode over to where Jordy and the guys from Hope House waited.

"Your lady friend and her son?" Jordy asked with a grin. "No wonder you fell head over heels. Looked like you were meeting the parents today, too. Big step!"

"It isn't what it looks like." Luke muted a groan. "We're working through some stuff right now."

Jordy hiked a brow. "Is she worth fighting for?"

Luke's throat clenched as he cast a yearning look toward the woman he loved. "Absolutely."

Inside the dog park, Shannon sat on a bench with Julia while Dad and Tate tried to keep up with Rowena, Daisy, and Dash. The dogs made some playful friends right away, including an energetic terrier mix from Luke's class.

Julia bumped shoulders with Shannon. "Something's on your mind, I can tell. Is it Luke? Earlier, you two seemed … I don't know … *off* somehow."

She'd prayed they hadn't noticed. "We're talking through some issues."

"He's been so good for you. I was hoping …" Julia shrugged.

"I know. Me, too."

After a moment, Julia said, "I'm a good listener if you need one."

"Thank you. Maybe soon, but not here."

Julia nodded as her gaze followed Luke across the play yard. "Of course."

"I'm seeing Dr. Yoshida on Monday, though. She's helping me figure out some things." Casting Julia a quick smile, Shannon rose from the bench. "I didn't see where Dad and Tate went. I should go find them."

At the first sign that Tate was running out of steam, she made an excuse about getting him home for a nap.

Dad helped her get Tate and Rowena into the car, then wrapped an arm around her. "You okay, hon? You've been awful quiet today."

"I'm fine, just tired. Please don't worry." With a squeeze around her dad's waist, she told him goodbye and promised to visit him and Julia at the cabin very soon.

Dad kissed her forehead. "If you need anything. Anything at all—"

"I know. And I promise you, when the time comes, I'll ask." She gave him a gentle shove out of the way and opened her car door. "I love you, Dad."

Driving away, she glimpsed Tate's enormous yawn in the rearview mirror. She tuned the radio to a Christian rock station and coaxed Tate to sing along with her in hopes of keeping him awake until they got home. Once he went down for a nice, long nap, she planned to spend some time with her Bible and the Lord.

Strange, how she'd never felt so strong or so weak, so capable or so helpless. For perhaps the first time, she understood what Paul meant when he wrote to the Corinthians, *For when I am weak, then I am strong.*

It wasn't about not needing people—it was knowing where her own strength ended and when to lean on others for the help they offered.

Chapter Thirty-One

Dr. Ingalls had invited Anika and Luke to come for another session with their father. Anika pleaded with Luke to go with her, but he said he was still working through his feelings about everything. "I'm not ready to see him again yet, but I'm working on it."

Anika wasn't certain she was ready herself. But when the doctor stated that Dad had initiated the request, she dared to hope he was finally prepared to confront the consequences of his actions.

At ten o'clock on Monday morning, she followed the attendant to Dr. Ingalls's office, where Dad was already waiting. Both men stood as she entered the room.

"Good morning, Anika," the doctor greeted with a smile. "Thank you for coming." He looked past her. "Luke didn't join you?"

"Sorry, not this time."

"That's perfectly all right. This will give you and your father a chance to speak one-on-one." He showed her to the seating area.

Her father barely glanced at her as she edged past, but

she couldn't help noticing his red-rimmed eyes. In all her life, she'd seen him cry genuine tears only once—the day he and Mom came home from seeing her doctor and informed the kids her lupus had caused heart problems. Although they hadn't offered details, Mom's look of resignation and Dad's quick exit from the room were proof enough of the seriousness of the development.

Mom had passed away less than two years later.

Dr. Ingalls's muted cough drew Anika's thoughts to the present. She took the chair opposite her father and forced herself to breathe.

The doctor steepled his fingers. "Vic, would you like to speak first?"

Dad's throat worked. He took a sip of water from the glass on a side table. "I, uh, I've had a lot of time to think," he began, his voice rough and raspy. "I know I've done some bad stuff, been a lousy father. And I—I'm a—"

When it appeared he was about to break down, Dr. Ingalls passed him a tissue but said nothing.

Hands clenched, Anika held herself rigid.

After one lengthy exhalation that seemed to come from the soles of his feet, Dad murmured, "I'm an alcoholic."

Dr. Ingalls closed his eyes briefly and nodded. "Thank you, Vic. Willingness to acknowledge the problem is the first step toward healing."

When he turned to Anika with an expectant look, she forced a swallow. "Yes, Daddy, thank you for finally facing the truth." She sat a little straighter and met her father's gaze. "You should also know that Luke found the shoebox."

He paled. A tiny squeak sounded from his throat.

Dr. Ingalls drew his brows together. "Vic, do we need to talk about this shoebox?"

Dad seemed to melt into the chair. He'd always been a

big man, but just now, he looked like a scared little boy. "Then you know everything now." A sob escaped. "You know what a lying, despicable wretch your daddy is."

Something shifted inside Anika, and the tears she'd expected from herself didn't materialize. She must remain strong for both their sakes, and only the power of God enabled her to do so.

She crossed the small space to her father's side and propped herself on the arm of his chair. Encircling him in a hug, she kissed the top of his head as he wept into his clenched fists.

"I'm sorry," he moaned. "I miss your mom more than I can say. If she hadn't gotten sick, if God hadn't let her die—"

"I know, Daddy. I know it's been hard." Shifting, Anika tilted his chin until he looked at her. "But you chose to pull away from us. You chose to drink. You chose the lies and deception. The hurt you've caused is all on you—not on Mom, and certainly not on God."

His lower lip trembled. "You're right, and I'm trying to own up to my mistakes." He looked over at the doctor. "Tell her, Doc. I'm doing the steps, working the program."

"He is," Dr. Ingalls agreed. "Sure, there've been ups and downs, but every day is progress."

Anika's thoughts returned to the day she'd found the box. She would never forget how Shannon's face had gone stark white, eyes wide and jaw dropping as she seemed to cave in on herself. Only after Shannon had fled from the cabin had Anika put the pieces together.

She slipped to the carpeted floor and knelt gripping her father's hand. "Daddy, listen to me. If you're serious about making amends, then you know there's someone else you need to come clean with. A widow—the sweet, kind woman your son has fallen in love with—has been grieving for the last five years because of your recklessness and lies."

Her father heaved a gravelly sigh. He shared a look with Dr. Ingalls, then gave a silent nod. To Anika, he said, "Tell Luke I'm sorry. Tell him I'll make it right."

The doctor stood. "I think that's enough for today. Your father and I should talk privately now. I'll let you know when another visit would be appropriate."

It was a relief to escape. Anika leaned against her car for several minutes and tilted her head back to catch the sun's rays and fill her lungs with clean, refreshing autumn air.

A prayer rose from her heart. *Dear Father in heaven, heal my earthly daddy. Because no matter what he's done or failed to do, I still love him, and I know You do, too. Show him Your forgiveness and mercy, and help him forgive himself so he can be whole again.*

Chapter Thirty-Two

L uke felt bad for not accompanying Anika to see their dad. As much as he'd been talking to God, working on his relationship with Shannon, and getting a grip on his feelings toward Dad, he hoped next time he'd be ready.

Through the barn office window, he glimpsed a dust cloud trailing Anika's car up the dirt lane. Instead of turning in at the house, she swerved toward the barn and parked out front.

Luke met her as she emerged from the car. "How'd it go?"

"It was rough—I won't lie. But at least I now have hope." She strode past him toward the office. "Any coffee left in the pot? I feel a headache coming on and need some caffeine."

Exactly what he'd worried about. He followed her inside. "It's been sitting there all morning. Should be nice and strong."

When Fletch sat up in his bed and yipped, Anika gave him a friendly pat before filling a mug. She dug through her purse for the vial of migraine tablets she never left home without and swallowed two pills with a gulp of coffee.

Luke leaned against the desk. "Feel like talking?"

"Not really, but ..." Settling into a chair, Anika stretched out her legs and gave her temples a massage. "Today seemed all about being honest with himself and with us." She sat forward, hands clasped, and looked up at him. "Luke, he seemed sincerely sorry about everything. And he made me promise to tell you he's going to make things right."

Eyes narrowed, Luke asked, "What does that mean?"

"I don't know exactly, but I had the impression he was talking about you and Shannon."

Luke scratched his jaw as he returned to the desk chair. He sat down with a thud. "Wish I'd gone with you to witness this for myself."

"Well, you had your chance." She took another swallow of coffee and grimaced. "This is awful."

"I warned you."

"And I warned *you* about letting Shannon get away. She's so right for you, Luke. There has to be a way to win her back."

"I'm working on it." Luke's gaze drifted toward the window as a shaky smile formed. "I didn't want to get your hopes up, but we've been talking on the phone nearly every night. And Saturday I saw her at the dog park."

"You did?" Beaming, Anika sat forward. "How is she?"

"Still sorting things out. She needs to talk to Steven's mother but hasn't found the right time yet, and it's eating at her."

"I can only imagine. Remember how hard it was for Mom and Dad to find the courage to tell us how sick she was?"

"Dad couldn't even get the words out," Luke said, recalling how his father had fled the room in tears. "Mom had to be strong for both of them. And for us."

"Shannon's strong, too, so don't lose hope." Anika came around the desk to squeeze Luke's shoulder. "I'm going to keep trusting God to bring resolution and healing to all of us. And I'm going to keep praying for you and Shannon to find the happiness together that you both deserve."

"Thanks. I've prayed more in the last few weeks than I have in my entire life." He laughed softly. "Being back in church has felt weird, but in a good way. I forgot how nice it was when we used to go every Sunday with Mom."

Anika's smile grew wistful. "She must be celebrating with the angels over your return."

He had no doubt.

"I'm heading to the house to lie down for a bit. This morning was exhausting." Covering a yawn, Anika stood. "Come over in an hour and I'll fix us some lunch. Then we can dive into the ranch books again. I still have questions, but I'm starting to get the hang of it."

Luke cast his sister an admiring grin. "Did you know you're pretty amazing?"

"Glad you finally noticed." Tossing a wink over her shoulder, she left the office.

He'd always known Anika was amazing. Why had it taken him so long to realize she had a real knack for ranch business—even more, that she actually wanted a role in running the place?

Maybe because you were too busy trying to shield and protect her instead of trusting the Lord.

Fletch limped over and rested his head on Luke's knee. Those big brown eyes held devotion and compassion, even if the dog couldn't grasp all the life changes his master was dealing with. Getting to know Shannon had opened Luke's eyes and heart to how much he'd been missing—and how much more he wanted.

He stroked Fletch's ears. "Guess you really can teach an old dog new tricks."

After returning from lunch, Shannon escorted an older gentleman and his Persian cat to an exam room. On her way back to the reception desk, her cell phone vibrated in the pocket of her slacks. Reading Dr. Yoshida's name on the display, she ducked into the break room to answer.

"I have news," the doctor said. "Mr. Daniels has asked to see you."

She squeezed her eyes shut and pressed one hand to her abdomen. "That was fast."

"It came as a surprise to me as well. I have been given permission to tell you that Mr. Daniels strongly wishes to begin making amends to those he has hurt. He and his doctor would like you to suggest a time that best fits your schedule."

Last night on the phone, Luke had mentioned Anika's visit with their father had taken a hopeful turn. They'd also talked about Shannon's increasing sense of urgency about confronting the man, which Luke fully understood.

Even so, she hadn't expected things to happen so fast. But now that it was, panic rose in her chest. She felt her way to the nearest chair. "Can we talk about it at my appointment this afternoon?"

"Absolutely. I'll see you soon."

She'd arranged with Brad to leave work at four. The

next couple of hours crawled by as she checked patients in and took calls for appointments. Her stomach was in knots by the time she climbed into her VW and headed toward Mercy Cottage.

Dr. Yoshida's calming presence and gentle guidance allowed Shannon to freely express her hurt and grief and anger, at times weeping inconsolably or pacing the room as she released her pent-up rage—and not just for Victor Daniels's part in Steven's death, but because learning the truth had almost destroyed her hopes for happiness with Luke.

"You understand Luke is not his father, don't you?" the doctor asked.

"Of course I do." Shannon blew her nose into a soggy tissue. "I believe it with all my heart. But is loving him enough for me to get past what his father did?"

Dr. Yoshida passed Shannon a box of tissues. "That's a question only you can answer."

"I know." Heaving a tremulous sigh, Shannon leaned into the chair cushion and shifted her gaze toward the window behind her. "Nothing about my life comes close to the way I'd envisioned it." She gave her head a quick shake as a smile formed. "That isn't entirely true. I'm a mom to the most precious little boy ever."

"A blessing indeed. And all the more reason you need to ..." The doctor paused for Shannon to complete the statement.

"Accept, adapt, and advance. The Three A's—how could I forget?" She smirked. "You should have those printed on a T-shirt to give to all your patients."

"Hmm, that's a great suggestion. I'll keep it in mind." Dr. Yoshida turned a page in her notebook. "Are you ready to schedule a time to meet with Mr. Daniels?"

A shudder raced up Shannon's spine. "I doubt I ever will be, but I'm not letting that stop me. When can we do it?"

Dr. Yoshida went to her desk and placed a call. Within minutes, she arranged for Shannon to sit down with Luke's father on Wednesday morning at ten o'clock. "Both Mr. Daniels's doctor and I will be present, but we won't intrude upon the conversation unless it appears necessary for either or both your sakes. Is that acceptable to you?"

Shannon nodded.

With the details completed, she offered Dr. Yoshida her sincere thanks and hurried out to her car. She sat there for a long time, just breathing in and out.

Accept.

Adapt.

Advance.

A cycle she must repeat with each new experience God allowed into her life. No more standing still. No more getting stuck.

No more allowing external circumstances to have sole power over her actions and reactions. From now on, she would try her best to entrust every moment to the Lord's loving direction.

That evening after Tate was asleep, Shannon phoned Dorothy to ask if she and Martin would mind keeping Tate for a couple of days. Things would be difficult enough without the added stress of avoiding her perceptive little boy's inevitable questions.

Dorothy must have sensed something deeper behind her words. "Are you all right, honey?"

Shannon suppressed a sigh. "I think I will be. But I've been dealing with some ... unsettling news lately."

"I sensed something was wrong. You know we'll help any way we can."

"Thanks. I promise I'll tell you more soon. For now, I just need a little time to myself. And your prayers, of course."

"We're always happy to keep Tate, and you always have our prayers."

Over breakfast the next morning, Shannon presented the plan to her son.

He cast her a suspicious look. "Where are you gonna be while I'm there?"

"Here at home, taking care of a few things."

"You're not gonna go to work?"

"Part of the time." She planned to ask Brad for Wednesday off, figuring she'd need the full day for the meeting with Mr. Daniels and then the aftermath. Tweaking Tate's chin, she gave him her most reassuring smile. "This is another one of those grown-up things that will be hard for you to understand until you're older. When the time is right, though, I'll answer all your questions."

Her brave boy gave a firm nod. "Okay, Mommy. Should I pack some extra stuff for me and Weena before you take us to GiGi's house?"

"That would be very helpful. Thank you."

At the clinic, she approached Brad about taking Wednesday off. When it came to her scheduling needs as a single mom, he'd been more accommodating than she could have hoped for. He also knew enough about her personal history that he recognized the importance of tending to her emotional health.

It felt strange going home to an empty house that

evening. She took advantage of the alone time to complete the proofreading job Ravi had sent yesterday. Tomorrow, she doubted she'd have the mental capacity for correcting commas and dangling modifiers.

After shutting down her computer and straightening a few things around the house, she filled the tub and tossed in a lavender-scented bath bomb, then soaked for half an hour while praise music played through the Bluetooth speaker on the counter. The lyrics tuned her heart to the Lord, inspiring a litany of prayers for herself, for Julia, for Luke and Anika, and for their father.

Feeling calm and better prepared for tomorrow, she propped herself up in bed and placed a FaceTime call to Luke.

"Hey." He shot her a surprised grin. "I was just about to phone you and apologize for not calling last night. We had an emergency with one of the cows."

"I hope everything's okay."

"I won't bore you with the grim details, but she'll be fine." He reached for something in front of him, and the TV noises shut off. "Everything okay with you?"

She took a steadying breath. "Luke, I—I'm meeting with your father in the morning."

"Really?" He looked as panicked as she'd felt yesterday when she'd first received the news. "When did this come about?"

"Dr. Yoshida finalized the arrangements late yesterday at my appointment." She hesitated. "I wasn't sure how to tell you ... or if I even should."

Hurt filled his expression. "I thought we were getting to the point where we could tell each other anything."

"We are. I just don't know how this is going to go. What I'll say. What *he'll* say."

After a moment of thoughtful silence, he smiled and said, "Tell me how any of that matters to *us*."

Swallowing hard, she replied, "Not one bit."

"I was hoping you'd say that." He winked. "I'm going to say goodnight now, but I'll be praying."

I'll be praying. Those words were comfort enough, and sleep came much more easily than she'd expected. She awoke the next morning filled with the God-given peace that passes all understanding.

At five minutes before ten, Dr. Yoshida came for Shannon in the Mercy Cottage lobby. "Are you ready?"

"As I'll ever be." She inhaled deeply, then let the air out in a rush.

The doctor escorted her to a small conference room she'd used a few times during her stay at Mercy Cottage when Dad and Julia had brought Tate for a visit.

"Dr. Ingalls and Mr. Daniels will join us shortly," the doctor said. "There's coffee and tea on the sideboard if you'd care for some."

"Maybe just water for now." Shannon filled a glass from the pitcher in the center of the table, then settled into a moss-green padded chair.

Across from her, the door eased open, and a thin, bearded man entered. He acknowledged Dr. Yoshida with a smile and nod, then turned a pleasant look toward Shannon. "Hello, I'm Dr. Ingalls. You must be Mrs. Halsey."

She smiled back, her mouth suddenly dry. She desperately wanted a sip of water, but her hands seemed glued to the armrests.

Dr. Ingalls turned toward the corridor. "Vic, would you like to come in now?"

A nervous cough sounded from beyond the doorway, then a man's throaty reply. "Guess so."

At her first glimpse of Victor Daniels, Shannon's heart hammered. Maybe she wasn't as prepared for this encounter as she'd hoped.

Dr. Yoshida, standing behind her, lightly touched her shoulder, a silent reminder to stay calm. She tried to pull in a full breath, but her lungs didn't want to cooperate.

The man stood across the table from her, eyes lowered, hands knotted. He met her gaze, a single tear escaping from the corner of his eye. "I'm sorry," he whispered, then repeated more forcefully and through shaky sobs, "I'm sorry!"

Shannon rose stiffly to face Victor Daniels, the man who had stolen the future she should have had. The man she'd tried to hate. The man whose criminal irresponsibility she wanted to heap back upon him a hundredfold.

But all she saw before her was a man broken by shame and sorrow, a sinful human being begging for a lifeline. A man desperate for the one thing she alone could offer in this moment.

Through no power of her own, her steps brought her to the other side of the table. She tenderly put her arms around him and whispered, "I forgive you."

Luke had awakened Wednesday morning with the conviction that he needed to go to Mercy Cottage. A big reason was his need to be there for Shannon, but he also knew it was time to see his dad. After taking care of a few barn chores, he got in his truck and drove over.

He couldn't miss Shannon's bright yellow VW parked

near the entrance. His heart twisted at the agony she'd suffered these past few weeks. Was she holding up okay in this meeting? How would his father respond?

At the reception desk, he introduced himself as Victor Daniels's son. "I know I'm supposed to clear it with his doctor first, but I'd like to see my father as soon as possible."

The receptionist checked something on her computer screen. "Your father and Dr. Ingalls are currently in session."

"Yeah, I'm aware."

The woman's brows lifted slightly. "All right. If you don't mind waiting, I can check for you when they're finished."

"Thanks. I'll just hang out over here." He turned toward the seating area.

He'd paged through one magazine and was about to select another when the inner door opened. Shannon appeared, and his heart slammed into his chest.

She froze. "Luke."

"Hi." He surged to his feet. "You okay?"

"I am." She took a step closer, a smile turning up the corners of her mouth. "I'm better than okay, actually."

The look shining in her eyes made his insides tingle. "I'm glad. You're all I've been able to think about ever since you told me about the meeting."

She closed her eyes briefly. "I saw your father, and I've forgiven him."

A swallow caught in Luke's throat. "Just like that? *How*?"

"It wasn't *just like that*. I can promise you it was one of the hardest things I've ever done. But I had to forgive him because ..." With an incredulous sigh, she pointed behind her to the plaque above the door: *Mercy unto you, and peace, and love, be multiplied.* "Because that's what it's all about, extending the same forgiveness and mercy God has already given me, more times than I can count."

Hesitantly, he took her hand. "Shannon Halsey, do you have any idea what a remarkable woman you are?"

She blushed and dipped her chin.

"No, I mean it. Your strength, your courage, your faith —you inspire me. You make me ..." He inched closer, his voice growing husky. "You make me want to be a better man. A man who's worthy of loving you. Worthy of your love in return."

Eyes sparkling, she looked up at him. "I already love you, Luke. I think I started falling for you the first day we met."

His arms crept around her. He leaned in with a grin. "In spite of my klutziness trying to manage Anika's booth at the fair?"

"I think maybe *because* of how cute you were when you realized you were in over your head."

"I am in *way* over my head right now, in case you haven't noticed." His heart thudded. "Because if I don't kiss you in the next five seconds—"

The receptionist called his name. He jerked as if someone had shoved him.

"Sorry for interrupting," she said with an apologetic smile. "I just confirmed with Dr. Ingalls. Give him a few minutes, and he'll invite you in to see your father."

"Thank you." Now his pulse was racing for a different reason. He looked back at Shannon. "I haven't been here in weeks, but something told me it was time."

"I'm glad." She drew him over to a small sofa near the window. "Your dad has made mistakes—horrible ones— but he's trying now to make amends. Let him, okay? Listen to him, hear what's on his heart. And when you respond, be gentle. Be merciful."

He touched his forehead to hers. "My mom used to tell me that God can bring something wonderful out of the worst imaginable circumstances. I don't think I believed her until now."

"He's pretty clever about that kind of thing." When she tilted her head, her lips grazed his.

A shiver raced through his limbs. He angled his mouth over hers and kissed her deeply, longingly, thoroughly. Didn't matter that the receptionist was probably watching. Didn't matter that they sat near a window in full view of the parking area. Didn't matter that soon Luke would face the man he'd held in contempt for all these years and would finally try to forgive him.

Because he wouldn't be here at all if not for the woman in his arms. She'd changed him. Challenged him. Healed him. *Loved* him.

And he would cherish her with every beat of his heart for as long as he lived.

Chapter Thirty-Three

L uke walked Shannon out to her car, where they shared another hope-filled kiss. As she drove away, Luke sighed and turned toward the building. The time had come to face his father.

Lord, there's no way I can do this without You. Please give me strength.

An attendant met him in the waiting room and escorted him to Dr. Ingalls's office. Well before they reached the door, Luke's heart was hammering. He paused in the corridor and scraped his clammy hands up and down his jeans.

The door opened, and the doctor greeted him with a warm smile. "Come in, Luke."

Across the room, his father stood. Chin quivering, he briefly met Luke's gaze. "Son."

Luke choked down a swallow. "Hi, Dad."

Once they'd taken their seats, Dr. Ingalls began the conversation. "Thank you for initiating this visit, Luke. I know it means a lot to your father that you wanted to see him."

"I should have come sooner, but I ... I needed to deal with a whole lot of anger and resentment first."

Dad used a fistful of tissues to mop wetness from beneath his reddened eyes. He roughly cleared his throat. "Can't blame you. I deserve every bit of it."

"That's what I thought, too, before ..." The knot in Luke's chest made it hard to breathe. "Before God got ahold of me and started changing my perspective."

"He's changed me, too, son. I hope you believe me." Choking back tears, Dad seized Luke's hand. "I *need* you to believe me."

"I'm working on it one day at a time." Luke firmed his jaw. "For now, it's enough for me that Anika believes you. Shannon, too."

"Shannon." Dad spoke her name in a shuddering, awe-filled whisper. His shoulders shook as more tears fell. "Even after everything I took from her, she said she forgives me."

"I know, Dad. She told me." He scooted closer and returned his father's grip. "Next to Mom, she's the most incredible woman I've ever known, and I'm in love with her."

"That's wonderful, son. I'm happy for you. More than I can say."

In the silence that followed, pieces began falling into place in Luke's mind. Brow furrowed, he studied his father. "When you took off for the cabin before ... all this"—his gesture encompassed the room and everything that had brought them to this point—"you knew it was the anniversary of when Shannon's husband died."

Dad closed his eyes and nodded. "When Anika told me Shannon's name and how you were starting to feel about her and that she was coming out to the ranch, I couldn't risk being there. How could I possibly face her?" His voice broke. He sniffed hard. "All the senseless, reckless, unforgivable things I've done over a lifetime, including nearly getting your sister killed and then lying to both of you—it all caught up to me at the cabin, and I just wanted to die."

As more sobs erupted, Dr. Ingalls clasped Dad's shoulder. "Vic, do you need to take some time?"

"No, no." He straightened and grabbed another handful of tissues. "I need to clear the air with my son."

"It's okay, Dad. It's okay," Luke said, meaning it. He could feel the forgiveness and love welling up in him like a cleansing ocean wave. When it broke on the shore of his heart, the last remnants of bitterness and disgust washed away.

Rising, he pulled his father to his feet and locked him in a mighty embrace. "I love you, Dad. Always have, despite how I've been acting. I want you to get better, and I'll be here for you every step of the way."

"Thank you ... thank you."

After a few moments, Dr. Ingalls cut in. "Luke, this has been a monumental day for your father, but he needs time now to rest and reflect. I suspect you do, too," he added with an understanding smile.

Luke only then realized how drained he felt, despite his exhilaration. He gave his dad another hug. "I'll come see you again real soon, okay? Anika and I both will."

The doctor called for an attendant to escort Luke's father to his room. When they'd gone, he turned to Luke with a knowing smile. "Your father has wrestled through some soul-deep changes these past few weeks. But I see now that's true of you as well. Please remember I'm available if I can help with any issues you or your sister continue to struggle with."

"I appreciate that." Luke shook the man's hand. "I was

a real jerk at first, and I'm sorry. Things'll be different from now on."

Dr. Ingalls cast a pointed look upward. "That's the wondrous power of faith and prayer."

Wondrous. That about summed it up, because only the Lord could have caused the transformation Luke had witnessed today ... in his father, and in himself.

A light snow fell on Saturday afternoon as Shannon directed Luke up the winding mountain road to her father's cabin. He'd asked if he could be with her when she told Julia and her father the truth about Steven's accident.

She'd left Tate with his great-grandparents again, but only after giving him an explanation his not-quite-five-year-old mind could absorb. She told him how much it upset her to learn that Luke's father was the driver whose recklessness had caused Steven to crash his motorcycle. She also told her son how sorry Mr. Daniels was and that she'd forgiven him, because that's what God wanted her to do, and she wasn't angry anymore.

Tate had solemnly taken it all in, but afterward, his face erupted into a huge grin. "I'm sad about my daddy, but I'm glad we're still friends with Luke and Anika. Can we go see them at the ranch now?"

Her heart swelled as she replied, "Every chance we get."

Now, she reached across the truck console and squeezed Luke's arm. "Thanks for coming with me today."

The love shining from his eyes kindled a flame in her chest. Not since the first blush of love with Steven had Shannon experienced the depth of happiness these past few days had brought. The growing sense that her late husband's blessing lay upon this relationship comforted her beyond measure.

"The gate's just ahead." Pointing through the windshield to the right, she said, "Turn in here."

She got out and held open the green metal gate while Luke drove through, then latched it behind him and climbed back in. Dad and Julia waved from the deck. With Daisy and Dash yipping and prancing at their heels, they started down the steps as Luke parked nearby.

Greeting Shannon with a hug, Julia whispered, "Does this special visit from the two of you mean what I hope it means?"

"Maybe," she answered with a shy grin. Turning serious, she linked arms with Julia. "But first, there's something else I need to tell you and Dad."

"Sounds ominous. Should we be worried?"

Shivering, Shannon flicked a snowflake off her eyelashes. "Let's go inside and talk where it's warm."

In the living room, Shannon's father added a log to the potbelly stove, then coaxed Daisy and Dash to snuggle into their plush bed nearby. As Luke and Shannon settled onto the sofa, Julia brought out steaming mugs of hot chocolate. She and Dad took the easy chairs on the other side of the coffee table.

Shannon took a sip of cocoa and then set her mug on a ceramic coaster. "First, I want you both to know that everything is okay. *I'm* okay."

"Ooookay," Julia drawled. Now I really am worried."

Dad reached over for Julia's hand and gave it a squeeze. "Honey, let's wait and hear what Shannon has to say."

As they gave her their attention, Shannon inhaled a steadying breath. "It's about Steven's accident." Praying for the words to come, she went on, "We've only ever known that something or someone caused him to swerve into that pillar, but no one could say for sure how or why. I needed to wait for the right time to tell you this, but I recently learned the truth about the accident."

Julia's brow furrowed. "I don't understand. How?"

Luke clasped his hands between his knees. "I'm sorry, Dr. Frasier. It was my father. He was on the same stretch of road that night and driving under the influence."

For a moment, Julia only stared, mouth agape. Shannon watched the same emotions she'd experienced flash across her stepmother's face.

Dad moved to the arm of Julia's chair and whispered soothing words to her before looking between Shannon and Luke. "Maybe you'd better explain."

"My father doesn't recall everything about that night," Luke said, "but he has a vague memory of veering to avoid a motorcycle, then seeing the crash in his rearview mirror. At that point, he panicked and sped away. Later, he started scouring news reports, and when he realized no one could identify him or his truck, he tried to forget it ever happened."

Luke then described finding the hidden stash of repair receipts and news clippings. As the facts emerged, all he wanted was to put as much distance between himself and his father as possible ... "Until I realized I was running from the truth, just like my dad."

Shannon squeezed his hand as she took up the story, explaining she'd gone to the ranch to be with Anika after Luke disappeared—only to see for herself what the shoebox held and realize what it all meant.

"After Shannon found out, I was terrified she'd hate me —hate my entire family." Luke wove his fingers through hers, his eyes filling. "And I didn't know how I'd survive without her."

Sniffing back tears, Julia rose and paced to the window. Shannon's father followed, encircling her in his arms as she pressed her forehead into the crook of his shoulder.

Shannon used the momentary silence to soothe her aching throat with a sip of lukewarm cocoa. She didn't have to imagine the blow this news was to Julia and wished she could have spared her the pain.

After a few moments, her father crossed to the coatrack and retrieved his and Julia's jackets. "We're going for a walk," he said, then added softly, "Don't worry, she just needs a little space."

When they'd gone, Luke leaned close and smoothed a strand of hair behind Shannon's ear. "You okay?"

"I've had time to work through this. Julia hasn't." She shifted to caress his cheek, her gaze softening. "How are *you* doing?"

"None of this is easy. But the talks I've had with my dad since Wednesday have been healing in so many ways." He sighed and tucked her close. "Plus, with you in my arms, how could I ever *not* be okay?"

When his lips brushed her temple, Shannon released a tremulous sigh. "Things haven't felt this right in a long time."

"I feel that way, too. Which is why ..." Still holding her, he shifted until their gazes met. His voice grew husky with emotion. "Why I want this—*us*—to last forever. Shannon, is there any chance you could find it in your heart someday —maybe not right away, but one day down the road, after things are ..." He gave a nervous laugh. "I'm not saying this very well. Where is Tobias when I need him?"

"Your message is coming through just fine." Heart brimming, Shannon snuggled closer. "Besides, if Tobias were here, I wouldn't be doing this." She nibbled on his earlobe. "Or this." She grazed her lips across his cheek. "Or this."

In the electrifying kiss that followed, she offered a wordless promise of hope for tomorrow and love for a lifetime.

Epilogue

When Shannon married Steven, they'd been struggling college students and couldn't afford the whole gown-and-veil, walk-down-the-aisle church wedding with a catered reception and dance. Besides, they hadn't been ready to tell their parents yet and had married in secret with only the minister's wife and church secretary as witnesses.

All these years later, and with a feisty five-year-old son added to the mix, Shannon couldn't imagine all that fuss and bother. A quiet ceremony surrounded by family and close friends suited her just fine.

For the past several weeks, she and Luke had been worshipping together at Elk Valley Community of Faith, where Shannon's father and Julia attended, as did the Wittenbauers. Shannon felt much more at home among the small, welcoming congregation than she had at the church she'd attended with Tate's great-grandparents.

Today, she and Luke would complete their final premarital counseling session with Pastor Jim Peters. Then in just over a week, on New Year's Day, Shannon would don the simple ivory tea-length dress Julia had helped her shop for and meet her husband-to-be at the altar to begin the rest of their lives together.

As she sat outside Pastor Peters's office waiting for Luke to arrive, a shiver of joyful anticipation coursed through her. So much had changed since that fateful day last August when her car broke down and her tenuous hold on hope threatened to break.

But God had other plans. Only He could have orchestrated everything that followed. Not only had Shannon met the man who would unlock her shuttered heart, but working for Ravi had reawakened her love of the written word. When he assigned her to proofread articles for a Montana-based parenting e-zine, the editor liked Shannon's work so much that she hired her to write a weekly column covering fun but low-cost activities and outings for children.

That job, plus the proofreading assignments Ravi continued to send her way, had allowed her to give notice at the veterinary clinic. After returning from a honeymoon in picturesque Walla Walla, Washington, Shannon and Tate would move into Luke's cabin at the ranch, and her eight-to-five days answering the phone and greeting clients would be over.

The inner door opened, and Pastor Peters glanced around the seating area. "Still waiting for Luke?"

Shannon checked the Friend Finder app on her phone. "He should be here any minute."

Moments after she spoke the words, Luke burst in amid a flurry of snowflakes. He slammed the door against the brisk winter wind. "Sorry I ran late. We were hurrying to get the last of the shelter dogs picked up for fostering over Christmas."

With Anika now taking an active role in managing the ranch, Luke had been spending more time doing what he loved most—volunteering at the Elk Valley Animal Shelter and teaching obedience and herding dog classes. Anika mentioned often that she'd never seen her brother this happy, finally at ease in his own skin. Floating on a cloud of happiness all her own, Shannon couldn't disagree. With every moment she spent with Luke, she fell more deeply in love.

Rising, she nestled into her fiancé's arms and tilted her head for a kiss that was much too brief. There'd soon be time for longer kisses ... and more. Smiling into Luke's eyes, she whispered, "I can't wait to be your wife."

"All right, you two." Pastor Peters grinned and ushered them into his office. "Let's remember what we're here for."

"That's all I think about," Luke said. "Well, not really. I do think a lot about what comes *after* January first."

Even though she'd just hinted at the same thing, Shannon felt herself blushing. The next several days couldn't go by fast enough.

With premarital counseling behind him, Luke only had to get through Christmas and the following week before his happiness would be complete.

That is, until he and Shannon decided together to grow their family. In the meantime, Luke would get plenty of parenting practice as he strove to be a good father to Shannon's son. Tate had already asked if, after the wedding, he could start calling Luke "Dad." Only one other person— the little guy's incredible mom—had ever stirred his heart so deeply.

He worried, though. He hadn't grown up with the best example of what a father should be. If anything, he'd learned plenty of ways he *didn't* want to be like his father. It still amazed him that Shannon had unreservedly forgiven the man for his part in her husband's death.

It amazed him even more that he'd come to a place of forgiveness himself—which never would have happened if not for the patience of both Shannon and Anika as they modeled what true forgiveness looked like.

He'd learned from them that forgiving someone didn't mean excusing the hurtful behavior. It didn't necessarily mean trusting the person again or pretending the bad things never happened. And it definitely didn't mean the wrongdoer wouldn't face consequences.

What it did mean was relinquishing any personal desire to exact punishment. It meant releasing the bitterness and anger. It meant letting go of the past and living in the present.

Above all, it meant walking in utmost dependence on the Lord ... and trusting Him fully for the outcome.

Luke's father had most certainly suffered the consequences of his actions—emotionally and spiritually, if not judicially. He'd wanted to turn himself in to the authorities, but the family attorney assured him that after so much time, and without convicting physical evidence, he wasn't likely to be prosecuted. Instead, he vowed that once he got out of rehab, he'd find a way to atone. He'd be a better man, a better father, a better friend.

Yes, if ever a life gone wrong could be redeemed, Luke saw the proof in his father. Dad had shared more openly with Luke and Anika in the past several weeks than he had in their entire lives. The stories he told about his early years with their mother and how much he'd loved her brought a clutch to Luke's heart every time. He began to understand how watching Mom suffer for years and then losing her had set his father on a path of self-destruction.

Luke worried he could easily fall down the same dark hole if anything similar happened to Shannon. He said as much to his dad as he and Anika sat with him in the festively decorated Mercy Cottage rec room on Christmas Eve.

"No, son, I know you better than that." Dad gripped Luke's knee. "You're stronger than I ever was. And you've got your mom's faith. You and your sister both." His eyes welled as he reached for Anika's hand. "I couldn't be prouder of my kids."

"We're proud of you, too, Dad. You've come a long way since ..." Luke swallowed over the lump in his throat.

"I'm all too aware of the depths I'd sunk to." Dad sniffed. "You have no idea how much it means that you've asked me to be there for your wedding, Luke. If I thought for a minute that my presence would upset your lovely bride or her late husband's family—"

"Shannon wants you there, and so do I," Luke insisted. "We've had long talks with Julia and her parents, and everyone agrees it's time for forgiveness and new beginnings. That's a big reason why we chose to get married on New Year's Day."

Anika scooted closer on the sofa and tucked her arm around her father's shoulder. "We're all looking forward to a brighter future—together."

"Reckon we've already been through the worst, and I hope it's permanently in the rearview mirror." Tears streaming down his face, Dad returned Anika's hug as his gaze shifted between her and Luke. "I'd never have made it without you two. You could have turned your backs on me, but you didn't. Thank you."

Luke rose from his chair and squeezed in on Dad's other side. He stretched his arms around both his father and sister in a warm embrace. Six months ago—six *years* ago—he couldn't have imagined this day would ever come.

Thank You, God. Thank You for restoring this family and for the new one I'll soon be forming. And thank You for never giving up on me, either.

❧

Needing a few minutes alone in the bride's room before the ceremony, Shannon gave Julia, Maddie, and Anika quick hugs and sent them to check on the men.

She stood before the full-length mirror and smoothed the skirt of her lace-covered dress. She had her "something borrowed," Julia's teardrop pearl necklace, and "something blue," a tiny sky-blue satin bow Maddie had pinned to an inner seam of her bodice.

Raising her left hand to a sunbeam angling through the window, she admired her sparkling engagement ring—her "something new." It wasn't large or showy, just a narrow gold band set with a dainty emerald-cut diamond. She couldn't have been more pleased with what Luke had chosen.

She wore her "something old" on her right ring finger, the antique Rose of Sharon ring Steven had given her when he'd proposed. It felt right today to wear this symbol of her late husband's love, a dream cut short but an assurance that true love never dies.

Warm tingles swept across her shoulders and down her limbs. It was almost as if Steven were standing behind her, enveloping her in a tender embrace and whispering in her ear: *"My sweet, brave Shannon, I'm so proud of you. Remember me, but have no regrets. And make sure our little boy knows how much I would have loved being his daddy. Go now with my blessing. Your new family is waiting."*

A knock sounded. "Shannon? It's Dad. You about ready?"

"Coming." She blotted her tear-dampened cheeks with a tissue. After a quick check of her hair and makeup, she pulled in a breath and let it out slowly, then twice more for good measure.

Stepping into the corridor, she gasped at the sight of her handsome father and son. Both wore maroon western shirts with bolo ties, new black jeans, and boots—wedding attire specially chosen by Luke in homage to her son's fascination with everything cowboy. Tate also sported the kid-size tan felt Stetson Luke had given him for Christmas. He carried a heart-shaped satin pillow bearing two gold wedding bands.

Shannon knelt before her son and tapped the brim of his hat. "Well, howdy, pard. All you need now is a horse."

"Luke says I can have my very own horse when we live at the ranch."

A promise her soon-to-be husband would no doubt quickly fulfill.

Shannon's father helped her to her feet, then pressed something into her hand. She peered at the shiny copper penny.

"It's the one your mother had in her shoe on our wedding day." Dad turned the penny over in her palm and pointed. "See? It was minted that same year. Thought it could be a symbol of her presence on this wonderful day."

"Thank you, Daddy. It's perfect." After giving him a

hug, she slipped the penny into the toe of her sling-back ivory pump. "Now I'm officially ready to get married."

Her future happiness certainly didn't depend upon longstanding wedding traditions, not when the Creator of the universe watched over her and her loved ones. But the token reminders, linking past and present, made the day even more meaningful.

On her father's arm, she strode to the sanctuary entrance. An usher had already seated Julia, and as the organ music swelled, first Anika and then Maddie made their way toward the chancel, where Tobias and Witt stood with Luke. Tate went next, strutting like he'd been appointed the new sheriff in town, and everyone applauded.

When Shannon's gaze met Luke's, he beamed a mile-wide grin. Bouncing on his toes, he looked ready to charge down the aisle and sweep his bride into his arms—and probably would have if his groomsmen hadn't held him in place.

No longer able to contain her own excitement, Shannon hurried her father along at more of a jog than the stately stroll they'd practiced yesterday at the rehearsal. As the organist sped up her playing to match, titters of laughter sounded among the guests.

Pastor Peters stepped forward with a chuckle. "Since it looks like the bride and groom are eager to get this show on the road, let's not waste another minute."

Shannon's dad placed her hand in Luke's, then kissed her cheek. To Luke, he murmured, "Love her well," then added only half-teasingly, "because if you don't, you'll answer to me."

Fingers interlaced with Shannon's, Luke replied, "That won't be a problem, sir. I'm all in."

"Me, too," Shannon whispered, her throat tight with emotion.

Then everything and everyone else faded until only one face filled her vision. This man—this strong, tender, faith-filled man—oh, how she loved him! With the Lord's help and blessing, she intended to show him every single day for the rest of their lives.

Looking for other books
in the Montana Mercies series?

Each book can be read as a standalone or in sequence:
Meet Witt and Maddie in the first book,
A Steadfast Companion

Then read Julia and Lane's story in book two,
His Unexpected Grandchild

Follow Carl and Rae's romance in
One Glance of Your Eyes

Award-Winning Author
MYRA JOHNSON

If you enjoyed *If I Fall for You*, please spread the word among your reader friends and wherever you share about books on Facebook, Goodreads, Instagram, or other social media.

Reviews are always deeply appreciated. A review doesn't have to be lengthy or eloquent, just a few brief words sharing your honest impressions. Reviews and personal recommendations are the best ways to help authors get discovered by new readers.

To receive regular updates about Myra Johnson's books and special events, subscribe to her newsletter using the signup form on her website:

www.MyraJohnson.com

With gratitude ...

Bringing this book to publication often felt like one step forward, two steps back. Just as I'd get some momentum going, "life" would hand me a major interruption.

Not all the interruptions were negative. Early on, I had the privilege of speaking at a Montana Christian women's retreat alongside my daughter, followed by a rejuvenating week of sightseeing with our daughter and son-in-law through Montana, Wyoming, Idaho, and Washington.

The next big thing that happened, only a few weeks later, wasn't so fun. My husband required open-heart surgery for a triple bypass and valve replacement. His recovery went well, praise God, and I got back to the book.

By then, the Christmas holidays were upon us, and who gets much done between Christmas and New Year's?

Progress resumed after the first of the year ... until one fateful day the end of March. My husband, more energetic than ever after his heart surgery (his nickname around here is "Project Guy"), was working on something in the garage when he took a misstep, fell, and fractured his hip. The injury required a full hip replacement.

Once again, the writing came to a screeching halt. Between hospital visits, I prepared our home with all the requisite mobility gear. Then came driving him to PT appointments, picking up groceries, and managing other household duties he typically handles so I can write.

I'm relieved to say that's all behind us now. Life has

once again settled into a semblance of "normal," which allowed me to *finally* finish this book, send it to my editor, and ready it for publication.

Now for some words of thanks. To daughter Johanna, who flew to Texas to be with me during Dad's heart surgery. Your presence was such a comfort! (Sorry for the horribly long layover on your return!) Grandson Bryan, you were so sweet to spend a night with Grampers in the hospital.

To Project Guy's sister, Judy, and our brother-in-law, Jim, for your unwavering friendship and generosity. You know the best restaurants and fun games for game night!

To friends Marie, Tim and Jan, Dolores and Larry, and Bill and Dee for making sure we were well fed during the hospital stays and afterward.

To my friends from CenTex Christian Writers, especially Joyce, who's an absolute whiz at marketing and promo. Also to the authors from my mastermind group—Tanya, Donna, Laurie, Delia—for the wisdom you've shared and the encouragement you've given.

To my editor, Teresa Lynn, for working me in when the draft was finished, and for your keen eye for detail.

To author and critique partner Melissa Jagears, whose thoughtful scrutiny helped bring this story to its final form.

To my readers, who complete the circle. Your loyalty and notes of encouragement make it possible for me to keep doing this job that I love so much.

And finally, to my Project Guy! THANK YOU for following doctor's orders, working hard at PT, and getting well! Let's keep it that way, okay? I hope to spend many more active and *healthy* years with you!

Well, not exactly "finally." Eternal thanks to my heavenly Father, who never leaves me stranded and always finds a way to lift me up when I need it most.

About the Author

After a five-year sojourn in Oklahoma, then eight years in the beautiful Carolinas, native Texan Myra Johnson and her husband are happy to be home once again in the Lone Star State enjoying wildflowers, Tex-Mex, and real Texas barbecue! Myra has been writing stories for as long as she can remember. Her published novels have garnered many awards, including top honors in Christian Retailing's Best for historical fiction and the National Excellence in Romance Fiction Awards. Her books have also earned acclaim in the ACFW Carol Awards, Georgia Romance Writers Maggie Awards, Selah Awards, HOLT Medallion, and Faith, Hope and Love Christian Writers Reader's Choice Awards.

Married for 50-plus years, Myra and her husband have two beautiful daughters married to faithful Christian men, plus seven amazing grandchildren and a precious great-granddaughter. The Johnsons share their home with two pampered rescue dogs and a snobby but lovable cat who thinks he's the boss of everyone.

To receive regular updates about Myra's books and other news, be sure to subscribe to her newsletter (signup form on website).

Find Myra online:
www.myrajohnson.com

facebook.com/MyraJohnsonAuthor

instagram.com/mjwrites

threads.net/@mjwrites

bookbub.com/authors/myra-johnson

goodreads.com/MyraJohnsonAuthor

pinterest.com/mjwrites

x.com/MyraJohnson

Novels by Myra Johnson

THE RANCHERS OF GABRIEL BEND

The Rancher's Family Secret

The Rebel's Return

The Rancher's Family Legacy

MONTANA MERCIES

A Steadfast Companion

His Unexpected Grandchild

One Glance of Your Eyes

If I Fall for You

FLOWERS OF EDEN HISTORICAL SERIES

The Sweetest Rain

Castles in the Clouds

A Rose So Fair

TILL WE MEET AGAIN HISTORICAL SERIES

When the Clouds Roll By

Whisper Goodbye

Every Tear a Memory

CONTEMPORARY WOMEN'S FICTION

All She Sought

One Imperfect Christmas

The Soft Whisper of Roses

NOVELLAS

Settled Hearts

(originally published in

The Oregon Trail Romance Collection)

Designs on Love

Lifetime Investment